THE MARCHESA

THE MARCHESA

Sarah Dunant

First published in 2025 by Sarah Dunant
In partnership with Whitefox Publishing

www.wearewhitefox.com

EU GPSR Authorised Representative
LOGOS EUROPE, 9 rue Nicolas Poussin, 17000,
LA ROCHELLE, France
E-mail: Contact@logoseurope.eu

ISBN 978-1-917523-08-0
Also available as an eBook
ISBN 978-1-917523-09-7

Copyedited by Jennifer Davis
Proofread by Louise Tucker
Designed and typeset by seagulls.net
Cover design by Emma Ewbank
Project management by Whitefox

Isabella d'Este was the greatest female patron and art collector of the Italian Renaissance. Born in 1474, she ran a famed court, was an icon of fashion and a formidable political operator who, in partnership with her husband, Francesco Gonzaga, steered the city state of Mantua through the war-torn decades at the turn of the 15th/16th century.

At her death, she left behind a magnificent collection of paintings, sculptures, books, instruments and curiosities. Long since lost or dispersed, all that remains is her correspondence: thousands of letters and copybooks preserved in a deconsecrated convent and church that house the State Archive of Mantua.

PROLOGUE

I have always had the most sensitive nose. Even as a child I registered the way perfumes and bodies fused together. As an adult, I could identify each of my ladies with my eyes closed and smell my husband when he was two rooms away. Though as he grew older so could everyone else, for by then his body was rotting and even the strongest of my concoctions failed to disguise his rankness. Still, I am not to blame for that.

I was an expert in perfumes, designed and gifted scents for women of good families all over Italy and beyond. Though if I am honest rather than modest (a necessary distinction in a woman's life), I never met anyone who smelled sweeter than I did.

Alas, not any more. Now the only scent I carry is that of decay. It hangs in the air like an incense of dust. Disintegrating history. Shelf after shelf, stack after stack, reaching high into darkness; boxes and folders crammed with letters, dispatches, envoys' reports, the whole lumbering bureaucracy of government. There are things that have not been touched since they were put here. I once witnessed a bundle of documents - not my own, praise God - crumble to nothing in a scholar's hands. The insatiable appetite of the bookworm. For so long, such a banquet we provided. I, at least, have been saved from the worst of it. For I am often in demand.

I always know when I am called for: the bright clatter of wheels over stone floors as the archive trolley rolls through dark chambers until it arrives into this cavernous space, once the nave of a great church.

'*Good morning, Marchesa Isabella.*'

The archivist is ever cheerful. Like the ones before her she has grown old in my company, turning from a ripe young thing, heels tapping out neat drumbeats on stone floors, into a thick-waisted matron who moves like an old dog. She will retire soon. Over time, they all do.

'*You are asked for again.*'

Inside the State Archive of Mantua.

Together we trundle back through rooms stacked with centuries of church and civil court records (I swear at night I sometimes hear the mutterings of dead litigants desperate to press unsettled suits), before passing through the heavy door that marks the boundary of past and present and on to the archive reading room.

Oh, what a miserable space it is now. No self-respecting monastery should ever have been a palace, but there was a time when scholars sat amid warm panelling and decorated plaster, bent over wooden desks pitted with ink stains and – who would think it of erudite men? – scratched initials and dates. Alas, all that is long gone. This new undecorated chamber is painfully dull: grubby white walls, plain tiles and ever plainer desks.

The place is barely half full today. There has been another plague recently and scholars – in my experience, never the bravest of souls – are dragging their feet to return. Most of them I've seen before, so I know where I am heading long before the archivist reaches her desk.

I would have noticed her anyway (it is almost always women who come for me these days), as she is dressed with a certain flair: a fitted leaf-green top over Turkish-wide ochre trousers and a long crocus-yellow scarf. Ah, but how I miss colour. It was everywhere in our lives, painted ceilings, gilded wood, frescoed walls, pigments and dyes from every known corner of the earth. We dressed in rainbows: gold silks, velvets bright as new blood, blues luminous as Our Lady's cloak. It's a wonder to me that anyone can access such a past in a barren space like this.

I have her scent now: a common blossom, cheap, with something cloying underneath, from the Indies no doubt. I could have done better for her. Close to, she is older than the flamboyance of her wardrobe suggests. Still, she has an excellent head of hair, a storm of dark curls, caught up with a careful carelessness at the back of her head, a few strands straggling free.

I've been in the company of worse.

She sits for a moment, the bulging files in front of her. Do I detect a touch of nerves? As she loosens the cloth ties on the first one, a mountain of brittle paper explodes upwards, for all the world like some kind of living thing released from captivity. Her intake of breath gives away her excitement. She lifts up a single sheet to the light - wafer-thin, the creeping stain of wax seal, ink faded almost to nothing in places. Holding history in one's hand. It is a moment that never disappoints.

I am there long before her: a note from my agent in Venice (his expansive script gives him away), telling me of the arrival of a consignment of silks from the Indies and a silver bowl I have commissioned ready for dispatch. Isabella d'Este, the consummate consumer. Is that why she is here? She would not be the first. Shopping, it seems, has its own history these days, and there are few who did it better than I.

I could announce myself to her now if I wished. Fan open the leaves of her notebook, breathe hot or cold draughts into her ear. Over the years I have been known to resort to mischief: blow blots of ink over some scholar's derogatory sentence, nudge the elbow of those who dare to fall asleep over my papers, so that an arm slips off the desk and they wake in embarrassed panic.

When I was a child my mother told me that if I prayed hard enough, I might detect the beat of angels' wings as they moved above my head. I never felt them. But I poured so much of myself into the trying that at times I felt the air shimmering around me. Now, it seems, I am the invisible angel, fanning breath and breezes on to those who study my correspondence. Such a treasure it offers. Thousands of letters both from and to me, a few in my own hand, the rest dictated through my secretary to be transcribed later into copy books for safe-keeping. We poured out our lives in ink then, the scratch of goose quill on paper a constant music in our ears. Which makes it even stranger that I live inside such silence now, the only one, it seems, who wakes when I am called for.

In the beginning I felt sure there must be others. I thought once I heard my husband's rolling laughter, how he guffawed when recalling some lewd joke, or the sound of Federico's childish voice singing out my name. But I think now it was only the work of the invisible worm. Over time, I have grown accustomed to my solitude, as one does eventually to most things. I was born with a curious disposition, and it is not without interest being an observer on the way each succeeding present refashions the past. It is a slippery idea, this thing called history.

She puts the page back into its folder, then pulls the second box towards her. Gonzaga court correspondence from an earlier date. Ah, of course. I know where she is going. I've been here many times before.

May 1480. A dispatch from the city of Ferrara, written by the envoy of the Gonzaga family of Mantua sent to assess a possible young bride for his marquis-in-waiting.

> *Donna Isabella is a child of singular intelligence ... I marvelled that she could give such clever answers ...*

Poor man! What else could he say after being subjected to a memorised Latin recitation of an entire letter by Cicero?

Singular intelligence - at six years old.

Some - they are not among my admirers - would say I was already fully formed: precocious, entitled, even at such a tender age lacking in both modesty and grace. As easy to laugh at as to admire. Like honey to the bee, scholars lap it up.

Except for what it misses. Both in the child and the virtues that she lacked. Modesty and grace will be of limited use in my future; a woman running a state with enemy armies at her borders, juggling treaties, negotiating the survival of family and children. Such challenges require a different blend of skills: a bedrock of clever, concealed under a coating of fawning and guile.

No. Starting with the child will not do at all. We need something much more arresting.

She turns her head sharply, frowning and glancing behind her. What? Does she feel my presence? Surely not. I've done nothing. Not even the slightest beat of angel wings.

Still, now I have your attention ...

I

August, 1509. The Gonzaga palace, Mantua

I beg you madam, as humbly as a poor unworthy servant can beg a high and singular patron, to be my husband's advocate in this time of need ...

Not all dungeons resemble each other.

There are the pits where prisoners must cling to the sides for fear of falling into a sea of excrement, or spaces so black that men's eyes grow a film over them and, should they ever be released, daylight will blind them worse than darkness. But in the same way that a greater guest warrants a greater set of palace rooms, so there are graduations in housing one's enemies, particularly when the prisoner is the Marquis of Mantua.

Venice, however, is a vindictive jailor.

His cell, it seems, has only the smallest of windows, so that by day he roasts, and at night the mosquitoes banquet on him. And though he rages and howls, they will not send doctors to tend to his suppurating wounds. Francesco Gonzaga, once the soldier saviour of Italy, is now a common prisoner of war and already wolves are prowling the perimeters of our state boundaries.

*But for the hope I have in you, my lady and His Majesty
the King, I think I would have killed myself with my
own hands ...*

We are sore in need of allies now and with France the current
power broker in Italy, one sure way to target the king is to share
my womanly terror with his wife.

*... for it would be far better to be dead than to remain alive
without my lord. Indeed, when I think of my lord and how he
is suffering, I die a thousand times a day.*

My hand reveals a tremor - deliberate, of course - as I write the
words. The lace and razor language of diplomacy. Is a thousand
times too much? No. No. A hundred would be too small, and
anything else would sound absurd. I know the queen to be a
woman who enjoys romances (the French specialise in them),
and at such a time even despair must be poetic. We are not
strangers, she and I. I have sent her bolts of fabric - the best
of them embroidered with the French fleur de lys - and she
has asked for my designs for headdresses and outfits. Though
I remain her supplicant, I am not without status. No, surely my
plea will not fall on deaf ears. Because if it does ...

Through my study window the surface of the lake shines
golden in the sun. If I turn my head to the left now, I will be in
the company of Venus and Mars together on Mount Parnassus,
while to my right, the warrior goddess Minerva chases demons
from the lake of virtue. It has taken me close on twenty years
to commission and collect the paintings that glow off my walls.
What was it my mother once said to me? *Enemy soldiers take
particular pleasure in destroying art.*

'My lady?'

The door opens.

'If the letter is to go while it's still light, I should copy its words now.'

Benedetto Capilupi, my scribe, as lean as he is tall. Strange how he has always been an old man to me, though he can't have been more than thirty when we first met. In my life I have had two tutors in the art of diplomacy. And my mother is long dead.

I watch his face as he reads it.

'Excellent, my lady.'

Except I know from his voice it's not enough.

'But? What? You have news?'

'Nothing to be vouched for ... whispers through whispers, wind in the trees, that is all.'

'Whispers or not, if you have heard them, so should I.'

He closes his eyes for a second. It is a gesture I know well. 'There is talk - with no proof whatsoever - that Lord Francesco thinks we are not doing enough to secure his release.'

'*Not doing enough!* I -'

'Remember, Your Ladyship, we have no direct contact as yet. The only news he has comes through his jailors. And it suits them to pour poison into his ears.'

'Saying what? That we don't care for his well-being ... that we think we can rule better without him?'

He drops his eyes. Poison. Of course. But clever.

Such a fine consort, your marchesa. Not every wife is so eager to put on the trousers when her husband is away. I can hear the hissing words already: vicious, spiced with just the right amount of gossip. *And so good at getting what she wants. That famous 'collection' of hers. You should hope your ransom money isn't already promised for some new work of art.*

Oh yes. I could mix this brew myself. And, of course, he will react. He can't help himself. My volatile, susceptible husband. I can hear it in his roars. *Oh, Francesco, don't you know they're playing you for a fool?* When he's in pain or embattled there is a petulance to him that ill suits a great warrior.

I could wish he was more stalwart, but then my body is not erupting with fever and sores.

'My lady?'

'Sweet Mary, they are weasels. All my dowry jewels are pawned, and they turn down every offer of ransom we make. But no one tells him that, I'm sure.'

'As soon as there are proper channels of communication, this can be addressed. With your agreement, I will amend and copy the sentiments of this excellent letter to both the emperor and the pope so that they too have reason to intercede.'

'Don't forget the sultan,' I add quickly. 'We're still his best market for horses and whatever Venice may pretend, she needs his goodwill on her trade routes.'

'His name is already on my desk.'

He stands, preparing to leave, and though the air is charged with anxiety I feel, as I always do, a kind of calm that comes with his presence.

'There's something else?'

He hesitates. 'A request. Through the nurses from one of the children.'

'The children? They know nothing!'

He lifts his hands. Whispers, the sound of wind in the trees. There is no such thing as a secret in a palace. When I was a child, we always knew when there was a threat, if only from the false jollity that came in answer to our questions.

'Little Federico. Of course. He will be eager to go and rescue his father.'

'No, my lady. Donna Ippolita.'

*

'I've come to tell you, Mama, that you must not worry. Everything will be all right.'

I try not to smile. 'Yes, Ippolita. I know. But thank you.'

At seven years old, she is the least demonstrative of my children.

'No. I mean that God has told me Papa will be released.'

The least demonstrative and the least recognisable. Even as babies, the boys have something of their father's swarthiness, and Ippolita's elder sister is plump and plain, but she has always been sapling thin, skin so pale it feels as if she has been drawn into life rather than painted. If I didn't know better, I might suggest she came from other loins.

'Well, that is excellent news.'

'I need your permission to go and stay with the nuns of San Vincenzo. To join in the vigil they are holding for him.'

How does she know about that? The gossip is louder than I thought. 'That won't be necessary. God will hear your prayers quite well from here.'

'Still, I would like to go. It is my intention to enter the convent, you see.'

I stare at her. A nun? How long has this being going on? I should be watching her more carefully. We already have requests for her hand in marriage. Though where we would find money for another dowry now, I don't know.

'A laudable intention, but you are not to worry about your father.'

'I am not worried, Mama,' she says. 'That is what I told you. God will see to it. We have an agreement. Father will be set free and I shall enter the convent.'

'Ippolita, you are very young for such a decision.'

'You were only six,' she says without a beat of pause. 'But *you* knew. You told us yourself. You were six, yet when the envoy from father's family was sent to meet you, you convinced him that you were the right bride.'

Isabella at six. That singular child again.

'I am nearly eight,' Ippolita continues firmly. 'Which is old enough to know how my life should be spent.'

'You are barely seven,' I correct her drily. 'And as with all children, you will do what your parents bid you. Nothing is decided ...'

'Papa would let me!' she interrupts stubbornly.

'Your father would –' My voice is sharp. Her elder sister would crumble in the face of such sternness, but not her.

The truth is, she is right. He probably would agree. He's always been softer with the children, at least the girls, and they love him unconditionally. Not Federico, though, surely. No, my first-born son is mine, my little Gonzaga warrior ...

I take a breath. 'When your father returns home – which he will before long – this can be discussed. For now ...' I watch her about to interrupt. '*For now*, you will say your prayers and care for Federico and your other brothers. And that is an end to it. You may kiss me and go.'

She stands her ground for a moment, then does as she is bid. But at the door, she turns. 'I shall ask God to help you change your mind,' she says, disappearing before I can answer.

The last word. How strange that she, who looks so little like me, is the one to have inherited my will. Each time I see her, her eyes seem bigger in her face. Is she fasting? I must talk to her nurses, for that too encourages a certain stubbornness.

At her age, given a choice, might I have favoured God over a husband? Convents contain no sweaty marriage beds or bloody birthing chambers, and Ferrara had more than enough fine establishments with Este abbesses who left their mark on history. My own great-great-aunt was beatified. On the anniversary of her death, her entombed body gives off a holy liquid, which the nuns use to cure the sick. Running my own convent, I might have commissioned paintings, even new chapels and cloisters, for not every order is the Poor Clares.

Ah, but I could never have borne the lack of style. The serge-cloth uniforms, the shorn heads. So much praying. So much silence. And the food ... Oh, the food would never have done.

No. The truth is I was always hungry for the destiny that was presented to me, even when there were moments when it felt more like a death warrant.

The young Donna Isabella is a child of such singular intelligence, that even I would not have believed the extent of it ...

Like all diplomats, the envoy from Mantua was well trained in flattery. But his words were not without substance. Time now, I think, for my scholar to meet the six-year-old.

II

Even if it hadn't been important I would remember the encounter, if only for the fuss made over my appearance: the stifling weight of fabric in my skirts, the way my hair is scraped back so tight against my head that it makes my eyes sting.

'Remember, just be yourself,' my mother murmurs as she settles me for the audience. 'Though perhaps a little quieter.'

My loquaciousness is already family legend. Such is my determination to join in conversations, it seems, that even before I spoke proper words I made noises in response to what others were saying, judging the gaps so perfectly that everyone would laugh and make room to include me. Right from the start, my hunger for life made up for the egregious fault of not being a first-born boy.

The Mantuan envoy - like my own scribe later - is tall and thin (perhaps all diplomats are chosen for their stature - lean enough to slide through cracks under doors, the better to hear conversations from within). Yet as he bends down to greet me, there is something in his expression that reminds me of the bust of Cicero that my tutor keeps in his rooms. So that when he asks me about my studies, how can I resist? I could have picked a longer letter to recite to him, but I had yet to memorise the end of that one.

I asked her questions on many different subjects, to all of which she replied with such good sense and so ready a tongue, that I marvelled that a child of six could give such clever answers ...

'Ha! What did he expect? Some ordinary six-year-old! This is Este blood that runs in your veins!' My father roars with pleasure as he reads the words aloud to my mother and me. 'I tell you, the state of Mantua has won a jewel beyond compare. The union is sealed already.'

'I don't understand, Papa. Did he write that to you - or to his master in Mantua?'

'See!' He roars again. 'See how we've made a diplomat of you already. No - this was never meant for our eyes.' He pauses. 'There are many ways to see a letter before it reaches the recipient. I daresay Cicero did the same thing in his time, yes?' And he beams at me. 'But rest assured, sweet child, we will not give you up for a long while yet. For now, your betrothed will have to make do with a portrait. We will have Tura start on it immediately.'

It would be the first work of art ever to be associated with me. What do I remember? How hard it was to sit still, the dress still pinching and pricking at all angles. Our court painter, Cosmè Tura, was old by then and the smell of the paints could not cover that of his skin as he stared at me, or rather seemed to look through me, while his hand moved independently across the surface of the panel.

As for the result? Well, in his defence he painted what he saw: an over-dressed child with cheeks so fat they swallowed up her eyes when she smiled. Even the envoy, in his covering letter accompanying the dispatch (his words, once again, copied without him knowing), felt the need to stress that ...

... while you may see her face, I can assure you that Donna Isabella's extraordinary knowledge and intelligence are more worthy of admiration.

My father roared again as he read it, but I could tell a barbed compliment even then. The portrait - I would seek it out as soon as I arrived in Mantua - would be conveniently 'lost'.

With the contract signed, a meeting was arranged. But the gap in our ages - my betrothed was eight years older - was wider than the moat of both our castles and he was singularly uninterested in a six-year-old *jewel beyond compare*. He was already deep into his first love affair: horses, which my father indulged, arranging jousts and hunting parties, even a Palio through the city streets, which, to nobody's surprise, he won easily. Somewhere inside this madness, we spent an afternoon in each other's company and played some game or other. He would later claim I cheated, which is possible since I did not like to lose even then. It would be years before we met again.

*

What else can I tell you about my childhood? My mother would give birth again soon enough: three sons and another girl, as well as accepting a boy born from a dalliance by my father. But even before my sister was sent to our grandfather in Naples, I was the chosen one: growing like a plant in full sun under my father's adoration.

As fast as my tongue mastered Latin, so my eye became fluent in art.

My mother was my teacher here, for she had a keen sense of beauty. For me, there will never be a more aching Deposition than the one on the walls of her bedroom: Christ's broken body being lowered from the cross, so contorted, so broken and human, that He seemed more ready for the university dissecting table than resurrection and life everlasting. There were times when I wasn't sure if I loved or feared it. But I couldn't stop looking at it. It was as though the artist - even his name was exotic, Rogier van der Weyden - had mixed his colours with the blood of Christ and the tears of the wailing women.

'He came from the far north,' my mother would tell me inexplicably, when I asked about it. 'They feel the story of the scriptures differently there.'

Then there were all the other walls in all the other palaces. So many are lost now, but one, Palazzo Schifanoia, I think, still stands. Built by my Uncle Borso, duke before my father, it was shining new when I was young and its great chamber was covered in frescoes, astronomical signs above and below, a rolling frieze of the months and seasons of the year: March with farmers pruning the vines, dogs cavorting at their feet, April in a courtly spring garden, courtiers and pretty ladies flirting, the prettiest of whom seemed not to mind the man's hand sliding inside her bodice. Modesty, it seemed, had its limits even in the best of circles.

Borso d'Este.

As for Uncle Borso, he was everywhere; presiding over his court with smiley eyes and fat face, his multiple chins like an avalanche of molten rock. (Ah, those Este chins. Such a battle I would fight with them throughout my life.) I swear I knew my uncle better from the walls than I could ever have done in real life. That painters could recreate the world as if it was unfolding in front of one's eyes is a wonder that would never leave me, even when things were at their bleakest.

I was young when the earth first shook but the thought of it still brings a taste of wormwood to my mouth. My mother is grasping my hand, moving too quickly through darkness so that I am stumbling to keep up. A servant is carrying a baby - it must be Alfonso, the eldest of my brothers. There is a torch, but it gives off more smoke than light and fear is everywhere. Somewhere, far ahead of us, a door swings open, and once we are through and it is barred behind us, my mother starts to laugh. But there's no mirth in the sound and I am still frightened, though I have no idea of what.

That corridor will later be flooded with light, becoming a regular thoroughfare connecting the palace and the fortress of St Michele. But that night it was an alien place. My father was away, and in his absence his nephew, Niccolò, had raised a force and marched into the city declaring himself the rightful duke, inviting the citizens to join him with a promise to lighten their taxes.

He did not, however, immediately storm the palace, which was a grave mistake, for once inside the fortress we were impregnable. He had lost long before the people failed to join him. A few days later, he was beheaded in the courtyard of the palace, the gates left open so the whole city could see justice being done. None of this I remember, though I learned later that my mother watched the execution and wept for him, because despite his treachery he was still of Este blood. And after they held his severed head up for all to see, my father ordered that it be sewn back on to his body and that he be buried in the family tomb. Not all rulers would have afforded him such an honour.

As we grew up, my brother Alfonso would pester me for details about the night we almost died. Like all boys, he had come out of the womb mad for anything to do with war and couldn't bear the idea that he had been there and yet had no memory of it.

'Just think, Mama, what they would have done if they had caught us.' His eyes grow wide with horror, as he repeats my every word. 'Father would have come back to find our three heads on pikes on the city gates!'

'I have told you before, Alfonso, there was no danger.' My mother, mild as always, waves away the thought as if it is an insect hovering too close. 'Your father was already riding towards us.'

'But *Isabella* says Niccolò and his men were everywhere and you - you were all alone, with no one to protect you.' In his mind he is already crawling out of her arms, an unsheathed sword ready to take on every rebel.

'*Isabella says*,' my mother repeats drily. 'Isabella, like you, was far too young to remember anything. The only fear that night would have been if we *had* been alone. But we were not. We were, as always, in God's hands and I never for a moment doubted that He would care for us, as He cares for all those who love and serve him faithfully.'

It is more or less the same answer that she gave whenever she felt moral guidance was needed. Except, she was wrong about my memory.

'Since your brother seems to hang on your every word, perhaps you might suggest he gives more attention to his studies than your far-fetched tales,' she says drily later, when we are alone over our embroidery.

'But I do remember,' I counter stubbornly. 'You know I do. And it was not as easy as you make it.'

She looks at me for a moment. 'In which case, you should ask God to help you forget it. Very little comes from dwelling on such things.'

*

Was she trying to protect me? Or was she already aware of the current of violence moving towards us? Either way, I think she was wrong.

I have sat on the shoulders of dozens of scholars come in pilgrimage to meet me, watched their eyes light up at the stories of beauty: the art, the statues, the silk and velvets, the jewels, the whole shimmering civility of court life. But in the same way there is no heaven without hell, so a woman born into a good family could not live without some understanding of the bilious nature of politics. The great boot of Italy in which we lived was soaked crimson with blood. No family was immune from it. Conspiracies, betrayals, claims on other people's thrones, allies turning into enemies overnight and always, always, mercenary forces ready to side with the highest bidder. War was a way of life.

I was not yet ten years old when my father put on his armour to meet an invading Venetian army, and, along with my newly returned young sister, I was sent to the city of Modena for safe-keeping.

If my childhood was charmed, it ended now.

III

The laughter of Beatrice, the oozing sweetness of marzipan and the smell of my own vomit. Such are my memories of exile.

Growing up, I'd almost forgotten that I had a sister. She had been little more than a baby when my mother took us to visit her own father, King Ferrante, in Naples. But he favoured her immediately, that much I do recall. He sat her on his lap, stroking her hair and lavishing kisses on her. He had a thick black beard and rotten teeth and his breath smelt more of the cowshed than the court. I took an instant child's dislike to him and I am sure he felt the same about me, for he was not interested in any of my talents. A lascivious man, I think if she had not been of his blood he would have taken her to his bed before too long. He excelled at war and cruelty. But he worshipped Beatrice and pleaded with my mother to let him keep 'his little dark angel' for a few years, so that she could learn the ways of the great Aragonese court and light up his ageing life.

'He'd bring me into the room when he was meeting princes or important people like that.' In our free time between lessons in exile, she chattered endlessly about the life she had left. 'I sat on his lap and whenever there were sweets or sugared fruits, he would suck them first, then put them into my mouth.'

'Eugh. What did you do?'

She shrugged. 'I waited till he wasn't looking, then hid them in my kerchief. There were always more when I wanted them. And I never had to study so hard there. Grandfather said women's smiles opens men's hearts to them. So girls didn't need to know as much as them.'

What would my mother have said to that? Yet at other times she would describe how she'd been ignored, left to run wild with other children in the family (a brood of them, from both sides of the blanket), careering through unused rooms and castle corridors like rabbit warrens, whoops and war cries echoing off the walls.

At night, sometimes she would creep into my bed and sob in a way that nothing could soothe because she so missed it all.

'I thought you didn't like the way Grandfather treated you.'

'I didn't. But - well, he gave me presents, and said I was his favourite. Though he said that to the other girls too, I think.'

Right from the start, Beatrice was young - much younger than the two years that separated us - and so desperate to be liked that at any excuse she would laugh and throw her arms around me, call me her darling, darling sister.

And she had another weapon with which to win my love: an endless supply of marzipan.

If there is any sweetness to match that of Neapolitan cuisine, I have never tasted it. Even their meats are soaked in it. I swear if my grandfather had picked me over her, I would never have slipped his sugared fruits into my kerchief. I was born with a craving for sweetness. Maybe it was in my wet nurses' milk, for it seems before I was ten weeks old, I drank three of them dry. My mother did her best to temper my appetite. *You do not have to eat every single cherry in the basket, Isabella* was a familiar refrain.

Only now my sweet tooth ran riot. The marzipan fruits were the best. Exquisite tiny replicas of apples, pears, glistening cherries, all sculpted in coloured sugar paste. Her trunks were loaded with boxes of them. They were the reward in every game we played, and of course I won more often than she did. Though even if I hadn't, the outcome would have been the same. Because it was not just my appetite that undermined me. It was also the fact that Beatrice was a singularly beautiful child.

She was dark, which ought to have made me the prettier of the two (every Venus I've ever seen looks as if she's been dyeing her hair in the sun for days), but her mane had a thickness and shine to it, and when she took it out of its heavy plait it would fall abundantly round her heart-shaped face. And her eyes, deep brown with flecks of gold in them, had a depth that she herself lacked. Those years in Naples had incubated a beauty. And it was impossible not to notice it.

Giovanni Pietro Birago: Beatrice d'Este.

I hadn't given much thought to how I looked till then. That may sound hard to believe, given how famed I am for my vanity and fashion. But it's true. There were mirrors, of course, but they were much inferior to those that would flow out of the island of Murano later. (I wouldn't see myself full length till I was in middle age and the first wall mirrors arrived from the Veneto: fragile as porcelain, weighty as sarcophagi and brutal with the truth.) No. As a child I was trained to read my reflection in the eyes of others. And the message there was always perfection.

My mother, of course, discouraged female vanity. Yes, she loved fabric and fashion; *an agent in Venice who does not know his cloth is no use to any court* is a truth I took with me throughout my life, but only as an arm of statecraft, so that she was careful to separate the importance of appearance - by which she meant dressing for the occasion, posture, tidiness, nothing out of place - from any kind of female flaunting.

But when she arrived in Modena some weeks into our exile, my appearance became her direct concern.

Less pleating at the waist or *try more lace on the shoulders*, she would sigh, as my dressmakers attempted to pin and yank me into dresses I had already outgrown.

Then there was my posture.

'You must stand taller, Isabella! Keep your head up. It will not do to slouch at this point in your growing up. You're beginning to look like a dwarf. Imagine what your betrothed would say if he stood before you now, offering his hand in dance. He would not like to see his future wife such a ... a squat little creature.'

Was she worried about my spine as well as my expanding girth? There was a history of hunchbacks in the Gonzaga family, even I knew that. My husband-to-be's grandmother had given birth to two daughters with backs as curved as snail shells, which made for painful marriage negotiations.

Marriage negotiations. That was the other rift between Beatrice and me.

Since I'd always known whom I would marry, any thought of my husband's status meant little to me. In contrast, Beatrice, adored for her looks over her studies, had cultivated a fierce appetite for French romances in which beauty, chivalry and marriage all went together.

'A prince must fight for his princess, you know.'

With only ourselves for company, our future 'princes' soon became a topic of conversation.

'She must be his choice out of all others. As I was. My betrothed is a great statesman and a famous warrior known and feared by everyone. When we marry, I will give him enough boys to make an army and they will all wear my colours into battle. What about yours?'

But I, who knew more about everything else, had less to say about Francesco Gonzaga. He was neither a statesman nor a famous warrior. Just an older boy, with a passion for hunting and horses.

The story was simple. How when his daughters were very young, Ercole d'Este, Duke of Ferrara, made brilliant matches for them both. First, he wooed and won the Gonzaga family in the state of Mantua with the hand of his elder and already accomplished daughter, Isabella. Yet the ink was barely dry on the contract when an envoy arrived from Milan. Ludovico Sforza, regent to the child duke, was himself looking for a wife and he too had heard tales of this impressive Isabella.

Milan! Beside Venice, she was the greatest power in northern Italy. What could my father do? He couldn't renege on a promise without making the neighbour state of Mantua an enemy. Yet how could he turn down this suitor? So, he offered Milan Beatrice instead. Such diplomatic acumen! Knowing, as I do now, what a liability daughters can be, I applaud him as roundly as history does. Then, however ...

Sforza versus Gonzaga. Milan versus Mantua. Beauty versus cleverness.

No one ever dared make the obvious comment, that the more prestigious union had gone to my younger, lovelier sister.

*

It was this that became clear to me in Modena.

Beatrice, always the princess of her own story, chattered endlessly about her 'prince', with his palaces and his wealth (*Grandfather Ferrante says he has all the greatest artists at his court*) and how though he was only regent now, he would soon become the duke and so she, *she* would be Duchess of Milan. While I - she never said it, she didn't need to - would only ever be a marchesa of little Mantua.

Envy. Another sin I would struggle with all my life.

Meanwhile, the drumbeat of war grew louder. My mother was adamant that all was well, that our army was repulsing the Venetian attack. But she was too devout to master the art of lying and the imprint of her hand in mine in that long black corridor came back to haunt me.

One night I woke with piercing cramps in my stomach. Over the days that followed, it grew worse. Now I was burning up as if a furnace had been lit inside me. There was no pestilence in the town and no one else was sick. It didn't take long before my mother became worried. I, who had never experienced anything that caused me real pain, was beside myself. How could a body hurt so much? Was this what Socrates felt when he took the poison? Did this mean I was going to die?

The urgency with which Mother wrote for doctors to come immediately to Modena is clear from the fact that the letter was in her own hand.

The next few weeks are smoke and haze in my memory. Doctors - three or four - are standing over me, peering and prodding, bleeding me, applying foul-smelling poultices to my stomach. At the beginning, Beatrice is there, bringing marzipan offerings, which she tucks under my pillow. But even the thought of them brings bile to my mouth.

'The tutor is mean to me in Latin. You need to get better.'

Except, it seems, I don't.

One night I wake to find my mother by my bed, her face in the candlelight wet with tears.

'What is it? What is wrong? Am I dying?'

'No, no,' she says lightly. 'No, of course you are not dying.'

'Then why are you crying?'

'Because - it brings me sorrow to see you lain so low. You, who have always been so eagerly alive ...' And she trails off, swallowing the tears.

'How long have you been sitting here?'

'Not long.' By which I know she means the opposite. 'You have been talking in your sleep.'

'What did I say?'

'You spoke in Latin. *Little Tulia*, you said: *Gone for ever. So affectionate, so clever –*'

'– *And so loved.*' I finish it for her. 'Tulia. Cicero's daughter. He was overcome with grief when she died. As you and father would be if I died, wouldn't you?'

'You should not even contemplate such a thing. God would be angry to hear you speak so. A letter is come from your betrothed, Francesco. He is extremely worried and asks that you get better for his sake as well as your own.'

Yes, clearly I am dying. Why else would she have contacted him? Princes and their princesses. Mantua versus Milan. 'And if I don't get better? What would happen then? Will Beatrice have to marry him instead?'

'What? No, of course not. You are not to worry about such things. He would not take anyone but you.'

No, and you would not let him, I think. *Because Milan is by far the better catch.* But I say nothing, just close my eyes and let the fangs sink further in.

In the days that follow, the pain grows less and soon I am encouraged to eat. Yet for the first time in my life, not only am I not hungry but I cannot bear the thought of food. I am dying, after all. I feel curiously light, as if my body might lift off the mattress without my giving it permission. The air around me seems to move and shimmer, as if it is as dizzy as I am. Yet it is not unpleasant. I can almost feel the angel wings getting closer.

'What is wrong? Why won't she eat?'

The words rustle their way down the corridors to the kitchen, where the ovens billow out the sweetest smells: honey, caramel, the cooks have even mastered the sticky scent of marzipan to tempt me. But I will have none of it. Instead of being Isabella the clever, bossy one, I am become Isabella, the radiant, fasting creature, her well-being feared for by everyone,

28

her name in all their prayers. A different kind of attention, with a power all of its own.

Beatrice is no longer allowed to visit. My mother alone keeps vigil. Watching, watching. Until at last she loses patience.

'I don't understand what is happening, Isabella. You are no longer in pain. The fever is gone and yet you lie there like ... like a nun determined to live on the host rather than real food. For such a clever child, this is most stupid behaviour. How can I take you back to your father in this state? What would your future husband say if he knew? He asks constantly after you.'

'He could always find another wife.'

'What?'

'I told you - you could give him Beatrice. I am sure he would like that. Then if by - by some miracle - I did recover ... I could marry Ludovico Sforza instead.'

In my strangely elated state, my mind and my mouth have realigned to show off a different Isabella, one who no longer plays the good girl to make everyone admire her. I think this may be when I truly discovered the power of my own will, and there was a keen pleasure to be had in it.

Beatrice and my betrothed. Mantua and Milan. I have said it twice now. And, of course, she has heard it, my mother. She sits quietly, her hands folded tightly in her lap.

'I wonder,' she says at last. 'While you have been here without me, has anyone said anything to upset you? Beatrice, perhaps?'

'No. No one has said anything at all.'

'Well, something is troubling you.'

'What if it is?'

She pauses. 'If you cannot tell me, Isabella, then you had better confide in God. For this childishness does not suit you. Especially considering the seriousness of this moment.'

'I am ill,' I snap angrily.

'No,' she retorts. 'You *were* ill. This ... whatever it is, is something different.'

Well, there will never be a better time. 'Tell me, Mama, am I lovely?'

'Lovely?' she says, clearly confused. 'Of course you are lovely. Though you will certainly not be if you continue to waste away.'

I shake my head. 'You are wrong,' I say. 'Beatrice is lovely. Me? I am too clever and too large.'

'What you are saying? Who has put this nonsense into your head?'

'No one.' And I have never felt more stubborn. 'But I know what is in front of my eyes. As do my dressmakers.'

Whatever my mother is expecting, it is not this and for a moment she is at a loss as to what to say.

'I've seen paintings when you were young and married Father. You were lovely then. That's what they all show.'

She frowns. 'Cosmè Tura is the court painter,' she replies carefully, and I watch as she thinks it through. 'It is his job to make the Este family shine.'

'Are you saying he lied?'

'I am saying ...' She hesitates. '... that a woman's beauty is as much a reflection of what is inside her, and that is what matters. You of all people through your studies should know that.'

'Ah, yes. Plato!' I say in sullen triumph. 'In which case, I am not even lovely inside!'

'Isabella! What is this madness coming out of your mouth! Perhaps you *are* still ill.'

But I will not have any of it. In the same way that I can never let go of a Latin recitation until I master every word, so am I painfully stubborn on things that offend me. In this, alas, I would grow no wiser. 'When Tura painted *my* portrait, he didn't make me lovely.'

'What portrait? What are you talking about?'

'The one we sent to Mantua. The envoy said as much. *Her face is nothing compared to her mind.* Now I am grown, the truth is evident for all to see. That's why Beatrice will marry into Milan and I will go to Mantua. She is more beautiful.'

'Isabella!' And now my mother's anger rises up to meet mine. 'You will stop this talk immediately. You are too favoured and your destiny is too strong for such ... such tantrums. You have no idea what you are talking about. What has Beatrice said to you?'

'Nothing. I told you, she doesn't need to say anything. I know it anyway.'

She hesitates, staring at me - a tear-stained, angry girl, barely ten years old. I think this may be the moment when she understands that I am both much older and younger than she realised.

'Listen to me,' she says, and her voice is changed now, insistent in a different way. 'The union with Francesco Gonzaga is vital to the future of Ferrara. You will marry him because the state needs an alliance with Mantua on our borders, precisely so that we can stand up better against invaders like Venice, whose soldiers - and I tell you something I had not intended to - are even now attacking the palace of Belriguardo, outside the city gates.'

'But you said -'

She silences me with her hand. 'I said they would be repulsed. And they will. Your father will see to that. But the threat remains. Venice is hungry for more power and influence. Which is why you, the elder and more accomplished daughter, were offered to

Mantua. To create a blood alliance and power block to make both our states secure. Do you understand?'

'But why –'

'I have not finished, Isabella,' she says coldly. 'Whatever Beatrice is or is not, she is young for her age and her education, I fear, has favoured romance over reality. Ludovico Sforza is twenty years older than her. He is not the duke of Milan, only a regent. He has power but no legitimate title, and there will be nothing for her to do but provide decoration for a court that already exists. While your husband will be the ruler of his own state, one that for too long has been without the ministrations of a marchesa, so you will create your own court to promote Mantua's greatness. As first-born child of the Este family, it is the destiny you were born to fulfil. And you would be ungrateful and unworthy not to embrace it. So there will be no further talk of loveliness or the lack of it, do you hear? Or God will see this vanity and surely take you to Him, and your father and I will have wasted ten precious years in the cultivation of an ingrate.'

Ten precious years. In other times in history, I think children are allowed to stay young for longer. But not then, and not me.

I think it was the tone of my mother's voice as much as the weight of her words that jolted me from my rebellion. That and the fact that however stubborn I was, in the end I couldn't quite imagine life without marzipan.

*

I recovered fast, both in body and spirit, and in the weeks that followed, my mother moved from my nurse to my teacher. I was made to sit with her daily as she dictated letters to her scribe. Lessons in the etiquette of correspondence; the soft bribery of gifts, everything from buckets of live eels to decorated prayer books sent to anyone who mattered. How, when necessary, a letter can be both unctuous and demanding at the same time. And how many necessary's there are in a woman's life! I can name you a dozen cardinals who would still be holding bishoprics were it not for the intercession of mothers, aunts or sisters.

My appearance too, now became an urgent project: rinses to lighten my hair, false pieces to thicken its fall, new styles to suit my face and new designs to go with my reduced shape (I would grow stout again soon enough). I was an apprentice in the art of painting myself for others to see. And, as ever, I excelled in the learning. The harder part was to ignore the compliments that came with it. Where once I'd been encouraged to shine in public, now, it seemed, I must deflect praise, returning the warmth to the giver.

'What is endearing in a child is conceit in a woman. Particularly when it comes to her appearance.' My mother's voice is constantly in my ear. The art of being a good wife and consort: the better it is done, the more invisible the effort. I drank it all in eagerly. No longer her recalcitrant daughter, I was now the future Marchesa of Mantua.

Meanwhile, the Venetians made peace and started to withdraw their troops from our territory

'What of Belriguardo?' I ask when the news comes through. 'How is the palace?'

'It will need work. Enemy soldiers take particular pleasure in destroying art. Cosmè Tura is an old man now.' She gives me a sly look. 'I wonder, should we get his apprentice to repaint the frescoes of myself and my ladies, so we look less lovely? We are all old and spreading now.'

But her mocking is not unkind. 'I think Mantua's court painter will be of interest to you in this regard. It's he who decorated the marquis' state chamber with scenes of family history - a marvel on every level. It has a wondrous fresco of your husband's grand-father's court, with his wife, Barbara of Brandenburg. Now, her portrait is most "arresting".' She decorates the word with a little flourish and smiles. Such mischief is new to me. 'Everyone who met her agrees it is a powerful likeness. For she was a woman of considerable character and determination.'

Mantegna: Barbara of Brandenburg.

Character and determination. What delight those sly words offer.

'What did *she* think of it?'

'Ah ... She may have had a few reservations. But then the painter was expensive and she was a most careful housekeeper.'

'Did she dismiss him?'

She laughs. 'No one dismisses Andrea Mantegna. They are all too much in awe of his brush. Though he is, I think, a some-what ... difficult man.'

'Should I have him paint me?'

'Why don't you wait and see. I suspect you will bow before his brilliance. Even the pope is keen to have his services. Come, it's time for you to write to your betrothed. His ambassador visits regularly to enquire about your health and Francesco himself has suggested coming in person to see you. He needs to hear from you directly.'

So it was that I sat down at the desk and took up my quill. It would be best, she insisted, to write the letter in my own hand, so he could judge for himself how well I was recovered.

'What should I say?'

'You are Isabella d'Este, the future Marchesa of Mantua, addressing the man who will be your husband. Say what is fitting for you both. Though not too many Latin flourishes. He is more a soldier than a scholar.'

Such care I put into it. And when it was finished, I read its success in my mother's eyes, the smallest of curves playing around her lips as she tried not to laugh. How I did like to please her.

I can never convey the thanks I owe to Your Lordship for the visits made on your behalf by your ambassador, for as soon as I was told of his solicitations, I found myself completely cured …

... Yet when I learned that Your Lordship had in mind to come all the way to Modena to check if my illness might be lasting longer, I almost wanted to be sick again, just to able to see you!

In the reading room, my flamboyantly dressed scholar sits back from her desk shaking her head and laughing under her breath. This is a moment to savour: the first letter in the hand of Isabella d'Este to have survived. Ten years old and my script is still somewhat unformed, every letter decorated with self-conscious curlicues or flourishes, each phrase marinated in courtly sentiment, a mix of flirtation and flattery altogether too arch for my age. Except that is precisely what is so rewarding for anyone who reads it. For there is a whole history behind such coy dissembling. I see that now in her smile, though I could never have known it then. It is the way in which girls of families like mine were encouraged to grow up: precisely by pretending to be what we had yet to become. And in that training, the art of letter writing was a vital process, the mastery of artifice as much as any expression of intimacy.

As for its effect on my future husband? Well, if he replied - and he surely would have done - I remember nothing of it. Though it must have been suitably courteous, for he had the best of scribes to help him.

Still, I suspect by then his mind was on other things. Or perhaps I should say other bodies, for those eight years between us marked out different paths towards our marriage in so many ways.

IV

Mantegna: Francesco Gonzaga as a young man.

Francesco Gonzaga. The problem with telling a life already lived is that the future gets in the way of the past. When I think of him now, it is like watching a pack of tarot cards dealt out on to a table: some good, some bad, but the last, overwhelming all the others, is always a heavily disfigured man trapped in his room, self-pity igniting fury in his pain. It is not an image to go with a successful union. And successful it was, at least in the things that mattered. In which case, that final card must be erased to do him justice.

How to bring him alive then, this rough, difficult husband of mine? There are his letters. Over the years, I have read most of them; even the private ones have found their way on to scholars' desks. But words were never his forte. No, Francesco Gonzaga was always a man of action. The hunter and the soldier.

A few images still exist, I believe. And they are accurate enough in their way. Of course, likenesses of powerful men are not required to flatter. Borso d'Este's chins are evidence of that. Still, nothing I ever saw quite captures the magnetic ugliness of Francesco.

He was not tall - on the ground, barely an inch or so more than me - and a touch of that hereditary curve had passed into his spine, though his costumes and armour were designed to disguise it well enough. Close to, his features were too big for his face: his forehead bulged outwards; he had an ill-formed fleshy nose that lifted in a most unlikely manner at the tip; and his eyes seemed to push their way out of their sockets, like a fish. His hair was a helmet of raven black reaching to his shoulders and cut thick over his eyebrows, like a cliff. His beard and moustache were both equally dense and the back of his hands had tufts of black fuzz growing out of them. Ugly, yes, when put into words.

Yet, when you looked at him, or rather when he looked at you, that is not how it felt. In his prime, Francesco Gonzaga had an energy, a heat that came off him as if there was fire in his blood. And when it was directed at you, the air itself seemed to quiver as if a hail of tiny arrows was hitting your skin. There were those who considered it an assault, for he could be boorish with it. And men in particular could take offence, for like dogs they smell threat or competition easily. Yet he was not stupid, not by any means, and on a horse or in front of a group of soldiers he could weave a kind of magic.

And by this point in his life, I have no doubt it was working on women too.

*

With the war finally over and the palaces rebuilt, my father set out to show off Ferrara's power as a centre of culture. He commissioned a vernacular translation of a comedy by the Roman playwright Plautus: a public performance to take place in the palace courtyard for the whole city to watch - actors, costumes, stage sets, even musical interludes, the last of which I was to oversee. Did I mention yet my early prowess with the lute and the lyra da braccio? My musical skills were not inconsiderable.

And the guest of honour? My husband-in-waiting, now established as the reigning Marquis of Mantua.

*

'You've changed, Isabella d'Este.'

Placed next to him at the banqueting table, I smile winningly, as I've been trained to, and wait to receive further compliments. His attention, however, is already back on his food.

'You've changed too,' I say after a while. Has anyone ever told him? He must know, surely, how very ugly he is.

'I am the marquis of my own state now.' He grins, waiting for me to congratulate him. But I am still owed a little praise. Finally, he prods. 'So what would you say about me?'

'I would say ... that you seem to like girls better now.' (It does not help that he has been extravagantly charming to Beatrice that very afternoon. *He's most courteous, but, oh, did you see how his eyes stick out? Urgh!* Her own husband would be no prettier, but she has yet to meet him.)

'Or maybe it is that I like you,' he says airily, then turns again to his plate. I watch as he skewers a large lump of meat with his knife, pushing it into his mouth. A small dribble of juice appears at the edge of his lips. How much he enjoys eating! It is one thing we will share, though his manners, never perfect, will grow worse with soldiering. 'So,' he says, chewing loudly. 'Remind me again how old you are.'

'I am still eight years younger than you.'

'Almost thirteen then. There! See my prowess with mathematics!'

'How is your Latin?' I counter.

He laughs. 'I haven't met a soldier yet who speaks it.'

'Julius Caesar? Pompeii? Augustus? Sulla?'

'Never been on the field with any of them!'

'And Virgil?'

'Who did he fight?'

'No one! He is one of Rome's finest poets.'

'I know.' He grins. 'And he came from Mantua. I know that too. If you feel so strongly about him, you can always put up a statue to him. Now it's my turn. How is your horse-riding, Donna Isabella?'

'Much improved,' I say fiercely.

'Good. Then we will ride together. Tomorrow.'

'Tomorrow, I cannot. I have to work with the musicians. I am responsible for the musical interludes!'

He groans slightly.

'You're not looking forward to the play?'

'Don't tell your father.'

'You shouldn't worry. It has been very well translated.'

'I know, I have heard. I have also heard it's rather long.'

What would my mother have me say here? Accommodate without lying. 'No one knows. There's been no chance to time it.'

'In which case, it won't matter if the music is longer or shorter. I will speak to your father and we will ride tomorrow.'

*

Though endless poets will romance and flatter me, both to my face and on paper, that morning in the forest is the nearest I will come to a scene of courtship. In the winter dawn, a sweet Ferrarese mist whispers around our feet, thickening into fog as we leave the city gates, until it swallows everything around us so that we can barely see what is in front of our eyes.

He keeps me close by him. Immediately behind are three of his men and three of my mother's ladies, the echoes of their horses' hooves ghostly in the rising dawn. His mount, jet black and exceedingly handsome, seems to obey his commands without him ever giving any. My own, unnerved by the weather, or perhaps the beauty of its companion, is snorting and whinnying.

A few hundred yards on there is a break in the layer of fog, letting in enough light for the path to become clear, revealing an army of skeleton trees on both sides. We have planned to ride as far as Belriguardo. The palace is now rebuilt and I am going to show him its paintings, but we are barely a quarter of the way there when he gives a shout to his men and suddenly spurs his horse on, urging mine along with him.

We move into a fast trot and when I start to lag, he yells, 'I thought you said you could ride. Give her her head. She will enjoy it.'

We cover ground quickly, the air fierce on our faces, and when he finally brings us to a halt we are isolated inside a swirling cloud. No sign or sound of any one following. In the silence as we catch our breath, a solitary woodpecker taps out a staccato message of welcome.

'You have a good seat,' he says, openly pleased with himself. 'When you come to Mantua, I'll find you a proper horse. Yours is too timid a beast. So, here we are, betrothed and alone in a wild forest. Are you afraid?'

'Why should I be afraid?' My tone reveals my indignation, for all this was clearly planned before we left. 'I know the path much better than you.'

'Still, anything could happen. D'you remember the first time you and I met?'

'No,' I shrug. 'And I think neither do you.'

'Not true. We played a game together and you cheated so you could win. No, don't look like that. You did. I didn't like you much then. But now ...'

And he grins. Such a swagger there is to him. There are those who will say that ours was a good match, that I might have done damage to a weaker man, but all I could think then was that he will always be eight years older than me.

He pulls my horse close (the animal, infuriatingly, does everything he says) and leans wide over the saddle, putting his hand behind my head and pulling me towards him. His lips are fleshy and his hair harsh on my skin, so that I have no idea if I like it or not.

'There!' he says, evidently much pleased with himself. 'How was that?'

How many times have you done this before? I think. It's not fair I am so ignorant. 'Your beard needs cutting,' I say firmly, determined not to be intimidated. But he is in his element now.

'Let's try again. Differently.'

This time, he pushes his tongue between my lips. And as he does so, I get a smell off him - breath or saliva? - that offends my nose. I have a sudden image of King Ferrante with Beatrice on his lap and feel bile rising in my throat.

'There!' Does he notice? If he does, it doesn't bother him. He settles himself in his seat again with a bright smile. 'The whole of Mantua is waiting for you to arrive. It doesn't suit a city to be without a marchesa, and my mother, God rest her soul, is long dead. They tell such stories about you, Isabella d'Este. A prodigy of learning, so clever, so advanced. And now she knows how to kiss! A fine new skill, I think.'

'Not a fit one for a courtier when done in such an underhand manner!' I spit back.

He shouts with laughter. 'I've heard you have a temper. Another man might almost be worried. Don't glower at me, Isabella. I'm not as uncouth as you think. Ours will be an excellent alliance. Leave me to my horses and my soldiering and you will have the run of the palace. It needs a woman's touch. You might even learn how to handle the great Mantegna better than I do. Though I can offer one trick.'

'What is that?' Because though I want to be cross, I also want to know.

'Tell him that his brother-in-law, Bellini, is working on the same subject at the same moment, and he will flay himself alive to do it faster and better.'

'Giovanni Bellini? But he's the greatest painter in Venice,' I say, parroting my mother. 'We should have *him* as our court artist.'

'Not a chance. The man never leaves Venice, and they would kill each other in the same town. You must make do with grumpy Andrea. I think you'll find him good enough for your taste. And now - my Lady Isabella ...'

And he raises his voice as we hear the echo of horses' hooves through the mist. 'We must locate our companions from whom we were somehow separated in this *damn* fog.'

The horses catch up with us, the men grinning broadly, the ladies anxious. I sit tall in my saddle and greet them brightly.

Just a gallop in the morning mist, my smile says. Nothing to worry anyone. Certainly nothing to tell my mother about.

'A gentle trot home, I think.' Francesco takes the lead, me next to him. 'We mustn't hold up this performance we've come so far to enjoy.' And then, under his breath, 'If I fall asleep and snore, kick me hard. I am told I frighten soldiers in the battle camp with the sound.' And he laughs. Thus, I gain a valuable lesson to take into my marriage: when my husband gets his own way, he can be an enjoyable companion.

In the end, he boasts too much about his snores; they are no louder than anyone else's. Those scholars who gleefully mark it out as the first proper theatre performance of the age didn't have to sit through it. There was, I am sure, a clever story buried somewhere underneath: identical twin brothers separated at birth cause all manner of havoc by being mistaken for one another.

'A comedy of errors! As bawdy as it is profound,' my father declared as we took our seats.

It's possible the fault was in the translation, for Italian uses many more words than Latin. Or that the scene changes and the musical interludes took too long (which they did). Myself, I think the ancients had a different sense of humour. And time. By the fifth hour, even my father was starting to slump in his chair and the citizens had long gone home, as it was past nightfall by the time it finished. Those who were still awake applauded loudly, which woke the rest of us, and such was the relief that everyone announced it to be a great success.

'A lesson for any enlightened court,' my father confided in me a few days later. 'Not everything that is edifying will be appreciated by everyone. But that should not stop a great ruler from aspiring.'

As for my mother, she was too sharp-eyed for the things that mattered to dwell on failure. 'I think you and the marquis enjoyed each other's company, yes?'

'Yes,' I say, because her question contains the answer that I know she wanted.

She holds my eye. But I have no intention of going further. I am thirteen and whether I like it or not, that means I am almost ready for marriage.

She, however, knew better, and when official overtures were made to bring me to Mantua early, so that I could become *accustomed to court life* in readiness for my role as marchesa, her reply was a perfect construction of courtesy and guile, *suggesting* that it would surely place too heavy a burden on such a virile young man to resist the temptations of his virginal young bride-to-be living so close.

Later in life, I will take great joy in watching my lap dogs look after their young: gentle cuffing to protect them from danger and a rough tongue to care for their appearance. For such was the wonder of my mother.

MARRIAGE

V

The wedding of Isabella d'Este and Francesco Gonzaga.

How many times have I reached this moment with scholars?

There is no lack of documentation. Far from it. Envoy's dispatches, family letters, guest reports, the spectacle is all there for the retelling: ceremonies, processions, concerts, entertainments, banquets. Oh, so many banquets.

Of course, we did not invent such excess. I could name you dozens of unions and families richer than ours. Nevertheless, we embraced it. How could we not? What better way to celebrate status than through extravagance? I've seen historians so gorge themselves on this feast of facts that all they do is vomit back great gobbets of it, as if the weight of the fabric or the number of precious stones will somehow bring alive the people wearing them.

But for the curious, there's another story to tell about weddings. One that looks beneath the surface of show. Indeed, it rather appeals to the bargain hunter in me, for it teases out veins of hidden parsimony on both sides. My own wedding chests, for instance, thirteen of them, were packed with dresses, most of which came with flamboyant detachable sleeves, so that one outfit could cunningly turn into two or three others. Then there was my dowry (such a thing was always a test of a family's status).

My father spent years of canny diplomacy promising loudly more than he delivered. She has the envoy's letter on her desk now to prove it, dry wit singing out from bright words.

Their excellencies love their daughter so much they cannot do enough for her ... If you'd heard their eloquent excuses as they complained of the cost of war and depressed times, you'd be convinced they had every intention of giving much more ...

No. The truth is that the Duke of Ferrara married off his precious, clever daughter cheaply. And when rumour of that got around – which of course it did – it was hard to tell if he was more enraged or delighted that people knew.

The Gonzagas practised their own deception in return. Half of my husband's wardrobe for the wedding – the gold belts, medallions, jewel-encrusted scabbards and sashes – were not his own, borrowed instead from his richer brother-in-law in Urbino, while the blazing tapestries of the Fall of Troy that decorated the great chamber in which we banqueted would be packed up immediately afterwards and returned to my grandfather's court in Naples.

*

At home in Ferrara, I sensed a growing anxiety as the event grew closer. My mother, I know, was distressed about the loss of me, though we never spoke of it. But she was also worried about Beatrice. The marriage to Milan was being pushed ever further into the future and there was an uneasiness about the whole affair. Rumour moved like smoke through the castle: the lovely Beatrice was not wanted now. Ludovico Sforza had become so besotted with a new mistress that he could not bear to take his eyes off her, even to become a husband to a ripe young wife. Beatrice herself took the whole thing badly, moping about in her rooms like a lost princess in a French romance.

It seemed I was the luckier one after all.

The timing of my leaving, like every other important date in our lives, was in the gift of our court astrologer. A most decrepit man - when he dined with us, he put as much food into his beard as his mouth - he spent long days consulting the stars before announcing that February 21st 1490 would be the most auspicious day for me to travel by boat to Mantua, even though there was ice floating on the rivers and the churches were stacking dead bodies in the crypts till the ground thawed out enough to bury them.

Anyone who knows Venice knows of Bucintoro, the great gilded ship that carries the senators out to the lagoon every year to throw a ring into the water to mark the marriage of the state to the Mediterranean. In Ferrara we did not rule the sea, but we did have dominion over the Po river, and that day we travelled by our own gilded barge, rowed by two dozen galley men, prisoners picked for their strength and the honour of earning their freedom with a purse from my father at the end.

Mantua in the 1500s.

As we went, the mist lifted off the water, a winter sun painted the ice flows silver and everywhere along the banks crowds of people came out to cheer our progress, buoyed up by a cartload of free food and wine. Another lesson to be learned in statecraft.

By late afternoon, Mantua appeared in front of us like a jewel rising out of the shining water.

In the days and weeks that followed I was the centre of attention, people flattering me endlessly, extolling my beauty and my talents. Which, of course, I liked. Yet so much was happening, so fast, that there were moments, I know, when I grew fractious, even petulant.

And in the midst of all this celebration, the alliance between the Este and the Gonzaga dynasties was sealed with an act of sexual consummation.

VI

Raphael: Study for the Villa Farnesina.

These days, what intrigues me most about my encounters with the future is how each new present has a different curiosity towards the past.

For the longest time, what we did in bed was of no interest at all to those who came after us. Indeed, the earliest waves of scholars who sought out my papers when the archive first opened were a good deal more reticent about such things than we were.

My first sustained archive encounter - how well I remember her - was with a ferocious English woman in corseted skirts and feathered hats, who spoke fluent Italian as if half her mouth was sewn together. The male scholars laughed at her when they were alone, but never in her presence, for she had the stamina of a team of oxen. The reading room was upstairs then, its walls lined with wood panelling, which had absorbed years of the smell of unwashed monks' bodies. I noticed it long before she did. In time, she took to wearing more perfume - an overblown gardenia scent, I remember, a hint of which remained in my folders long after she'd finished with them. Julia Cartwright was her name, though on her archive ticket she spelled it Giulia (how English people do seem to love us Italians), and when she came to write my life - two whole volumes it took her - she flattered and soaked me in praise at every turn. More than I deserved, I would say now - for unspiced adulation makes for dull reading after a while.

However, it would never have occurred to *Giulia* Cartwright to venture past the bedroom door.

There had been times, before then, when some were even affronted by our portrayal of the human body. I remember once seeing copied images of Michelangelo's figures from the Sistine Chapel, each and every one of them with their genitals painted over! My first thought was that Lutheran heretics must have taken over Rome after my death, for they were always the most violent prudes. I realised only afterwards it was the work of our own good church, panicking - rather late - to address its reputation for corruption.

Recently, though, there has been a growing interest in what took place between the sheets. Most especially when it comes to women.

How much did we know? What pleasure did we feel? Or how much pain? I've witnessed dozens of scholars sifting through records of court cases, sniffing out sexual details and misdemeanours. What positions did the Church allow in marriage? How much sodomy took place? Men on men. Or men on women, as a way to stop children. Both actions were crimes, of course, though the policing of one was more lenient than the other. The business of courtesans, courtship by rape, public brothels, changing laws on prostitution ... it seems this present cannot get enough of it all. In the same way that people once scrutinised our spiritual lives, now they strive to get into bed with us.

What, then, will this new scholar of mine make of this moment?

There is nothing immediately in my correspondence to help her. A union as important as ours called for there to be witnesses of the deed, but my mother argued that on account of my age - I was still fifteen - we should be granted privacy. The next morning, a group of courtiers entered the room singing bawdy marriage songs, as was the custom of the day, and at some point the bed linen was taken away for inspection. Proof, though, was hardly necessary. Francesco's beaming face and my fierce smile were enough. Every night in a thousand beds all over Italy, new young husbands and wives were performing the same rite, albeit soiling less expensive sheets.

Still, if she were to consider what she already knows about me, I think she might try and imagine what did, or did not, happen in that marriage chamber.

Yes, I was young. But I was not ignorant, nor unprepared. I'd witnessed the violent dance of love in all kinds of animals, the strutting, the squawking, the braying. My mother had laid out the facts with clarity and, unlike in many unions, my husband and I were not strangers to each other. I knew - and if I didn't, that ride in the forest had told me - that just as I brought virginity to the marriage bed, so he would come with expertise. Or at the very least, practice. At eight years older, his education would have been remiss if he hadn't had some kind of tutor in the bedroom as well as the study.

A courtier poet I patronised - he became my secretary in later life - once composed a monograph on the nature of physical love and dedicated it to me! (It sounds unlikely, I know, but it is true - the man's name was Mario Equicola, I could direct her to the document now, it is surely somewhere in the archive.) In it, he writes about the superiority of women in such matters; how their bodies are made for more sexual pleasure than men, because they have more areas of flesh that respond to the touch.

Well, I am guilty of teasing now. So, let me say this clearly. What happened between Francesco and myself that night was not awful. Neither was it wonderful. Rather, it was ... well, unrewarding. For me, at least.

Would it assuage your curiosity if I took you with me into the chamber? I am not so prudish that I cannot return there.

There are a few candles, of course, to soften the darkness, and a number of sweetly perfumed globes hanging from the ceiling. Alas, they are little match for his smell. I had become aware of it earlier, during the ceremonies: how the sweat of flesh, marinated too long in heavy garments, overwhelms the spice of his perfume. But again, it is the saliva of his kisses, now mixed with a surfeit of rich food and wine, that offends most. Perhaps he too was nervous - he had, I remember, drunk a great deal - though he showed no sign of it.

Then there is his body. With his clothes released, the coarse black hair that crawled across the back of his hands now exploded all over his torso. The only naked male figures I had seen until then were smooth Roman statues, or images of Christ or the martyred St Sebastian, and their skin was always sweetly hairless. Nothing in life had prepared me for coupling with a minotaur.

Not that he acted like one. There was no violence. He didn't force me. Nor did he reject me or seem to find me in any way wanting. My nightshift, of the finest lawn and lace, was designed to draw attention to my full breasts, which he clearly enjoyed, kneading them like lumps of dough, and sucking at my nipples as if I was his wet nurse rather than his wife, followed by much gasping and growling in the act itself and then a collapsing in triumph. It was over not long after it had begun. He seemed pleased enough with both himself and me, and was half asleep before I could push him off.

As for pain? There was none. Or rather, none that I was not ready for. But when it comes to pleasure? Well, if I am honest, I had felt more translating Cicero or Ovid.

Perhaps if I had been more lovely? Or he more skilful? I know that there are men who seem to pleasure themselves by pleasuring women. But that was not my husband. He was young and impatient and had not been taught to think of anyone but himself. He may even have seen it as a compliment to me, that he was at ease enough to be himself: Francesco Gonzaga, twenty-four-year-old warrior and Marquis of Mantua. A man other women have been pleased enough to have in their bed. Why should his wife feel any differently?

Is this such a shocking story? I don't think so. Though poets might choose to imagine all of the fairer sex turning into Venus when the night falls, I believe most of us women know better.

Later, when I saw his 'others', it struck me that they were quite unlike me. Physically, he favoured the willowy type, fine long necks and billowing fair hair, women with a talent for simpering; flirty, with a touch of the claw underneath. It's possible they enjoyed doing it with him too. That sizzle of energy, the swagger, the confidence, all this they may have found irresistible, so that their hunger matched his. Alas, I never had anything in common with such women, though I usually employ one or two among my ladies to give zest to the court, watching with disbelief as even the cleverest of men follow them around with their tongues hanging out.

There are other things that this new scholar of mine might say about me as she gets to know me: that I was a young woman who had grown up too much in love with her own mind, had lived too long happily within it to yearn for the pleasures of the flesh. Or, with the passing of time, would it be more honest to put it another way? Did I ever feel jealous of those who enjoyed it more? To which the answer must be yes, sometimes. Men and women on fire for each other have a radiance that lights up everything around them. In poetry, it burns off the page. Our painters, who were giving such new life to the Virgin and all the saints, were also joyfully presiding over the birth of Venus, and you would need to be blind not to notice the way that men fell on their knees to *her* in a quite a different kind of worship.

I once came across a drawing in the collection of the artist Giulio Romano, done by his master, Raphaello Sanzio: a red chalk sketch of a naked woman, her hands held up around her as she turns halfway towards us as if in a dance. Young - not much older than I was then, she radiated such unconscious grace, such delight in her own body, that I couldn't imagine any man not wanting to lie down with her. But that was never who I was. And there is no good to be had from pretending any differently.

Throughout my life, I would be at my happiest outside the bedroom. I have made my peace with that and if those who study me are to be true to my voice, then they will too.

Over the coming nights, he came regularly to my bed, until, when the celebrations were finally over, he left on a hunting trip and I did not see him for days.

With the guests gone and everyone busy cleaning, unpacking and wanting my attention - *Where to put this, my lady? How does the new marchesa want to arrange that?* - I found sorrow creeping over me like a slow mist. My husband's life had not changed at all. But I was a stranger in a strange place and all those I loved and held most dear were no longer here.

It was now that I met my new secretary, Benedetto Capilupi. Such a beanpole he was, his long face seemingly impenetrable of feeling: another requisite of a good diplomat.

> *You will forgive me if I do not write now in my own hand, but I am much occupied ...*

He'd been chosen by my husband, so initially I feared he might be some kind of spy assigned to watch over my behaviour.

> *Here, my illustrious lord looks well on me and no pleasure is lacking ...*

Yet even in that first encounter, what I recall is his kindness. Because as the words flowed out of me in my letter to Beatrice - he wrote at least as fast as I could speak - any flowery politeness fast dissolved into pain.

*Yet I find I do not enjoy these things with the contentment
I would if Your Ladyship was near ...*

It is late in the day. Most of the desks in the archive are empty
and a certain somnambulance has settled over the room. Yet
the air around my serpent-haired scholar is charged with
concentration.

*... I so regret being deprived of your sweet company that it feels
as if my soul has left my body.*

She is on her second reading of the letter. From the speed of
her progress, I suspect Italian is not her mother tongue, though
even native speakers struggle with the mix of calligraphy and
what is now for them arcane language. Still, I cannot fault her
attention, for these words in particular reward study. Partly for
the bond they show between myself and Beatrice - how I missed
my sweet-natured sister in those first weeks - and partly because
their melancholy tone offers clues to that ... What shall we call it?
Unsatisfactory consummation?

If a new wife has been introduced to heaven in her
husband's arms, would she really be felled by such cruel stabs
of homesickness? For that is the pain I feel again as I read my
words over her shoulder. Surely, she must feel it too.

I can still see the room - a nondescript chamber - in which
Benedetto and I sat that morning. I think the fact I had yet to find
a place for myself in the castle was part of my early distress. The

dead marchesa's apartments had been made ready for my arrival, but it was an age since there had been a woman's taste at court and my husband's sense of fashion was not acute. Right from the start, I longed for rooms of my own, somewhere I could display works of art such as my mother had collected, a chamber to sit and play my lute, to read or study, the kind of place my father and other male rulers had. But that February day - it was cold and raining outside, I remember - there was no such comfort to be had.

My dismay at your departure was so great that I was quite beside myself ... and since I cannot visit you personally, I will do so continually in spirit and with letters. And I beg you to treat me similarly, for I could have no greater pleasure than to hear from you daily.

Capilupi's script is elegant but small. Like all scribes, he was trained to the profession young, so that by the time he came to me he was very practised and the letters that were duplicated into the copy books that she is reading now are as word-perfect as the originals.

Commend me to our illustrious mother, and each night when you go to receive her blessing, receive it also for me and kiss her hand in my name.

After I have finished, Benedetto gives me a few moments to compose myself, before reading my words back to me so I can check his accuracy. He chooses not to notice the glistening in my eyes. But when I tell him that I must now write to my brothers and cousins (it seems suddenly important to me that I stay in touch with everyone who reminds me of the life I have left), he says softly:

'If I may offer a word of advice, Your Ladyship? You have expressed yourself with great spirit here, and, as you say, you have many other calls on your time. Perhaps you might allow me to copy a few of these loving phrases to others. In this way, they can be dispatched faster. And so faster will come all their replies.'

She would do well to become fluent in Benedetto's style, for his quiet diplomatic skills, even some of his language, will weave their way into my own correspondence. His script on the page now, for instance, allows me to picture the man himself: his wry smile, his diamond-sharp attention. He gave his life to the Gonzaga family. He once showed me the pad of his writing thumb. It was discoloured and deformed, as if a spoon of flesh had been scooped out of it, the skin worn dark and hard as a nut from grasping the quill. We would be together many years (he should have retired long before he did, for his health was failing him) because I couldn't bear to lose him and I know he felt the same about me.

My dismay at your departure was so great, it feels as if my soul has left my body.

I watch over her bowed head as she copies parts of the letter carefully into her notebook. I like the intensity of her concentration, and I also like the neatness of her own script. The book's pages are unlined, so that she must construct her own invisible lines, just as we did.

I think people no longer have scribes. In fact, it's possible that some have given up using pencil or pen and ink altogether in favour of this new writing machine that is so popular now. It is one of the things that endears her to me, this new scholar of mine, that she does not use such a thing. For all that it is remark-able in the way the pressing of raised letters turns into words on a moving page, I find the endless tap-tap-tapping an irritating intrusion into centuries of quiet study. In our lives, whole worlds were contained within the covers of hand-copied books, and the libraries we laboriously collected were, in their way, sacred spaces, so that the scratch of pencil or ink on paper is for me almost a gateway into the past.

Sitting above her now, watching her hand move across the page, I notice how amid those tumbled curls there is the thinnest sliver of grey tugging at her roots.

Ah! Along with your scent, I could help you there, I think.

But not yet.

No. I am far too young still to care about such things.

VII

It is the destiny you were born to fulfil.

I was never one to wallow in despair, and even if I had been my mother's voice remained loud in my ear.

You will create your own court to promote Mantua's greatness.

My own court! If the marriage chamber was a labour I would never take to, then here was my compensation, the work I had been trained for. I'd brought with me new cooks, new seamstresses and new musicians, all of whom needed settling. I was in need of more ladies. Local ones this time. Once again, my mother's voice guided me. I picked from only the best families: looks, wit, loyalty the obvious qualifications. There were certain others as well, but I will get to them in good time.

I made a short tour of the lands that comprised my new state, and everywhere I went people lined the route, cheering and welcoming me. Mantua had been without a marchesa for too long and they wanted to love me.

With the household in place, I started on my life's work. I found what I was looking for soon enough: two small semi-derelict chambers within the castle, one on top of the other, connected by a steep small staircase. My allowance - carefully managed - would cover the art I intended to buy. But to take over the rooms themselves, I would need my husband's permission.

I picked my moment carefully. The court was in the highest of spirits: Francesco had been approached by the Venetian senate to become commander-in-chief of its army, bringing with it a most generous purse. At twenty-four years old, it marked him out as Italy's foremost soldier.

'Before I accept I must visit your father, the duke, to make sure of his good will. Then there will be business to sort out in Venice. You will be content here on your own?'

'Of course. Though I shall miss you,' I add quickly, hearing the echo of my mother's applause in the background.

'I am sure there is more than enough to keep you busy. And when I get back, perhaps you will have news for me, yes?'

News. My smile does not waver.

By which, of course, he means am I with child. Which I am not, because that very day I have started bleeding. But he does not need to know that. Or rather, I do not know how to tell him.

'Perhaps,' I say brightly.

'Before our marriage, I would leave my brother in charge of affairs when I was gone.' He hesitates. Oh, but I have been waiting for this moment.

'Certainly you must consult with my father,' I say firmly. 'But he will offer no protest, of that I can assure you. The Estes and the Gonzagas stand together on all such things now. The fact that Venice needs you - and there is no better soldier in Italy - means she will be an ally to both families rather than a foe. As to the daily business of government here, obviously, my lord, you must decide. However ...' I shrug. 'My mother took care of the running of the state whenever my father was away. There was never anything he did not know, as she wrote to him daily, and every decision waited on his approval first.' *Though*, I think, but do not add, *he sometimes made mistakes.* 'So I could ...'

I stop, but only because I can see how much he is enjoying the performance.

'Ha! It seems I have not only a wife, but a chief minister too. And how serious she is about it all!' He grins and that dark energy crackles around him again. 'Very well. The job is yours. Just don't make your letters too long. It's hard to read screeds when you are in the saddle! Now -'

'Before you go, my lord, there is one thing ...'

Isabella's first grotta, Castello di San Giorgio (Ducal Palace).

'My God, but the place is a ruin,' he says, picking his way across crumbling floorboards. 'What will you do here?'

'The chamber beneath here will be my *grotta*. Where I shall put objects of beauty I intend to collect: works of art, antiquities, old statues and the like.'

'Old statues and the like! I hope my wife doesn't feel the need to surround herself with naked Apollos so soon after her marriage. Some might question the virility of the captain general of the Venetian army!' And he laughs noisily, for of course such an inference is ludicrous to him.

'You needn't worry,' I counter gaily. 'The only naked Apollo worth having is in the collection of Cardinal della Rovere and he would rather die than part with it. No, I am thinking more of busts, medallions, curiosities, that kind of thing. Treasures that I might show to visitors, as a feature of the Gonzaga court.'

'I see,' he says, amused by my fervent seriousness. 'And this room we are in now?'

'This room?' I turn on the spot. 'In this room, I shall commission special paintings for the walls - five or six of them, I think - and my desk will be here at the window overlooking the lake, where I will write letters, play music with my ladies, read or study, poetry and Latin.'

'You are intending to create a studiolo for yourself!'

'Oh no, not really, not that at all.'

Isabella's studiolo. Every scholar who studies me knows the word, though it means little enough now. Just as these days women sit next to men in the archive, so doubtless they have rooms of their own for contemplation or study. But then ... oh, then the very idea of a woman wanting such a thing was a kind of heresy. Throughout my life - usually behind my back - people will cite it as evidence of arrogance, my lack of womanly virtue. But to his credit, Francesco will never be one of them.

'Well, whatever it is to be, you'll have a splendid view,' he says, crossing to the window. 'You recognise it, yes? The backdrop to Mantegna's painting in the chapel, the Death of the Virgin: she is lying on a bier underneath this very window, so that as you look at her, you look out on to the lake of Mantua itself.'

'Oh, I didn't realise -'

'No, well, you didn't spend half your life desperate for something to distract you while the priest droned on. I used to imagine myself on one of the boats, decked out for war, setting sail on a crusade to fight the infidels with a cargo of the best Gonzaga horses.' He grins. 'At least I still have the horses.'

'And you are Italy's foremost soldier,' I say, but the same compliment paid twice never quite shines as brightly.

'Well, it seems you've made your choice.' He turns from the window. 'It'll need a lot of work.'

A sudden scrabbling erupts from under the floor and two fat mice rear up from a hole, darting across the broken boards, running over my feet as they head for another cavity.

'Ah!'

He laughs as I fall into his arms. 'What, my fierce scholar of a wife is frightened of mice! Who would have thought it, eh?'

And we are both laughing now, enjoying each other's company - a newly married young couple with a lifetime of collaboration ahead of them.

'Though I must say, I rather like it,' he says thickly as his embrace closes around me. I feel a shiver pass between us. Venice, Ferrara, the call of the road, suddenly it can all wait. Another kind of conquest is on offer.

He pushes the door shut with a backward kick of his foot and pulls me even closer. I feel him harden against my skirts as his mouth moves towards mine. How many times have we done this already in the bedchamber? Yet those encounters are in the dark so that I don't have to stare into those bulging eyes.

What? Are we to couple now, here in this room? No, no. This is to be my space, where I will be myself, Isabella alone. No place here for his grunting and groaning.

I let out a little gasp of relief, putting my hands against his chest, laughing as I push him away, as if I am all a flutter with it still. For a second my response confuses him and he resists, then, deliberately, lets me go and stands watching me as I dust off my skirts.

Beneath our feet, the mice continue their noisy games. I give a further little gasp, but this time I do not jump and he does not offer. How much does he realise, this stupid, clever husband of mine? Much more, I think, than I gave him credit for then. In my defence, I was still very young.

'And when it is finished, you will be able to imagine me sitting here,' I say breathlessly, turning to the window in an attempt to bring us back together, '... looking out on to the lake as I write my daily letters to you, everything you need to know about government. Though I will make sure they are never too long,' I add playfully. 'Since you will be reading them in the saddle.'

*

That same afternoon, we say our goodbyes. In the courtyard, his men are saddled and waiting, their laughter already much coarser in nature than when they were in the company of ladies.

He joins them eagerly and the household comes out to wave them off.

The Marquis of Mantua is the professional soldier again. And Isabella d'Este, his new court wife. Our letters over the coming weeks will be full of cheer as well as business, for we are both in our element now.

Which, though it may sound like an excuse, is not. It was the partnership we were born to create.

Any further 'news' would have to wait.

*

Not long after, Beatrice was finally wedded to her regent duke, and with my ladies I travelled to Milan to celebrate the union.

As a bride, my little sister was as lovely as ever, her radiance like the bloom on ripe fruit, yet in temperament she remained frustratingly childish. She flung her arms around me, pulling me around her apartments, eager to show off every jewel and precious gift. Everywhere she went, she was surrounded by admirers and magnificence, all of which she accepted with glee, though she was prone to tears as easily as laughter.

When she was in the company of her husband, however, she became coy, almost skittish, growing visibly nervous if he got too close or in any way touched her. More than once I caught my mother's eye moving between both of us. What was she thinking? That she had raised one daughter too old for her years and another too young?

Whatever the problem, it didn't seem to bother her husband. On the contrary, Ludovico Sforza treated his young bride with an air of amused gentleness. He was a most peculiar looking man; thick-set build with skin as dark as a Turk and a mane of hair to rival that of my husband. His treatment of his young nephew, the rightful heir whom he kept in soft imprisonment in a nearby palace, had earned him the reputation of a cunning thug. Yet face to face he had a wit and a warmth that made him hard to dislike. And taste. Oh yes! Ludovico Sforza had taste. As well as the money to go with it. His palace at Pavia overflowed with the most beautiful art and objects, which he was only too happy to show to anyone with an interest.

'I see you have appetite for such things, sister. As I would expect, for I hear you are a collector yourself?'

I shrug. How quickly gossip moves when the subject is questionable female behaviour. 'Very modest, I assure you.'

'Still, it's as well my wife doesn't share the same aspiration. What would dealers do if they had to choose between the two lovely Este sisters?'

'I daresay they would go for the bigger purse.' And though I mean the words to be light, they come tart off my tongue. I had steeled myself against any return of envy, and yet ...

'You may be right,' he laughs. 'But the fact that you say it tells me you are already a woman who knows what she wants. And, I suspect, how to get it.'

There are those who will say later that I liked Ludovico Sforza too much. But then it's easy to slander women over such things. His enemies - there were many of them - would say he was just a tyrant who knew how to flatter. And there is some truth in that. But I never met a woman who didn't have a good word for him. I knew then that Beatrice would not resist him for long. He was one of those rare men who liked women as well as loved them, and they also seemed to like him back. Even without the title of duke, he had everything a man could want: power, wealth, taste, a lovely young wife, and a mistress as enchanting as a naiad, who everyone knew was already fat with his child. And when he was not with her, he could always feast upon her snow-white flesh as he held the most sublime portrait of her in his private apartments.

That was his other great achievement: to have brought to Milan a painter/ engineer from Florence whom everyone now wanted as their resident artist, one Leonardo from Vinci.

In this, at least, I could hold my head half high, since I too was now patron to a great court painter.

The news from Mantua was that Andrea Mantegna had returned from Rome. I was about to commission my first work of art.

VIII

Mantegna's Oculus: Camera Picta, Castello di San Giorgio (Ducal Palace).

The very first time I stood inside Mantegna's painted chamber, I grew giddy from twisting and turning to take it all in. I returned later on my own and lay down on my back on the floor, because that was the only way to take in the marvel of his trompe l'oeil cupola. He had painted the ceiling as if it was a dome open to the sky, bright blue with scudding clouds above and ladies peering down over the circular balustrade; each and every element perfectly in perspective, from the naked putti with their heads stuck through the stone opening to the plant pot cunningly perched on the edge as if it might at any moment fall upon you. A miracle in paint.

Below, and around, the walls were covered with scenes of the Gonzaga court, even down to faithful representations of the favourite family horses and hunting dogs.

And then there was Barbara of Brandenburg.

An arresting portrait. My mother always chose her words well. He had captured her in middle age, the impact of a dozen pregnancies on her thick form, her face flat as a pancake, her gaze staring directly out at you, penetrating and severe. Around her he had painted half a dozen younger, prettier women, but she was the one you couldn't take your eyes off.

Fifteen ducats a month and all the food, wine and firewood he could consume: that's what it had taken to secure the services of the young Mantegna thirty years earlier. A hefty sum even then. A marchesa with a nose for good housekeeping might be forgiven for expecting an element of flattery in return for such an outlay. Or did she perhaps recognise herself on that wall, and see it as another kind of compliment?

*

By the time I return from Milan, he is already cloistered in a chamber in the far reaches of the castle, working on *The Triumphs of Caesar*, entrance barred to everyone except the men who brought him food and drink. Even unfinished, the project is legendary: nine enormous canvases following a great procession of victory - soldiers, horses, chariots, banners and all the spoils of war.

I would have liked to go to him - he would never dare bar me entrance - but it was unacceptable that I, his marchesa, should be the supplicant. Instead, I issue Mantegna a formal sharp request for his presence.

I receive him in my half-finished studiolo, the gilded ceiling shining new, the floor ready to be tiled, the walls marked out for where the paintings will go. I am dressed for the occasion and admit to a certain level of nerves. He, however, makes no such effort with his appearance. The first impression is of a man older than Methuselah. His face and hands are swollen and cracked like overcooked loaves of bread with blotches and streaks of paint dyed into every line and crevice. If Mantua's court painter owns such a thing as a mirror, he can never have looked at himself in it.

'I gather you are most busy with Caesar's victories, Maestro Mantegna.' I launch in bright and breezy, because if I am nervous, I am also excited. 'I must say, such a work is a fitting allegory for the military glory of the Gonzagas.'

I offer a few further clever observations on his work, older than my years, to impress him, to which he says nothing. My studiolo is already the subject of considerable court gossip, yet he shows no interest whatsoever in its empty walls, clearly prepared for the works I will hang here.

'Our meeting takes place because I am sore in need of your talents. As you see, a number of works will be required for my ... my room here, though I appreciate you can't do them all at once.'

I pause. Is he listening? If he is, there is no sign of it. 'I have thought much about it and I know it will speak to you because the themes are classical: a study of virtue overcoming vice.' I say, warming to my subject. 'I have a few ideas ... A depiction of Mars and Venus together on Mount Parnassus, or perhaps the goddess Minerva driving devils out of the garden of Virtue. That kind of thing - all perfect material for your brush.'

I stop because my nerves are turning my mouth slack and it is outrageous that he has yet to speak.

'I've no time,' he mutters, not even bothering to look at the walls.

'Yes, I know you are busy. Still, I am sure we can come to some arrangement.'

'I have no time,' he says again.

I take a breath. 'I am aware of the wonders you are creating for our family, maestro. Between the Gonzaga patronage and your talent, Mantua has become a jewel in Italy's great crown of art. And as her new marchesa, I assure you, such things are at least as important to me as they are to you.'

'Which is why I have no time,' he repeats, shaking his head so that a hank of greasy grey hair now falls over his eyes. 'Caesar's Triumphs take all my attention.'

'You have been at them a good while,' I say mildly.

'Quite the opposite.' He blows out his lips angrily. 'I've wasted almost two years away from them.'

'In the service of a pope,' I remind him gently.

'A pope who had no taste, and wanted everything yesterday, but didn't pay till the year after. If at all!' he growls.

I leave a beat of pause. 'I think it is unwise to speak ill of the dead. Especially His Holiness.'

How long had Pope Innocent been in his grave? At least six months now.

'I'd say the same about the new one.'

And despite myself I feel a certain thrill at such temerity.

'Really? Yet I hear he has excellent taste. He has just given a considerable commission to the Roman painter Pinturicchio, to decorate his new rooms in the Vatican.'

Ah, all those hours writing letters bring their own reward, for gossip is golden. There isn't a ruler in Italy - indeed, most of Europe now - who hasn't heard a few stories of Alexander VI, the Spanish Borgia cardinal who bought his way into the papal crown but still has a river of money to spare. 'Pinturicchio, it seems ...' I add, warming to the sparring, 'is now the most sought-after artist in the whole of Rome.'

'They deserve each other,' Mantegna retorts sourly. 'The man can only paint simpering courtiers and overdressed saints. I wouldn't pay him to decorate my outhouse.'

All this jostling for position and talk of money! All my life I would long for the company of great artists, as if they were a race elevated above the fray. Yet the more dealings I will have with them, the more I find them to be like ill-mannered children: peevish and grasping.

'So, what are you saying? That you cannot accept my commission?'

'No.'

'I see.' And my smile is glued to my face. 'Well, then perhaps I should approach your brother-in-law, Giovanni Bellini. He is exceedingly accomplished when it comes to classical allegory, yes? Even more than you, perhaps?'

To my delight, I watch a ripple of pure fury go through him, though his jaws remain clamped shut. In time, I will discover that both of them can be equally recalcitrant. But I am new to this business and still learning.

'Of course, I understand it must seem a ... er ... challenging commission.'

He scowls further, his expression like that of the school boy waiting to be set free from some dreadful lesson. He thinks he has won. But he is not going anywhere yet.

'So, why don't we go for something simpler. I'm in need of

a portrait of myself. The one from my childhood - by Cosmè Tura - is fine enough but, sadly, it has been mislaid.' (Already buried in some cupboard or other.) 'I would like a new one by your good self.'

He shrugs, as my smile grows wider. I've already decided there will be only one winner in this encounter.

'And don't tell me you cannot do it, Maestro Mantegna, because I will not take no on this. It's hardly a *Triumphs of Caesar* I am asking for. Rather something to mark the arrival of the new marchesa. Something suitably ... splendid.' Was there another word for flattering? 'A reflection of "status" as much as likeness.'

There is a silence. It's impossible to know what Mantegna is thinking, since his face never changes. I wonder, would it crack apart if he were to smile?

'Good,' I say sweetly. 'That's settled then.'

'I have no time to paint it.'

'Which is perfect, since I have virtually no time to sit for you either.' And again Barbara of Brandenburg's flat-iron face wavers in front of my eyes. He wouldn't dare ...

I wave my hand in a bright gesture to show the audience is at an end. 'I will send one of my ladies dressed as myself so you can capture the richness of costume and hairstyle. As for my face, I am sure you can add something ... suitably fine, to celebrate your new marchesa.'

He mutters something angrily under his breath.

'Exactly,' I say firmly. 'I feel the same sense of privilege to be working with you. We will both be rewarded by history for it. Though in your case, I am sure the treasury will go further, something "extra" on top of your generous monthly stipend.'

Mantegna: self-portrait, concealed in Camera Picta.

I leave a small pause, and watch his eyelids flicker. That at least has made an impact. 'God speed your brush for the glory of the Gonzagas.'

God, however, had painfully little influence over the timetable of Andrea Mantegna.

It would be months before I sat even once for him. And close on a year before he delivered the portrait. Though by then, I had more pressing matters on my mind than art.

I was finally with child.

IX

Any news? Francesco launches the question every time our paths cross. Such is his belief in his own virility that it seems astonishing to him that I have not conceived the minute he touched me.

The bloodhound in all of this, though, was my mother.

Obviously, there has been gossip; it flows as effortlessly as the waters that joined our two cities. No doubt she too has added up all the time that either my husband or I are away travelling and begun to realise that her clever daughter has found ways to minimise what she does not like doing in life.

'I trust you're not draining the Mantuan treasury too quickly,' she comments as I describe the work being done on my studiolo and grotta. 'You know that such rooms are a highly unusual venue for a young woman.'

'I don't see why. I like to study as much as my husband - probably more. It is all within my dowry allowance. I was well schooled in such matters by my own mother.'

She smiles wearily. I know my leaving has caused her pain; letters from my old tutor tell sweet stories of how she has ordered my rooms closed up, keeping the only key for herself. Yet face to face no such sentimentality is on display.

'I take no credit for you, Isabella. I have never known a child I could teach less. In some things at least. So, how are relations between you and your husband?'

I tell her what I think she wants to know: what a fine job I am doing reorganising the household and running the state in his absence. And how much I enjoy it. All of which is true. I cannot get enough of governing. And, to my joy, I am good at it. 'A flood of dispatches go out under my seal every day. You'd be proud of me.'

'And Francesco?'

'– is supportive of every judgement I make. His letters are full of praise for my good sense.' Also true. There are ways in which this thing called marriage is suiting both of us well enough.

But she is not to be put off the scent.

'And when you are together?'

'He's more away than he is home.'

'All the more reason that when he *is*, you should care for him as a wife must.'

'I do,' I reply, stiff-lipped. Sitting in this room with her, I feel like a child again.

She waits as I wrestle with myself.

'He has a passionate nature, your husband,' she continues eventually. 'Like many professional soldiers.'

A passionate nature. Which makes mine what? Cold? Dull?

Except it is not that simple. I am back in the castle court-yard, a few months before. I wasn't snooping, merely passing on my way somewhere else, but the noises had genuine distress to them: nervous cries, entreaties, matched by a darker bass tone underneath. There had been trouble with the boy pages recently: certain intimacies being taken with the prettier ones by elder men, causing friction and, in one case, an outright fight. The moral fibre of a court has contagion built into it. When things slip too far ...

'Who's there?'

Only now I was met with sudden silence. No doubt they have recognised my voice.

'I know someone's in there. You are to come out now.'

Further silence. Then, eventually, a scuffling ... and from the darkness a girl emerges, a pretty scrap of a thing, clutching her torn clothes to her breast, eyes down, darting past me like a scuttling field mouse released from the claws of a cat.

Not the serving boys then. I stood, waiting. Why didn't I walk away? Did I really need to know?

I heard a sigh from the darkness, then someone clearing their throat.

'Who is there? This is your marchesa speaking.'

'Yes, yes, Isabella. There's nothing to fear.' Francesco emerged, buttoning himself up and running a hand through that mane of black hair. 'A simple afternoon dalliance, that's all.' He grinned. 'It's finished now. What are you doing here anyway?'

That was it. Not even a shred of embarrassment.

'Who is she?'

'No one! It's nothing, I told you.' And he sounds almost weary with the effort of talking. 'I'm due at the stables anyway. Why don't you go back to your rooms?'

I remain rooted to the spot.

'You don't need to know, Isabella,' he says more sharply. 'It's not your business. Nothing here is your business, do you understand? Go back to your rooms.'

I did as I was told, my face hot from the humiliation. We spent the next few days prowling around each other, and when he finally came to my bed, he was as energetic and careless as ever, as if nothing had taken place. Among his many talents, my husband was good at ignoring what he did not want to see, so that after a while he could pretend it hadn't happened at all.

But that was not my way. Not then, at least.

My mother is still looking at me.

'I sometimes think, Isabella, that your cleverness has made it harder for you to accept things that are quite "ordinary" in the world.'

I shake my head brusquely, not trusting myself to speak. She gives another little sigh. 'You are too young, I think, to remember our visit to Naples.'

'That's not true. I remember the smell of my grandfather's beard. And how much he favoured Beatrice.'

'Ah, yes - your prodigious memory! Then perhaps you will also remember that a short while after we returned, we welcomed a new baby into the family.'

'Of course, Giulio. My half-brother.'

'Your half-brother, yes.' She pauses. 'You were most loving to him, I recall.'

I shrug. Had it really been so easily accepted?

'So, you see, whatever ... discomfort you may be experiencing in your marriage, it is quite normal.'

'Has someone been spying on me?' I say angrily.

'Oh Isabella, I need no spies to read your face. I am trying to help.'

I don't need help, I think. Except I do. 'What happened to her? Giulio's mother, I mean?'

'Nothing. She was one of my ladies-in-waiting. A good-natured young woman, committed to the well-being of the Este family and ... attuned to doing as she was told.' She pauses.

She was so proper in many ways, my mother, that sometimes it was hard to know when her precision was being used as a weapon. I am not sure my father ever worked it out either. 'Sometime later, she entered a convent.'

'Every one of my ladies is utterly loyal to me!'

'Oh, I know that well enough. I chose most of them myself, you remember. But you and Francesco spend large amounts of time apart. It will be quite usual for him to get what he wants elsewhere, particularly if his wife is ... not always available.'

But I am not willing to go there. I take a breath. 'He tells me it's none of my business.'

'Then you should listen to him,' she says evenly. 'For he is right.'

We sit for a moment in silence. Would it have helped if we had had this conversation before my marriage? Too late to think of that now.

'Were you not upset?'

'And if I had been, what good would it have done?' she says simply. 'It was how it was. How it *is*. It's important that you understand this. Because holding things against each other will help neither of you. A wandering husband does not make for a bad marriage, Isabella. Indeed, some women ...' She pauses, holding my eye. 'Some women prefer it that way, as it gives them freedom to pursue their own interests.' She lets the silence sit for a while. 'In either case, the sooner you have children, the easier it will be, for both of you. Believe me, child, there is no other way.'

*

In the months that followed, her letters mixed affection with forthright advice. When Francesco fell ill, she urged me - no, more than that, *ordered* me to visit him daily, to serve him food with my own hand and offer *words and caresses, as a way to increase his love and win his blessings.*

Whatever it was she had not managed to teach me before my marriage, she was determined I would learn it now, and whoever her spy was - and I had some suspicion - they clearly knew my movements well. After the third letter, it was easier just to obey.

But it was Beatrice who played the trump card. Barely a year or so into her marriage, news came that she was already with child. Of course! No doubt they had charmed each other, and my lovely, loving sister now had a husband who worshipped her and to whom she would give the legitimate Sforza heir that his mistress could not.

Which, with my mother there as her birth companion, she duly did: a healthy boy born after a labour that they both agreed was a good deal easier than trying to make a cake in the heat of the summer.

Oh yes, those were the very words my mother used, no doubt in order to encourage me! My scholar has the letter there, right now, on her desk in front of her, a smile on her face as she reads the phrase. *Easier than baking a cake in the heat of the summer.* Ha! Something, I am sure, neither my mother nor Beatrice had ever done!

Relief. Fury. Rejoicing. Bitterness. Such a storm of feelings it threw up in me. On paper, my congratulations were effusive. But I spent the whole of the next day in the chapel, praying. For what? The good health of my sister? Of course. God knows, I did not wish her ill. But also for the speedy conception of my own heir.

*

My husband was due back imminently from a tour of his troops. In the days before his arrival, I oversaw the laying of majolica tiles for the floor.

How I loved them. They were an experiment, an attempt to preserve the brilliance of colour with a glaze hard enough to withstand the test of feet over time. Each carried a heraldic image from the Gonzaga family: the fortress, the eagle, the faithful hound. The history of Mantua lay beneath my feet.

Majolica tiles from Isabella's studiolo.

Yet with every step I was reminded of what was needed to keep the family triumphant. My mother, as ever, was right. Without children, there was no marriage. I welcomed Francesco home with my sweetest-smelling perfume and the coyest smile I could manage.

I was never afraid of work. And work was what was needed now. Once he cleaned off the mud from the road, he responded with an almost childlike delight.

The castle was a rumour mill within weeks. In the world outside, the political earth was starting to tremble under our feet. The talk was of a dangerous new alliance between Milan and the French king. Had we had more of an ear to the ground, we might have detected the sound of an army beginning to gather on the other side of the Alps. But the only news worth following in Mantua was what might be going on in the body of its marchesa.

How I hated those first months. Everywhere I went, there were eyes on me, checking what food I asked for, what I refused, if I was sick, if I was well, how tired a journey might make me, scrutinising each and every variation of my moods. Of which, I admit, there were a good many.

There are women, I know, who when their next flow is lighter than the last immediately start crowing their fertility to the skies. But that was never me. So many of them are proved foolish. A man's seed doesn't always flourish inside a woman. The heat of her womb can be too little - or too much. How many unformed little blood bundles have been expelled in the first months? It happened to my own mother more than once and who was I to say it would not happen to me. No. I would be with child publicly only when I was ready, when I felt it start to move inside me. The quickening of life. Proof beyond doubt. And no one but me would know that moment.

My ladies fluttered like a flock of anxious starlings around me. Even my treasured secretary was changed in my presence: solicitous, attentive, as if I were a showpiece of Murano glass.

'Tell me, Senor Capilupi,' I said. 'Do you ever write letters to anyone without my approval?'

'Your seal is only ever put on a letter that you yourself have dictated to me, my lady,' he said with clear horror.

'And what about your own seal? Does that sometimes go out with news to anyone else?'

He had the decency to look confused. 'News? To whom?'

I smiled, and I am sure my eyes disappeared into my cheeks, for they were quite plump by now. 'My mother, for example?'

He hesitated for a few seconds, then he said with admirable simplicity, 'I believe it would be a dereliction of duty not to reply if I am written to.'

*

She arrived herself a few weeks later, laden with boxes of fruit and fresh fish and bolts of fabrics for new dresses that might be required. Her eyes told me what she was thinking the minute she saw me. No doubt she was looking again at that difficult young girl she had tutored through adolescence, her body sprouting in all directions.

Except I was not the only one changed. If I was swelling, she had shrunk. Her skin was sallow and she had a cough that would not go away. There was something wrong with her. But only one interrogator was allowed in this meeting.

'It is nothing. A leftover from a Ferrarese spring fever.'

'In August?'

'The months have sped by for both of us. You are much altered.'

'Am I?'

'I think you know you are. Your face is fuller and you have put on a good deal of weight. Do not scowl at me, Isabella. It suits a woman well enough. Though you must be careful not to get too tired. I hear you were most fatigued on your recent shopping trip to Venice.'

'What? Were you on the boat with me, or have certain nervous little birds been singing to you?'

'I am not here to fight with you. I am here to help you rejoice. You are some months with child.'

'That may or may not be so, but I am not sure of it yet.' I put my hands over my stomach. 'I feel nothing.'

She looked at me. 'I assure you that will change soon enough. You yourself were a most lively fish in the womb.'

'I was a girl,' I muttered grimly. 'I have heard that boys conserve their energy better.'

She smiled. 'Ah! So you are sure about that?'

'No,' I said, my humour deserting me. 'Though I pray.' Because, of course, I did.

'As you should.' She stood up. 'Oh my, what a stubborn creature you are,' she sighed as she gestured for me to come her towards her. 'The world - and your husband in particular - is waiting to celebrate, Isabella. You look quite lovely, you know.'

I shook my head angrily. For I was sure that was not true.

She opened her arms and I came inside. Except, I no longer fitted.

'Will you be with me? For the birth?'

'Of course.'

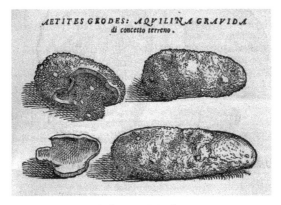

Eagle stone. Woodcut.

In the event, she was not. Instead, when I saw her off on the boat, she pressed a talisman in my hand, a gnarled hollow stone that looked more like a nut and rattled when I shook it.

'It is an eagle stone. From the Indies. Your father paid a small fortune for it. Listen. Hear how it carries new life inside it? It possesses sympathetic properties. You must keep it strapped to your thigh in the last months of pregnancy and hold it to your belly when the pains start to come. Just in case I am not able to be with you. It will help you birth safely and with less distress.'

'Did my sister use it?'

'No. She did not need it.'

'And you?'

'Ah - always another question, Isabella! I think it helped, yes.'

'It will not be like making a cake,' I said firmly. 'I shall scream.'

'I have no doubt of that. Most women do. Come now, a last kiss because I am tired.'

My final memory is of her moving away from the deck into the cabin below, and the sound of her coughing, a sound that grew fainter as the boat set free from its moorings and moved off into the middle of the lake.

She died two months later.

They did not want to tell me when it happened. But I knew. Our letters crossed every week, so that when hers did not arrive, no excuse of business would convince me. And I was becoming more adept at reading Benedetto Capilupi's face when he denied things.

They were worried that I might lose the child, of course.

But that did not happen. We bred sturdy fishes, Francesco Gonzaga and I. Not a single one would be dislodged early. When they eventually told me, I cried, but I was growing fast by then and an inexplicable sense of well-being was stealing over me, as if I were a well-fed cat lying in the sun, too full and content to bother with much at all. The real tears would have to wait.

Those last months, there was never a day when I was not in chapel. I spoke to the baby with such love and conviction. 'A most lively fish you are.' I had been repeating my mother's words as soon as the kicking began. 'A soldier, I am sure.'

But I did not give birth to a soldier. When she - Eleonora, named after my mother - was delivered (there will be many labours to come and they are not worth entering unless one feasts on pain: suffice it to say the eagle stone did little for me), I knew it immediately, not simply from her cry, but from the way the midwives greeted her arrival with too much jollity.

Four years into my marriage, I had given birth to a girl. And I could not even appeal to my mother for help.

A girl!

'I am sorry.'

'What do you mean? She is lovely. Look at her. Flesh of my flesh!'

Francesco was beside himself with pride. How many of his hunting dogs had he welcomed after the whelping, the bloody little creatures licking his hands? It was all easy nature to him. He'd long forgotten the scuttling in the storeroom, and my steely disapproval.

'Don't be dispirited. She is a beauty, Isabella. There's all the time in the world to give her an army of brothers. Where is the silver cot your mother sent? We shall put her in it immediately.'

'No!'

'What?'

'No. The silver cot was made for the next Marquis of Mantua. And it will wait for him. She can have a wooden crib. It will do her well enough.'

He frowned. 'But why? I would not mind. She is -'

'Well, I mind,' I said, and my voice was high pitched. 'It was not made for a girl.'

A girl! A day and a night in thrashing agony, my body splitting in half to expel a creature with a head the size of a melon. I was half crazed with the exhaustion and shock. She did not care. She had all she needed in the swollen midwife, while I lay, breasts tightly bound and throbbing to suppress the milk. In the days that followed, I felt so lost I could barely find Isabella inside myself. I thought of my studiolo, the view from the window. I imagined myself with my lute, plucking rainbows of melody from its strings. I heard the tap of my ladies' feet as we began a dance rhythm. I traced the contours of Cicero's face in my mind. Cicero. Plato, Livy ... the greatest of the ancients never suffered thus inside their own torn flesh. And all for a girl.

I would grow to feel better about my daughter. But I would not love her in the way I would do my son. I know it would serve my reputation better if I could pretend differently, but there's no point in trying, since the proof is there for anyone to see: the briefest of letters composed in reply to my brother's wife, Anna Sforza.

I thank Your Ladyship for your sweet and loving words.
I know that you, like me, would have wanted me to have a boy,
as almost everyone desired ...

... But we must deem everything God does for the best and be
satisfied with what pleases His Divine Majesty.

At her desk, she is copying the letter, word for pithy word, into
her notebook. The worlds she and I inhabit are different in so
many ways. Her very presence here, along with all the other
women who now study me, are testament to different possible futures for children born with a pleat rather than a penis.
And if I know that, then she must also know how different it
was for me.

What can I tell her then that she doesn't know? What else is
buried inside these brief lines? Because while the stilted, courteous words may seem cold at first reading, they also contain an
unspoken understanding between us women.

Yes, my sister-in-law Anna's words had been *sweet and loving*,
but the fact is her letter to me was also too brief, which in itself
showed that she *like me, would have wanted me to have a boy, as
almost everyone desired.*

In my life, how many such letters would I compose to women
who had failed in this first and foremost duty of marriage: the
production of an heir? Not even the acceptance of God's will
could make up for that. Not long after this moment, Anna herself
would fail with her first-born, though in her case God would
take her as well as a girl child. And in my condolences to my
brother, Alfonso, I too will claim to be comforted by *what pleases
His Divine Majesty.*

Easy words to write.

Not so easy to feel. Read in that light, this letter of mine reveals something else: that there is no time for further lamentation on the matter. No dynastic marriage could be secure until there are at least two healthy boys in the nest. I had failed. And just like my mother, that meant I would have to do it again. And again.

It is that sense of determination that is also imbedded in my words.

As soon as I had healed, I welcomed my husband back into my bed. And it may surprise my scholar to learn - and in this she will have to use her imagination, for it is not the stuff of my correspondence - that he treated me with a little more gentleness than I had grown used to. One question at least was answered. I was not barren and I had survived the birth of a girl. I was barely twenty years old and, God willing, had a long fertile life ahead of me. Of course, I would be pregnant again soon enough and nothing would be gained by dwelling on the past.

My scholar, it seems, is in agreement, as the archivist has already arrived at her desk with the next set of folders. They exchange smiles and, as she thanks her, I hear her voice for the first time, and find it pleasantly rich in timbre. Which is just as well, because I much dislike - how shall I put it? - 'squeaky voiced' women. Though that is still in the future.

*

She plunges into the first folder, sifting through dates until she finds what she is looking for. Oh yes, it seems we are of the same mind.

The birthing room is only a few months behind me and Eleonora still fixed like a leech to her wet nurse's breasts when our world starts to collapse around us and I am left once again running the state as my husband leads the biggest army Italy has ever seen into battle.

Over her shoulder, I read the words the scholar now writes in her notebook:

'*If childbirth belongs to women, war is men's work.*'

I could not have put it better myself.

WAR

X

Pisanello: unfinished fresco (detail), Ducal Palace, Mantua.

Yet if war is men's work, then on this of all days I would give anything to share it with him.

I have tried so hard to imagine it. In one of the many great chambers of the palace, there is a frescoed wall teeming with violence: a jumble of rearing, stumbling horses, men in full armour, cunningly foreshortened, upturned on the ground, flailing like giant woodlice. It is a half-finished work by a long-dead artist. But no less truthful for that. Except, however long I stare at it, I cannot feel the agony of a lance piercing through a visor, or hear the screams of the horses as their entrails spew out on to the ground.

As a child, the only pain I ever really wished to enter was that of Christ and I was always a poor student in this regard. I once came upon my mother on her knees in front of her crucifix, tears streaming down her face. She had journeyed with Him through the unfolding Passion - the scourging, the carrying of the cross, the hammering of the nails and the cruel slow ebbing of life - yet I could feel her elation in their shared suffering. I know some who've gone further. Mantua's own visionary Osanna Andreasi, the tertiary nun who has guided the Gonzaga family for many years, received the stigmata when she was barely fourteen, a pain so intense that they say it took her into an ecstasy of swooning. She lives closeted in her father's house, a strange wizened little creature to whom God has given the gift of prophesy. I have visited her often these last weeks, hoping for a sign of what might be to come. But not even she has been allowed to see this battlefield, to count the bodies, or read the faces of the dead.

*

July 6th 1495, The Battle of Fornovo.

It will go down in history as a clash of nations that soaked the earth with blood. On one side, a French army, loaded with booty on the long march north from the captured city of Naples, reached the Taro valley, near Parma, to find their way blocked by a force combining soldiers from Milan, the Papacy and other city states. And at the head of it, Venice, with its appointed general, Francesco Gonzaga, Marquis of Mantua. The first great battle of my husband's military career. How strange, then, that as I sit in my studiolo with sunset turning to night over the lake, it is over already, yet I do not know who has won.

I have been here all day, a merciless sun baking the air until it seems there is none left to breathe. My only companion is my lap dog, Aura, curled asleep safe under my skirts as ever. I dismissed my ladies early, their fake good humour pulling across my nerves like a razor. In contrast, the discordant chorus of frogs lifting off the water as dusk comes in feels almost comforting. There is no fear of death in their song.

As a bird flies, Fornovo is seventy miles away, which means we will learn nothing until the first riders reach our city gates sometime tomorrow. For all I know, I could be a widow already, a twenty-one-year-old woman running a state she was not born into, with no heir to ensure her future and most of her dowry jewels pawned to raise money for her husband's troops.

Yet I am not afraid. No. I might not have the sweetest or most faithful of husbands (certainly, I could wish he was better at the filigree work of diplomacy; these last few months I have found myself constantly mopping up after his careless tongue), but give him a sword and a horse and his furnace energy would fire up any army to follow him. At least, that is the story I tell myself.

Whatever the outcome, when they come to count their dead, the French will have only themselves to blame. In the year since they poured over the Alps on to the Lombardy plain heading south for the kingdom of Naples, they have inflicted devastation wherever they marched, for an army on the move is a plague regardless of whether it unsheathes a sword or fires a cannon.

At first, no one was willing to go against them. All those entwined branches of family trees meant that there were some who were content to see Naples fall. My regent brother-in-law,

Ludovico Sforza, had made a public pact with the devil here. His path to becoming Duke of Milan was blocked by his young nephew, whose wife was from the royal family of Naples, so that when the King of France announced a claim on the Neapolitan throne, it suited Ludovico to support the army that might depose them.

Other states chose not to fight a battle that wasn't theirs. Then there were those, like us, caught in the middle: a brother-in-law in bed with the French, myself a granddaughter of the house of Naples. While Francesco was hot for glorious battle from the start, I fought a proxy war through paper and ink, streams of letters going out to all sides, flattering, promising, prevaricating, showing ourselves to be friends to all and enemies to none.

In the end, it had been France's very victory that undermined her. With Naples fallen, the occupying army had given itself up to pleasure, growing soft and distracted on conquest and plunder, so that the longer it dallied, the more time there was for an opposition to grow. Until this moment now.

*

Our marriage never worked so well as it did in times of crisis. The birth of Eleonora had helped. At home, Francesco was a besotted father, and away his letters are full of praise for my guardianship of the state. *We approve of your every action ... for we know you to be prudent and wise thanks to experience and intelligence.*

My studiolo is now the centre of government, dispatches arriving and departing daily like flocks of birds. Today alone, I have ordered every church in the city to say mass and hold vigils for its marquis's safety, and overseen the distribution of free bread and wine - war brings unrest, however stable the state.

How I love this room - the burnished gold of the ceiling, the busy brightness of the floor tiles. And on the walls, Mantegna's first completed painting: Venus and Mars poised on the summit Mount Parnassus, a chorus of dancing nymphs at their feet next to the winged horse Pegasus, a perfect portrait of a Gonzaga stallion. The work marks my own triumph in battle. Since our first bruising encounter and the arrival of an insult of a portrait, a fat-faced girl with eyes like currants in an uncooked bun (I do not exaggerate! There isn't a woman in history who would have chosen to put such a thing on a wall), I have learned better how to woo my enemies.

Not with flattery - Mantegna's temper makes him allergic to that - but with money and additional deliveries of wood, fish and fruit. Even maestros have their weakness and I have discovered his. His eldest son is a violent reprobate who does nothing but spend his father's fortune, so that the household is always in need. And since he does not have the grace (or maybe the time) to thank me properly, our great painter has gradually become more 'amenable' to my commissions.

Benedetto assures me that if I can handle Mantegna, then most of the rulers of Italy will cause me no problem. My secretary has, I have discovered, a dry vein of humour, which has got us through many long days together. The running of the city - adjudicating disputes, reading submissions, pleas for pardons, all this has been easy enough and though modesty precludes me from saying more, I think I am a good judge, steely when needed, yet clement in my way: even now there is a young thief walking the streets of Mantua who would have no hands at all to lift a spoon to his mouth if I had not intervened to save one of them from amputation.

Since I cannot be on the battlefield, I must take pleasure in such smaller achievements. Especially on nights like tonight.

The frogs fall silent as the darkness takes over. There is a story I have been told many times now: how years ago the city had the honour of hosting a pope for an extended visit, but he and his senior clerics left early, complaining that all Mantua had to offer was fever and frogs. Francesco's grandfather drained large tracts of marshland after that, which some say helped with the fevers, though it seems to have had little impact on the frogs.

July 6th. Such a midsummer night will be short enough. Yet this one already feels as if it will go on for ever. The oil lamps are lit and I am delivered a tray of honey cakes and sweet wine. I would prefer my regular dish of marzipan but war has disrupted the supply lines from Naples and my own kitchen has yet to match its quality. The cakes will do well enough for they remind me of childhood, the way they make my teeth sing as I suck out the honey. From under my skirts, Aura, whose sense of smell is even more acute than mine, emerges in anticipation of the moment when she can lick the honey from my fingertips. If warriors flourish on roasted flesh and ale, then Isabella d'Este and her lap dog thrive on sweetness, and there is a limit to how much one can deny oneself comfort at such a time.

Francesco's last letter sits on the table in front of me. It tells how an advance guard of French troops had entered the valley early one morning to reconnoitre the land, and his men, camped nearby, had launched a surprise attack on them, killing three dozen and taking a number of prisoners and booty. It reads like a romance story, filled with careless courage and comradeship, the main discomfort being the call to arms, which had come so early he had had to forgo breakfast. Later, I would find out he offered a reward to the first man to bring him back a French head on a lance, embracing him until they were both covered in blood. But he writes none of that to me. *And don't forget to kiss the child for me. Tell her she has a great general for a father.*

Is this how men get through battle? By turning the horror into stories?

*

I have no idea of the hour when a knock comes on the door.

Benedetto stands in the threshold. I rise -

'No, no, my lady. No news yet. We will not hear till after daybreak.'

'How long after?' I say, though I know I have asked this question before.

'If the result is decisive, and the marquis puts pen to paper straightway, as I am sure he will do - then sometime around morning mass. You have not slept?'

I shake my head. I don't need to return the question, since the answer is in his face.

'You might profitably do so for a few hours now, my lady. I will wake you as soon ...'

I shake my head again and we both smile.

'Then perhaps ...' He hesitates. 'I wonder ... is there is any outstanding correspondence that might take your mind off the waiting?'

'What do you suggest?' I say as I beckon him to his seat. 'Two different letters, to suit the news? One to the Venetian senate and the pope, congratulating them on a great victory. The other a paean of praise and flattery to the French king for his prowess and mercy in preparation for the ransom we will have to pay for my husband.'

'The marquis would not allow himself to be captured, my lady,' Benedetto says firmly.

'I know that. Tell me, have you yourself been in war, Benedetto?'

'I have been in the camp, not on the battlefield. A secretary's hands are considered too important to risk putting weapons in them.'

'And?'

He is silent for a moment. 'I would say that there is no stranger place. After the army leaves there is, for a while, an unearthly quiet, then later there is only madness. And both feel as if they will never end.'

'I cannot imagine,' I say quietly. 'Though these past few days I have tried.'

'I think if women could imagine battle, then men would not feel the same yearning to return home when it is over.' He pauses. 'As I know His Lordship must feel at this moment.'

'You are a consummate diplomat, Benedetto. And please do not tell me that it is simply what you were trained to do. For I know it is a profession of instinct as much as learning and that you have it in your very bones.'

He is caught off guard by my compliment and shifts his eyes a little. Diplomats do best operating in the shadows.

'So! If not war, then what shall we talk about?' I say gaily, for I don't like to see him uneasy.

He glances around the room. 'I was wondering, what are your thoughts about the bust of Homer?'

'You know as much as I do.' I smile. It is kind of him to go so far to distract me. He has little interest in art, or the purchase of furs and fabrics (though he already knows more about women's fashions than most men), but ancient things dug out of the ground capture his imagination. 'Nothing has changed since the last letter went. But we have high hopes.'

'Your agent in Rhodes seems most able.'

'Greedy, too. Though his commission is less than it would have been here.'

It has been an excellent strategy. The price of antiquities in Rome inflates with the elevation of every new cardinal (of which there are a good number, since the Borgia pope creams off a small fortune on the selling of each one). But further afield, on the Dalmatian coast or the islands of the Mediterranean, there were once ancient cities too, and with the right man in place when a farmer plunges his spade into the earth and hits marble or carved stone, I have first call on the bidding. The bust of Homer is temptation itself. Of course, one cannot be sure it *is* Homer, but my agent's sketch shows a fine head, albeit with a large chip of the nose missing - the plough has done its work too well here. Which is why it is such a bargain. The likeness of Homer, nose or no nose, buried for fifteen hundred years, soon to be sitting here in my presence! A shiver goes through me every time I think of it. It will be my last such purchase for a while. Even if we win, it will take time to redeem my jewels from the pawnbrokers of Venice.

And if we lose ...

'We will not lose, my lady.'

I turn. I was not aware that I had spoken out loud.

'No. No ... of course not. But if we do ...' I follow the thought.

'Eleonora could not inherit. And though I am sure she would be well cared for, there would be no place for a foreign marchesa widow here. I suppose I would return to my father.' I pause. 'Or go into a convent.'

'I think, my lady, you would not find yourself well suited to a convent.'

I laugh. 'We have already agreed you are a superior diplomat.'

'That does not mean I can't tell the truth.'

'The truth? Very well. Tell me then, Benedetto. How have we done, you and I, in this little room together, running the state of Mantua? And be aware, I can spot flattery. Even if I like it.'

There is the beat of a pause. 'You have governed like a ruler.'

'You mean I have grown used to taking your advice, even when it is does not come in words.'

He smiles. 'As I say - like a ruler.'

'Then make me a promise. If - or when - we come through this, in the future if you ever think I falter, you will tell me, yes?'

He nods. We watch in silence as the darkness fades and a gauzy dawn light slides into the room, both of us, I think, a little embarrassed by the intimacy between us.

After a while, the bells start to sound out for early mass.

'We should go,' I say, 'I must change my dress.'

'I will call for your ladies.' But as he opens the door, there is a sudden rising commotion down below, a servant halfway up the stairs.

I glance at him. 'Surely it's too early?'

But as we descend, we both know it is not. The castle is alive; the news is there is news. A rider is at the gates. No time for me to change now.

I join my ladies and make my way to the painted chamber that has become my formal visiting room these last months. I take my seat, spreading my skirts and holding my hands tight in my lap, waiting for the man to be announced into my presence. Above me sits the court of Lodovico Gonzaga with the iron-faced Barbara at his side. If I turned my head now, I would see him leaning out of his chair, almost pushing himself out of the painting, as some momentous news is being whispered to him by his secretary, the interchange so real that you wonder why you cannot hear the words. But not even Mantegna would dare to celebrate a disaster, and in the next panel Ludovico and his grandsons (my husband, young and sweet as honeysuckle) gather outside the city to greet the family's newly appointed cardinal, while a Gonzaga horse and hounds look on from the adjoining panel. Those wind-swift Barbary horses. Surely this rider would have merited one of those.

The man, ushered into the room, stops a few yards away from me and attempts a bow, but his legs shake too much from the novelty of being out of the saddle. The space between us is thick with the smell of the road and his sweat. I reach out my hand and he gives me the pouch. I would like to say I read its content in his eyes, but his face is too thick with dust. I dismiss him to the kitchens and break the seal. Except my own hands are trembling now and as I falter Benedetto takes it and opens it, moving his eyes swiftly across the pages. No one reads diplomatic letters faster than the men who are trained to write them.

'The day has gone to our great marquis!' he says loudly. 'The French have fled the field and our lord is safe and well.'

And somehow it is not just the room but the whole castle that hears him, for an echoing shout seems to rise up everywhere at once.

'God be praised,' I say, laughing. But then, as I look at him, I see something in his face that is not about triumph.

'God be praised,' I repeat firmly. I give orders for the church bells to start ringing again and the fireworks we have prepared in readiness to be let off. Then I banish everyone from the room.

'You have barely had time to read all he says, Benedetto. So now you can do so again, out loud for me.'

Which he does, and the words do not sound like my husband at all.

The day is theirs, he writes. Yet the battle was exceedingly cruel. A night of torrential rain had turned the earth to mud, so that both men and horses staggered and sank into the ground, unable to face each other like proper fighters. Any rules of chivalry were trodden underfoot as the French launched into battle yelling: *To the death. No quarter, no quarter, take no prisoners,* so that he must name some of his finest warriors and noble friends among the dead. Men he never thought he would see fall.

The day is theirs, he writes, yet no thanks to certain fighters. His squadron had attacked the rear part of the army at a narrow crossing by the river, and successfully cut off the baggage train. But rather than going after the French, some of them - God knows not his own men, but Greek and Albanian mercenaries employed by the Venetians - fell on the spoils rather than pursuing the enemy. And though he rode among them roaring commands and slashing at them with his whip, they could not be turned from profit to glory. Which means that though the day is ours, his words are full of fury and shame.

I sit staring at the pages in my secretary's hands. 'Help me here, Benedetto,' I say at last. 'He says they took the day. He says that more than once. Yet this does not feel like a victory.'

'This is not a battle any Italian will be used to fighting. *To the death* is not a cry our soldiers are accustomed to hearing. They make their livings from war, which means it is better to survive to fight the next one, and the taking and ransoming of prisoners is the natural way of things. In this way, there is some profit, even in defeat. But the marquis says here that he himself captured two noted French generals, which will be much to his credit. I would not be surprised if the king himself sends an emissary to negotiate with him.'

'But he talks of so much slaughter. Can you tell from his words who lost the most men?'

'I think that is less important than the fact that the French fled the field.'

'Yet they are still heading north towards home. We've not stopped their retreat.'

'That is true,' Benedetto says carefully. 'But it will be done with more ignominy now they are separated from their booty. To have lost such a rich baggage train is a heavy blow. No, Your Ladyship, the day is ours.'

'Still, I feel little triumph in my husband's voice.'

'You asked about what being in a battle is like, Your Ladyship.' He hands the letter to me. 'I think you are hearing it in his words.'

The pages in my hand are crumpled and stained from hours spent pressed close to the rider's body. Men's work. All of it. Even those who do not fight understand it better than I do. But I can learn.

'Perhaps it's best for now that we keep this letter to ourselves,' I say softly. 'Let the Greeks and Albanians stew in their shame, we need hear no more of them. I am sure with a little sleep my husband will feel the pulse of victory flowing more strongly. You are right, it is not nothing to have taken from them all their spoils.'

He nods.

'And, as you say, they are fleeing with their tails between their legs. That is the story we need to tell. How the Marquis of Mantua led his men into a fierce battle that banished the enemy and gave us back our dignity and liberty.'

'Indeed, Your Ladyship. And I am sure that is what His Lordship will be telling you himself soon enough.'

I rise from my chair. *What would I do without you, Benedetto Capilupi?* 'So! We have letters to write. I hope your hand is strong.'

'Never stronger,' he says with a broad smile. And it feels as if in some way we too have survived a battle.

When we have finished, I join in the celebrations. I order a bust of my husband to be carried through the streets with garlands round his neck; and as it comes through the main piazza bordering the palace, I stand out on the balcony with little Eleonora in my arms and the people cheer and cheer, and will not let us go back inside. And before the letter to my husband is dispatched, I add, in my own hand, a postscript in the voice of his daughter, telling him all the world is hailing her father as the great general who has secured the liberty of his country.

Because, despite the fact that the earth of Fornovo is soaked with the blood of more Italians than Frenchmen, that is how it will go down into history. More than we need the truth, we need a story of victory. And with it a hero of the people.

*

In the reading room, the archive is closing for the day. Hers is the only desk still occupied. She has lived a whole night and a day with me, oblivious of the world around her. The chief archivist coughs gently and, when she catches my scholar's attention, raises her eyes to the clock.

She makes a face, closing up the folder and her books quickly and mouthing the word *Sorry*. They both smile. Lost in history. Is there a better place?

XI

Sperandio Savelli: commemorative medallion of Francesco Gonzaga II.

I would say if my husband's honour was undeserved.

The truth is that he acquitted himself with singular glory on the battlefield. Everyone who fought with him that day is clear on that. He was the first into the fray and the last to leave, and he took risks that some might say were foolish rather than brave, but because he did not die they became part of the triumph.

The day after the battle, as Benedetto had predicted, the king's own emissary arrived to negotiate a ransom for his captured generals and, magnanimously, to congratulate him on his victory. Which pleased him as much as the two thousand gold ducats the Venetian senate awarded him a week later, with an extra thousand for his faithful consort marchesa. The bust of Homer was within my reach.

The king now offered to entertain him in person to negotiate a treaty, so he might lead the rest of his soldiers home in peace. There are those who saw Francesco's acceptance as an unwise move, for though he led the army, he was still employed by the Venetian state, and if there was any negotiating to be done it was their diplomats who should be doing it. But by then the very wind in the trees was singing out my husband's name, so when his request came through to send outfits and jewels for the meeting, I said nothing.

Instead, I had medallions cast in his honour and appointed a painter to go straightway to Fornovo to make sketches for a fresco of the battle, which would cover a wall of the palace. Few know his name now, for the work is long gone and his brush had none of Mantegna's power, but his will was more compliant and speed was of the essence. The maestro himself we commissioned to produce a new altarpiece: the Madonna of Victory - my husband in full armour receiving Our Lady's blessing. There was some discussion as to who should kneel opposite him, but I refused to subject myself to that unblinking gaze again, and it was decided to put our holy visionary Osanna as Saint Elizabeth in my place. He could hardly make her look any worse. The work would be installed in a brand-new church built to mark the occasion.

Did we gild the lily too much? I think not. Ours was an age when most rulers considered themselves exempt from modesty. And as I have learned over the years, history is less to do with the event than the way it is written down and remembered. In which case, we cannot be chastised.

As for that baggage train of spoils? Like the casting of lots for Christ's clothes, it was divvied up among the victors - though the richest object when it came to embarrassing the French had little monetary worth. In one of His Majesty's private chests was found a book: a kind of diary he had kept, detailing every personal conquest he had made within the rungs of Italian womanhood.

Along with - can you believe this? - sketches done by his travelling artist so that he might remember each lady better. I never
saw it - it was hardly fitting for a woman's eyes - but those who
did claimed to be torn between admiration for his appetite and
astonishment at his lack of taste.

My own favourites were the tapestries, which showed
considerably more artistic judgement than His Majesty's taste in
women. As spoils of victory they were the rightful property of my
husband, so when Ludovico Sforza asked if *he* might have them
for his palace in Pavia (oh yes, the man had the most exquisite
taste), I dressed my refusal in a wrapping of courteous excuses.
Which he, equally cordially, accepted.

As it was, my sweet-tongued brother-in-law emerged
remarkably well from his gamble with the devil. Not only did
his alliance with the French mean they left Milan unscathed, but
as the war unfolded that troublesome young nephew who stood
between him and his dukedom died from a sudden violent stomach illness. While he had often been sickly, he had never been
as sick as this. But with the King of Naples fallen, there was no
one from his widow's family left to point the finger, and so the
clever Ludovico Sforza got away with whatever he may, or may
not, have done.

And he and my sister now became Duke and Duchess of Milan.

In all our meetings, he never failed to make himself agreeable
to me. When you had his attention, it was hard to imagine he
would give it to anyone else, so that while everyone knew he had
other women, he never made my sister feel small or unappreci-
ated. I think he had grown to worship her bright spirit. So yes,
there were moments when, once again, I felt a stab of envy for
the marriage I had never had. What a fine couple we would have

made, he and I, and with the Sforza purse I would be halfway to amassing one of the greatest collections of the age. *Isabella d'Este, Duchess of Milan.* I whispered it sometimes under my breath.

Had I been blessed with the holy Osanna's gift of future sight, I would not have been so besotted.

But we were all blinded by victory for a while, which made it easy to miss the underlying lessons to be learned. The land of Italy had proved ripe fruit for any foreign monarch with an army who could lay claim to one or other of its states. And inside that tangle of family roots there was always a lost connection to be dug up.

Perhaps I might have seen it more clearly if Benedetto and I had still been dealing with such matters. But the daily thrust of politics was no longer my domain. My husband now ran the state again, and I returned to bargaining over the chip in Homer's nose and issuing invitations to poets and musicians for our smaller, but ever more regarded, court.

*

Then there was the question of an heir.

It was only fitting for the glory of the house of Gonzaga that the baby I carried that autumn would be a boy. Francesco had no doubt of it. 'A warrior son sired by the warrior on the night of his return!' he exclaimed to anyone who would listen as I swelled. He may have been right about the timing, for as Benedetto predicted, a victorious soldier pleased to be home is a joyful thing for everyone concerned and a little of that joy for once found its way into our bed.

This time, I did not hide my condition. It was my civic duty to publicise my husband's potency. War had hit the people hard, and there were pockets of unrest in the city, so that it helped to keep a sense of celebration going.

Yet even early on, as my stomach rose up into my mouth, I had a chill sense of foreboding. With each passing month I grew more certain. Everything I felt in body and mood, down to the moment of the quickening and how high the baby rode, pressing on my lungs till I could barely breathe, was identical to the journey I had been on before.

The only way it which it differed was the delivery. They told me that the labour would be easier, since I had experience now of birth. And so it was.

But that was less to do with the power of muscle memory than the size of the sad little body I expelled.

Not to announce an event that will be welcome to your excellency or to me, but to do my duty, I inform you that at an hour and half before sunset I have given birth to a girl.

As she already knows, brief letters often follow the birth of a daughter. But the one I wrote to Francesco that night is brevity soaked in bitterness ...

The chill which has come over me, the whole house and the city I leave to your Excellency's imagination. I commend myself, as always, to your good graces.

Chill. The very word prefigures an unhappy ending. In the reading room, I feel her distress as she lifts her eyes from the page.

There is more if she has the appetite to hear it. The baby was far too small, right from the start, as if while growing inside me she had known she was a mistake. Her skin was a bruised blue too long after the birth, and her cry had none of that insistent angry-bee tone that I remembered from Eleonora's first days. In the eight weeks that she lived, Margarita - for that was the name we gave her - never learned to smile, just slept feverishly or lay limply in the crib, as if to not cause us any trouble. Everyone knew she would not survive.

I had failed again.

There are some who sit with this letter who might think I willed her to die. But that was not how it was. I think she willed herself. All I could do, all we could all do, was watch her take her slow leave.

That same chill that came over me at her birth grew colder and darker with every passing day, so that in the end I left the city to try and regain my composure. She waited until I had gone before putting herself into God's hands. The news was broken to me by my brother-in-law, Cardinal Sigismondo Gonzaga, who was residing at court. It was kindly done ...

At this time, the baby died like a chick and flew to heaven ...
I have decided to bury her in the peace of the Lord tomorrow
during daybreak.

... but then he was a kind man and his faith in God was deep.

And so I conveyed the news to my husband.

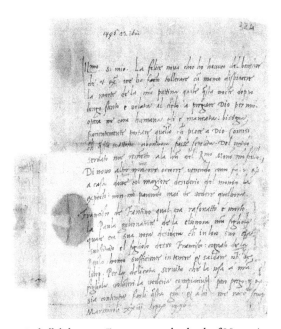

Isabella's letter to Francesco on the death of Margarita, 1496.

At her desk, I note the shine of a tear in my scholar's eye.

She is not the first to be felled by the cruelty of this story. I once sat over a young woman so ill at ease with the texts that she sometimes mouthed the words under her breath as she read them, who when she finally deciphered Sigismondo's news, muttered: 'Ooh, how cruel. Why didn't you stay with her?'

The wind I blew across her desk lifted half a dozen pages clean on to the floor. I still remember her startled glance. Well, why not? How dare she judge me? How dare any of them? Yes, I had faults. Some of them I knew at the time, others I have come to admit later. But this, this was different.

Would I have stayed longer if she had been a boy? Is that the question the future wants me to answer? Very well. Then, here it is. Yes. If she had been a boy, I daresay I would. And if that is evidence of a hard heart, then so be it. But it is not why I left. No, I left because it hurt too much to stay, to witness the slow ebbing of that feeble little spirit. I had failed again and at that moment everything felt intolerable.

The loss of babies, in or out of the womb, was plaited deep into all of our lives. And dwelling on it could only inflict further damage. Whenever it happens, however, the sand never stops passing through the hour glass. Another year, another pregnancy, another nine months of sickness, growth, rising exhaustion, everyone watching out for your every move: *Don't do this, Your Ladyship! Be careful of that! No riding now, remember what the doctors say!* While under their breath they are all thinking the same. *Would God favour the Gonzaga/Este union this time?* The very air in that birthing room had been so thick with prayer, it had been hard to breathe. And all for a tiny, sickly girl.

None of this had anything to do with Francesco. His role was played out easily enough. Away on military affairs, he was not there for the birth, nor the death. There are those who praise him for the sanguinity with which he accepted the news. But then, why should he not? He was still the adored liberator of Italy on a lap of victory, the virile warrior who could give the world an army of boys. And I did not need the drip feed of gossip to know that he sired a good few of them as he went on his way.

The chill which has come over me ... I leave to your Excellency's imagination ...

No, the chill and the shame were mine alone. And if that makes me a monster, then so be it. Any scholar who wants to do me justice will have to embrace my anger as well as my distress, for there are moments when the two grow too viciously intertwined for me to control.

I wonder, does she know that already?

XII

It was not long after Margarita's passing that the letter came from Beatrice, now Duchess of Milan and already a mother of two healthy boys, with news that she was pregnant again. My confessor is long dead, so there is no point in concealing things I am ashamed of. Pregnant again! I could taste the bitterness in my own saliva, because I knew, *knew*, that once again it would be a boy. How could I not wish her well, this sweet-natured sister of mine? Except I didn't.

The warm words I sent in readiness for her confinement were wrung out of me. I might excuse myself by saying that Margarita's death had made me careless with my affections. How the more I struggled with the loss, the angrier it seemed to make me. The fact is, I was not bred for failure, especially one that my will could not overcome.

Looking back now, I think the damage was more in my daring to predict the future. Whatever my status, I had not been singled out for stigmata or visions of holiness. Though I was to be proved right about the sex of the child.

*

January 1497 roars in with snow and bitter frosts, which no fires could quite dispel. Inside a gloomy castle, we are wrapped in furs, vowing never to curse the heat of summer again. Francesco is back and life has returned to something close to normal. The weather and the state of the roads makes the movement of mail more precarious and on the day in question the dispatch riders have come and gone with no letters for me.

I am gathered with my ladies reading romance poetry, my lap dogs - I have more of them now, four plump parcels of warmth and fur - lazing at our feet. Such is their loyalty to me that they are the only four-legged creatures my husband cannot charm, so that as the door opens on him, they rise up yapping and growling. The dislike is mutual, which is one of the reasons he does not often venture into my *lair*, as he calls it. No doubt he finds it too female and claustrophobic.

Ignoring them, he glances round as if he would also like to dismiss my ladies, but doesn't quite know how.

'Isabella,' he says. I hush the dogs, for I know from the tone of his voice that something is wrong. 'I have news that will bring you sorrow and I would like you to be prepared.'

'Ferrara. My father!' I say immediately, for his great age is with me day and night.

'No, no. This comes from Milan.'

'The baby?'

'Is born, yes. But dead.'

'Ah, how sad. It was a boy?'

'Yes, a boy,' he says, then pauses, looking at me carefully. 'There is more. It was a difficult birth. The doctors could not stem the bleeding. Beatrice ... well, Beatrice did not survive it. The letter is from Ludovico. He thought it best to write to me first, knowing how upsetting this news would be for you, so that I should be the one to break it.'

Does he say anything else? If he does, I don't remember it. Something sharp skewers inside me and I can no longer quite breathe.

'Beatrice? Is dead?'

I see him send a worried glance to my ladies. He is not used to me being the slower one.

'Yes. She is dead. They did all they could. The duke is beside himself with grief.'

He holds out the letter to me. At my feet, Aura, always the bravest, lets out a burst of further yapping, but I cannot hear it properly under the thudding of my own heart.

She is here, standing in front of me. I see her so clearly: my lovely, fecund, adored sister, her thick snake braid plaited with gold and silver threads. No artifice, no guile. Just a pretty young duchess, so in love with life that you wonder that any man would need women other than his wife.

But her death is not to be laid at his door.

'This is my fault.'

'What did she say?'

My ladies shake their heads. If they have heard, it is not to be repeated.

'It is my fault,' I say again.

My mother, my sister and two newborn babies. Three generations, all now flown to heaven. *Flown to heaven.* Those had been Sigismondo's words. They will be together now. While I - I am still here. *I have heard that Isabella did not always think kindly of me,* my sister is saying, and I see my mother nodding wisely.

'But I loved you. You know I did. Loved you so much.'

And now I have everyone in the room alarmed. Francesco comes towards me but I wave him away.

'It's all right. I am fine. Fine. I must write immediately to the duke. And also, yes, to my father. He must hear it from me.'

But when I try to move, I can't stand up unaided. And the dogs are barking wildly again.

'Should I send for the doctor?'

Poor Francesco. He has seen legs and arms blown off by cannon balls, yet he is unmanned by a woman's grief.

'I have no need of a doctor. I want to see Osanna.'

'My lady, we cannot hear you. What is it that you want?'

First I am too loud, now I am too soft. It must be the hammering in my ears. I turn my attention to the dogs and hush them sternly into silence.

'I do not want a doctor,' I say slowly and clearly, when there is silence again. 'What I want is to be left alone. And a carriage to be got ready to take me to the house of Osanna Andreasi. Do you understood me now?'

*

As I relive it now, I am not so sunk into the same quicksand of pain. Which is just as well, since if I were to enter it further I think it likely I might appear self-pitying. I was not the one who had died with a child stuck in my pelvis. Of course, fear stalks every birth: the rising panic of the midwives, the sight of one's own bed sheets soaked in blood. Birth and death; how smoothly the words go together. But it had not happened to me. Miserable little Margarita had slid out all too easily, as if apologising for her own existence. And I had turned my back on her, refusing to feel, jettisoning her to her fate. In the same way, I had nursed an ice chip in my heart for my sister's good fortune. Now she was gone. They were both gone. And I was the one in pain.

That is the gangrene in the wound I took to Osanna in her humble house across the city. Not only the sense of abandonment - I know now that all grief has that in it. But rather the knowledge that had I done better, they might somehow be alive.

The treads of the narrow staircase to her room are worn thin from the feet of the sick and ailing who come for her blessing. My wide skirts scrape the walls. She could have lived in grander quarters - by birth, she was of good blood - but instead she had chosen the smallest chamber, as dark as our lady's womb.

Osanna's room, Casa Andreasi, Mantua.

Along with the power to look into the future, God had given Osanna Andreasi the ability to enter people's hearts, unlocking secrets they did not even know were there, so that though no one has told her of my visit, she is waiting for me, aware of everything that is inside me before I have a chance to confess.

'Ah, my lady Isabella. Let us pray together.'

She takes my hands in hers so tightly I can feel the ridges of scarred skin on her palms where the stigmata have never properly healed.

'The dear duchess is beyond pain now. She is bathed in His love and He will care for her through all eternity. His mercy and goodness is without bounds. And for that we must thank Him.'

'He will not hear my prayers.' I shake my head. 'There were times … I … there were times when I thought ill of her. I envied all that she had. I was angry it was not given to me.'

'He knows that already. We are all sinners. Every one of us. And He will forgive us all if we come to Him with our whole selves. Come, Your Ladyship, pray with me.' And she sinks on to the floor, pulling me down with a strength I can't resist. Fragility and iron. She was made of both.

'He won't hear my prayers,' I repeat. 'I have offended too much.'

'What? You think you are more undeserving than all the others who come to Him?' When she smiles, her lips collapse into her almost toothless mouth. 'You may be the Marchesa of Mantua, but in His sight, you are just another sinner asking forgiveness. It will not help to turn your guilt into the sin of pride. Come, let Him wash away your pain with His love.'

And so we pray together, my knees cushioned by my skirts, her bird bones hard upon the stone floor, as her mumbled words flow out on a single vibrato musical note. The air is thick with the smell she carries with her, a sickly perfume akin to lilies left too long in a vase, the scent of extreme holiness. There were times in her presence when I found it oppressive and sought to counteract it with pomades and scents, but that day I welcomed it as the sweetest perfume ever created, because I knew it came from God.

So many dead. My mother, my daughter, my sister. I was praying for all of them. And yet. And yet ... I know there was something else. A glimmer of that other Isabella, the one born to make bargains with the world. Even, it seems, with God.

I have done grievous wrong and I beg your forgiveness. I shall raise altars and great art in your name. Only grant one thing in return. I beg you, give me a boy child.

In this, I think, Osanna was not inside my head. Indeed, she did not seem to be there at all. I have no idea how long we knelt there. I only know that after a while, I became aware of a change around me. When I opened my eyes, she was exactly the same, fixed, hunched, her lips still moving, but her eyes, once closed, were now wide open and staring, staring without blinking into the air above my head, seeing nothing. Or rather, seeing things that I could not.

I called her name, but she did not reply. It happened this way sometimes when we visited, Francesco and I, how after a while she moved beyond us, leaving us alone in the room, so that we had to make our own way out, blessed by the closeness of her trance.

I started to rise, but her hands darted out and grabbed mine again. Only rather than holding them, this time she pushed them back against my body, pressing powerfully into the folds of my skirts, under which lay my womb. And her words, sung out in a high breathy voice, would stay with me, not just through the weeks of grief, but in the months, even years to come.

'Ah. I see something. Yes. A crib, a beautiful silver crib, next to your bed. And inside ... a healthy boy child.'

And a great wave of joy flowed over me, followed just as fast by an ice grip of terror.

'Oh, what else? What else do you see?'

But there was nothing more. Already, she was gone elsewhere.

That, I believe, was part of my penance.

Because from that moment on, birth would hold an extra fear for me: that in the arrival of a son foretold, the vision had said nothing about the well-being of the mother.

*

No written record remains of my visit to Osanna, though her prophesy was noted, as were all of her visions into the future. I offer it now as a glimpse into a different Isabella, one that is no longer the entitled capable consort of a national hero.

Yet, a shadow of that moment has found its way into the archive.

Though she has shown a brave and manly spirit in many other adverse situations, in this case she is so defeated and overcome with pain that I fear she has no resistance left.

In the archive room, my scholar has accessed a copy of my husband's reply written to Ludovico Sforza soon after and finds it worthy of copying word for word. I never knew of its existence then, but reading it over her shoulder now I realise that whatever our differences - and they were to become manifest soon enough - there was, at times, a chord of great tenderness between us.

Testimony, I think, to the partnership we shared.

XIII

I wonder, looking back, if Osanna saw more than she shared with me that night. Might it have helped my grief, for instance, to know that in some ways it was merciful that Beatrice died when she did?

Her span on earth was painfully short, that much is true. But it was also rewarding. She was the consort of a wealthy, powerful man who loved her, she gave birth to the heirs every state demands and presided as a duchess over a court rich with great art and great artists. I would have given much to have what she had, yet so soon it would all be washed away. I wonder, how would my pretty little sister have coped with the terror of flight, the disinheritance of her children, the destruction of her court? To live the rest of her life as an exile, depending on the charity of others, all the while knowing that her charming, rogue husband was rotting his life away in a French dungeon?

No, better, I think, that she died when she did. And that the gift of being able to lift the veil between the present and the future is given to only a blessed few. For the rest of us would surely be crushed by it.

As ever, business was the giddy dance of politics, that endless tangle of family roots and the temptations of Italian wealth.

French army marching on Milan: 16th-century woodcut.

Barely two years after Beatrice's death, a new King of France launched a new army of invasion. Only this time the state that France laid claimed to was Milan and its ruling dynasty, the Sforza.

There were those who saw it as just punishment, since it was Ludovico who had invited the French into Italy in the first place. Others found ways to justify it by profiting from the spoils. The states who fared best were the ones who followed where the wind was blowing early. In Mantua, however, we were caught yet again between power and family, a wound impossible to staunch. Beatrice was dead, yet her child sons were heirs to the duchy. How could we desert them? Yet how could we risk the wrath of a French king?

I might have been bred to love art and music, but anyone who reads the letters that pour from my hands will know how much of my life was spent marching to the drumbeat of war. And managing the temperament of my warrior husband. Because exactly those same qualities that made him so formidable on the battlefield - his charisma, his bravura, his recklessness (I am the first to glorify him in such things) - rendered him a liability when it came to the subtleties of diplomacy.

The glory that had come with his great victory at Fornovo was fading fast. Except, he couldn't let it go. In Francesco Gonzaga's eyes, he would for ever be 'the saviour of Italy', and therefore more important than any who employed him. Even when his paymaster was Venice.

His careless mouth in the negotiations after the Battle of Fornovo had already annoyed the senate once, but he still believed Venice was lucky to have him and was always on the lookout for better offers. So that as the French threat to Milan grew louder and Ludovico Sforza - secretly - started to woo him to take charge of his state's forces, Francesco, like a cock crowing at dawn, could not keep the news to himself. It wasn't long before the whole of Italy knew that the Marquis of Mantua's sword - and loyalty - was up for sale.

*

I did my best to contain him. But it was all useless against his loose tongue.

'There is no need to talk of this again, Isabella.'

High on wooden scaffolding in the banqueting hall of the palace, a few young apprentices are working on the final details of the Battle of Fornovo with Francesco himself, magnificent on his huge Barbary horse, dominating the scene. I have chosen the setting deliberately since my husband is always in the best humour when in his own company.

'I do not say this to criticise ...'

'– I know, I know, your concern is well meaning. But the fact is you know nothing of the ways of soldiering. Veteran commanders like myself speak a different language, chew the cud of politics in ways that are altogether more direct. That is how the world works for men.'

'I understand that. All I'm suggesting is that whatever is said in such "conversations" should be kept within the room where they take place. Venice is an exceedingly jealous mistress, with spies everywhere.'

'What? You think I am ignorant of that? You underestimate the power of my reputation. As the saviour of Italy, I say what I think to anyone's face. And I am respected for it. The more weasel language I leave to the diplomats. Along with the copious letter writing of my most capable wife.'

I return the backhanded compliment with a practised smile, learned, like so much else, from my mother, though delivered with less grace.

'Oh, don't look so worried, Isabella. It does no harm to our standing if Venice knows how highly I am valued by others. Anyway, you of all people should be open to the idea of protecting your brother-in-law.'

'Yes, and you know I am. But if – when – his position becomes impossible ... All I am saying is that it doesn't help for everyone to know our business before we do.'

'Aagh. Enough of this! Tell me, who is this "everyone" who spreads tales behind my back, eh?'

I take a breath.

I am not surprised that Francesco is ridiculed ...

The letter from our agent in Rome - a man loyal beyond question - was addressed to me alone. But then I alone had asked for his opinion.

> *... It is necessary for him to be wiser and more discreet, so that they are only scoundrels lying through their teeth, who say that wine makes every secret spill from his mouth ...*

'My lord ...' I know every word of it by heart - but what good would it do to repeat it now? 'My lord ... no one needs to tell me anything. Such things are carried on the wind.'

'Then you should treat them accordingly and brush them off. As I do.'

But I have pricked his pride now, so he cannot let it go.

'You know, when it comes to reputation, Isabella, there are things that are said about you too. Oh yes. Yet I do not bring them up to attack you.'

It would be better not to rise to it. But there is a thorn lodged in me and when pressed I cannot help but wince.

'You have nothing to reproach me with, Francesco. I am tireless in protecting our interests.'

I know what he is thinking: *tireless yes, in all but the most important thing.* Two years on from Osanna's prophesy, my womb is still empty, with no sign of an heir. I know how tongues wag behind my back: *if only Isabella d'Este behaved less like a man and laboured as hard in the bedroom as she does in her precious studiolo, the house of Gonzaga would be flourishing.*

Of course, he will not say such a thing to my face. Because if he does, I might reply that for a woman to be pregnant, her husband needs to spend time in the bed too, not galloping around the country plucking all the low-hanging fruit available to a hero.

It is what soldiers do, Isabella. My mother's words are never far from me and I've learned to close my ears to gossip, which runs like a vein of poison through every court. But when the Marquis of Mantua appears at a public tournament, barely sixty miles from his home, wearing the colours of a lady other than his wife, the slight cannot be ignored.

How could he imagine such an insult would not get back to me? That the woman came from a lesser family made it worse. Of course, when I ask about it, those close to me claim to know nothing. Benedetto won't even meet my eyes when I bring it up. Yet the diplomat in him understands the message it contains: such public flaunting of infidelity shows a carelessness to those to whom Francesco owes a duty, be it the state of Venice or his own wife.

But it would stick in my throat to speak of it now. At such times, my fury is like a thick stock, in need of diluting before it could be palatable, even to myself. There will be a moment when it will spill over regardless, when he walks into a room and his indiscriminate lust will be painted on his face and body. But with no heir, and the earth trembling underneath our feet, this is not it.

'My lord,' I say again, pouring honey into my voice. 'It will come as no surprise to anyone that Ludovico Sforza is lobbying for your services. You are Italy's greatest soldier. I simply say that for that very reason alone, it is best to at least appear to keep your options open.'

He looks at me sharply. He is not so lost in vanity that he doesn't know when he is being managed. But - and in this we share the fault - he can choose to ignore it when he wants.

'Keep our options open? Indeed, you are right. I tell you, our brother-in-law needs us a good deal more than we need him. And he would pay most handsomely for my services.'

And so his 'secret' negotiations continued. Until at last, he was ordered to appear before the senate in the doge's palace in Venice. And there, in the great hall, in front of the whole Venetian state, my proud husband was officially stripped of his title and salary as commander general of the Venetian army and sent on his way.

Venice would never forget nor forgive his disloyalty, and he would never forget nor forgive the ignominy of such a public dismissal, so that it became a scab that he could not resist picking, and thus never entirely healed. For all his energy and charisma, my warrior husband wounded more easily than many men weaker than himself.

*

It did not take long for matters to come to a head. The French army was already on the move when the pope and Venice, together the biggest power block in the north, allied themselves with the invaders.

It would have been suicide to fight against them. In the end, we could do nothing but watch the horror unfold.

XIV

September 1499.

The end of the Sforza dynasty sits like a dried bloodstain on any timeline of the past. Close on a hundred years of politics and culture smashed by cannon balls into fragments of history, a lesson to all that fortune is a capricious mistress who can turn her back on the most forceful and charismatic of men when the whim takes her.

As Ludovico and his entourage fled the city and the French soldiers poured in, ransacking those breathtaking palaces with all their art and beauty (*enemy soldiers take particular pleasure in destroying art*: how often would my mother's words return to me in life?), Benedetto and I sat up together through another night, composing courtly letters to Milan's new ruler, showering him with congratulations and gifts and declaring ourselves loyal Frenchmen into eternity.

> *You should know, Your Majesty, that here in Mantua we are all dressed in lilies —*

I dictate, in playful reverence to the French fleur de lys.

'What? You think it is too much?' I ask, seeing the slight smile on Benedetto's face.

'Not at all.'

The day after, I put in an order for bolts of the best imported silk from the Indies to be embroidered with the same flower and sent to the king, along with designs of my own for the queen's wardrobe.

I think possibly my pretty words and gifts made a difference, because the king himself invited Francesco to join him on his formal entry into the city. Like lovers the morning after a sexual conquest, victory makes some men magnanimous and my famed warrior husband (with or without Venetian approval), seated on his fiery Barbary horse, was a fine addition to any triumphal march.

If we could not save the dynasty, at least we could offer refuge to some of its artistic inheritance. They flowed in from the north as the last winter of the century drew the nights in faster: sculptors, musicians, artists, writers ... some carrying enough jewels in their saddle bags to make a new life, others with barely the clothes they stand up in. In this, Francesco is wiser than me. 'We can't house them all, Isabella, be careful whom you woo.'

Leonardo da Vinci: Cecilia Gallerani.

Of course, I went for beauty and the greatest talent. I'd long had a fondness for the mistress Ludovico could not bear to give up for his wife. There are those who swoon and weep over the portrait da Vinci would do of a Florentine cloth merchant's wife a few years later. But for me, no woman he ever painted came close to the brilliance of Lodovico's mistress, young Cecilia Gallerani, holding an ermine in her hands: an image of such grace and mischief that her very spirit seems to be escaping from the frame. I admired it from the first moment I saw it on one of my visits.

Later, when I came to know her better, I asked her to send it to me so that I might compare Leonardo's hand with that of Giovanni Bellini as a possible portraitist, and in this way her sweet face had been my companion for many months. And, of course, sweetly again she agreed.

By the winter of 1499 she was close on thirty years old and no longer radiant - that kind of beauty, like a meteor storm, dazzles precisely because it is over so fast - but her kindness and grace remained, so that as she walked in, bedraggled from the road, with a gift of a book of poetry for me, I knew she would be a fine adornment to the future, as well as a memory of the past. I think for all the pain she caused her once, even my sister would have taken her in in similar circumstances.

*

And the greatest talent? Is there any court in Europe that would have turned away Leonardo himself? By then, he had made himself into a work of art, presenting like an old-world prophet - tall and skeletal thin, with a mane of snowy hair and beard - though with the manners of a court dandy (there is nothing like humble birth to teach a man the art of dissembling). Everyone knew he kept a catamite as pretty as he was spoilt as his assistant, but we all chose to forget it, for the man's creativity was as deep as the ocean that separated us from the New World.

'However much you offer him, whatever you commission will remain half-finished.' Whatever his faults, my husband was a shrewd critic when it came to art. 'They say his *Last Supper* in Santa Maria delle Grazie is already flaking off the wall. The man will be attentive to your face and forget you the moment you are out of his sight. Believe me, Isabella, Leonardo will drive you more mad than Andrea Mantegna.'

Of course, I had to try. I engaged him in many conversations about art: the merit of painting versus poetry, nature versus artifice, things it was well known that he thought deeply about. Our exchanges, however, are hardly worth recalling (though scholars scour my letters for his name), as he had a great deal less to say than one might have hoped. Or rather, he gave off the air of a man not interested in debating with women. He was polite in praise of my collection (*polite!*), and in gratitude for our hospitality he dashed off a few sketches of me, one of which is quite pleasing but shows none of - what shall we call it? - the inner fire that he could give to a woman when he wanted.

He left soon after, first for Venice, then to his native Florence, and from there - well, he would go on to drink from the devil's cup, in the pay of the Borgias, whose bottomless purse would tempt him from art into the machinery of war again. I lobbied him endlessly for a finished portrait, but though he sent courteous words, he did nothing. So all I have to show for my efforts were two slapdash drawings, one of which, it seems (and she will surely understand how this pains me), has become infinitely more famous than its subject.

Leonardo da Vinci: Isabella d'Este.

Other artists, at least, were only too eager to serve us, including a master sculptor who would carve a magnificent marble doorway to my studiolo and the great Lorenzo da Pavia, the best instrument maker in the whole of Italy, now with time on his hands to take on other commissions. We even found room for Ludovico's head chef, a man who could marry taste and smell in a way that had every guest salivating long before they picked up their knives: the briny aroma of the river inside garlic fried eels, the sharpness of mint within the roasted sweetness of lamb, even the scent of flavoured ice statues as they melted slowly in the warmth of candlelight.

*

It is one of the great faults of this thing called history that it offers the future so little evidence of the senses. We are resurrected primarily through words. Everything else fades. Buildings decay or are destroyed, bronze sculptures are melted down for cannons, frescoes lose their colour, oil paint cracks, varnish darkens, the strongest perfumes lose their scent and the rich touch of velvet or brocade becomes food for generations of moths. Still, if I had to pick the sense I miss most in my eternal quiet, I think it would be sound. The chatter of voices, different languages, laughter, prayer, the claws of my lap dogs scrabbling across tiled floors, all and everything is swallowed up by silence. And then, of course, there is music. Oh, but if I could transport this scholar of mine anywhere into my past now, I know straightway where it would be: the banquet in our city palace on the night that marks the turn of the half millennium into the year 1500.

Such a celebration we mounted, the great hall filled with dozens of long tables, their freshly starched white linen already soiled with meat juices as the echoing hubbub quietens in time for the first musical interlude. I have just taken possession of one of the most beautiful lutes ever made - Lorenzo da Pavia's first commission to me - and when prevailed upon I offer up a short (but not, I think, inadequate) rendering of a work by our resident composer.

In this, you understand, I see myself only as an aperitif for the man himself, because Bartolomeo Tromboncino is the greatest exponent of the lute that our age produced, and he has a voice as haunting as his compositions. Had Eurydice heard Tromboncino first, I swear she would have followed him out of Hades instead. Better for her in some ways, as he would never have bothered to look back, for the man was a most unsatisfactory husband. He cared not a jot for his own wife until he found her in bed with another man, at which point he let the lover go before soaking the sheets with her blood. If we had longer I would tell you what happened to him, for it is the richest gossip (how could we do without his talent?), but that would take us away from the moment.

As the last notes of the lute fade away, the air grows thick with applause and cheers.

Now comes more food, the heady mix of smell and taste, followed by a recitation from one of our resident court writers: a work dedicated to the Gonzaga family, of course, which is only fair since we have paid their bed and board for the - sometimes considerable - time it takes them to compose it. Then, as the candelabra are lit, the room is prepared for dancing and laughter and chatter rise up again as the night comes in.

There are a number of special guests here tonight, cardinals, foreign diplomats and the like. A few of them have drunk too much, which has the dual effect of loosening their tongues at the same time as they try to loosen the ribbons on the bodices of my prettiest ladies. Which, of course, is why I have placed them next to each other.

Isabella's Ladies. If they were not so occupied I might introduce you to a few now, for they are worth knowing. Eleonora Brogna, for instance, or little Brognina as we called her, sitting with the Neapolitan ambassador; still a girl rather than a woman at this point, but as sweet as she is lovely and already smart enough to winkle state secrets out of a man quicker than the rack or the strappado. Then there is Livia in the green velvet, or Mariana to her right: one with the voice of an angel, the other the energy to dance till dawn. Each chosen personally by me, recruited at that moment when the flower is poised to burst from the bud (I am quite unsentimental in this. Had I met myself at that age, I would have turned me down). All well born and well educated, I dress, house and train them in the highest of court manners. In return, because I cannot be everywhere at once, they are my ears and eyes, alert for gossip, rumour or subterfuge, which, like nectar, they gather up and bring back to me. In short, an army without weapons unless you count the ability to flirt, along with a sharp wit to protect themselves. Most men, I have noticed, relish a touch of thorn with the flower, and used judiciously it can stop anything but a raging bull.

Isabella's Ladies. Known otherwise to some as Isabella's whores. Like all the other insults, it is the slander of envy. Who would not have such an intelligence service? And if they do ever overstep the bounds of respectability ... then I assure you, it is as much their choice as mine. Whatever the outcome, there will always be an eligible husband for them, along with a generous dowry. That too is in the contract between us, which never needs to be signed. In return, all I require is unshakeable loyalty. Which I get. Save for one - but she is not here tonight.

No. During the full moon of that new year when another half millennium began, our court was the most wondrous thing. And there was another reason. For I was newly with child.

The fall of Milan had shaken us all in so many ways. My virile husband, still smarting from his slight by the state of Venice, spent more time at home than with his troops. And with Osanna's words still in my heart, I swallowed any grievance I might have felt in the past, and welcomed, indeed invited him regularly to my bed, opening my night shift to him eagerly - even on the odd occasion when I suspect he might have chosen sleep instead.

When did you last bleed?

Do you have any soreness of the breasts, Isabella?

Are you more tired than before?

My mother's questions had long become my own. I knew I was with child before the sickness was due to start. Only this time there was none. No bile in my mouth, no desire for strange tastes, no terrible bouts of enervation. Instead, my energy knew no bounds and the quickening arrived earlier and stronger than ever. I was carrying a warrior. Of that there was no doubt. How I wish my mother might be here to meet him.

I took her eagle stone out from my jewel chest and strapped it to my thigh. I had not bothered with it during the carrying of Margarita, but now I checked the binding every day and never took it off, even to bathe. When I came close to my term, I ordered the silver cot my mother had commissioned all those years ago to be taken out of storage and put in my chamber. Francesco, whose faith in Osanna was, if anything, greater than mine, did not stir from the palace, except for the hunt. Yet the closer it came to my due time, the more my sister visited me in my dreams, lovelier than ever, clad in a white silk gown, her dark hair tumbling around her shoulders and a smile on her face. Only when I went towards her, she turned and walked away, and I saw that the bottom half of her gown was drenched in blood, so that she trailed crimson rivulets on the floor behind her.

I told no one of the dream, not Francesco, not even Osanna herself. If the words were spoken out loud then somehow everyone would know that Isabella d'Este was afraid. Towards the end I became so large that I could not ride or dance or even sit comfortably, and my face grew as round as my stomach. When labour started and the pains began to saw into my abdomen, I grabbed hold of my chief midwife's hand - after two births, there was little decorum between us now. 'If there is a choice between the baby and the mother, Frassina, you will favour the baby, do you hear me? Mantua - and I - will never forgive you otherwise.'

She had a florid face, her cheeks decorated with the tiniest veins of blood, which she used to say represented every baby she had safely delivered, and she laughed as she patted my hand down on to the covers. 'My lady, I have seen you do this twice before. You have the muscles of a great snake and the stamina of an ox.' Then a frown crossed her face in case I should take offence at the image, but I was laughing too. Until I was not.

Five hours later, my son emerged from the darkness into the light: the most beautiful, ugliest baby one would ever see. I knew, before any words were spoken, that I had done it. The way the midwives drew in their first breath in readiness to shout, how their voices rose up in exultation, the joy slipping out through the cracks in the door, pouring into the corridor, down to the room where my husband was waiting, already on his feet. And from there, out through the windows of the palace into the streets, reaching the bell ringers and priests who announced it to the whole city. The Gonzaga dynasty had an heir. I, Isabella d'Este, was now the true Marchesa of Mantua and a woman worth celebrating.

XV

Isabella, Marchesa of Mantua: scholar, collector, diplomat, patron of art, music and writing, and now the mother of a boy child. A woman not only worth celebrating, but surely deserving a place in history.

Except (and I wonder how much my scholar understands this) for the longest time after my death, those who claimed an interest in history showed little interest in me. Or indeed women like me. Nor did they seem to care much about the wonder of our smaller city states: Mantua, Ferrara, Urbino. We may never have been as grand or as powerful as Venice or Rome or Florence, or as overflowing in art, but our great age - this thing that is now so valued and trumpeted as *the Renaissance* - would have been a much lesser affair without us.

So when did I first become worthy of serious study?

I can tell her exactly when it happened. When the Gonzaga papers were finally removed from the old ducal palace, where they had been feasted on by mould and bookworms for centuries, and brought here to the empty monastery building. The year was 1868. Italy, a land for so long broken up, invaded and ruled by others, had become a single nation at last. Histories of its past now demanded to be written. And Mantua's archive contained riches.

Ah, but this scholar of mine should have been here then! What a spectacle it was. It felt as if the whole world was celebrating, and we, the past, were a part of it: carts laden with chests moving across the great piazza, an army of men, backs bowed under the weight of memory, snaking through cobbled streets to what would now be known as the State Archive of Mantua.

Except the hastily converted monastery turned out to be too small for all that history, so that not everything could be kept. What to save and what to destroy? Such arguments there were over it. Until finally it was decided that no one would be interested in centuries of household accounts. Bonfires were lit in the main piazza; sacks of bone-dry documents feeding the flames as clouds of inky ash moved through the city.

Copy books and ledgers filled with endless lists and figures. How scholars bemoan such 'vandalism' now! It seems there were veins of gold inside those pages: the vagaries of fashion, supply and demand, the cost of everything: wine, food, wages, linen, spices, animals, furs, silverware, jewels, perfumed gloves, boots, dwarves, domestic slaves. How could one construct a history of trade or chart the rise and fall of great family fortunes and courts without it?

Here at last, history's misfortune was to my advantage. For not only did I buy everything, from everywhere, I also recorded the unfolding of every deal, describing, bargaining (oh, how I bargained), complaining, returning things that I did not like. Even works of art. Oh yes. Not every patron had a bottomless purse. And not every artist delivered what was asked of them. I have seen such wry smiles on the faces of art historians as they follow my correspondence with men now worshipped as demigods. Leonardo may have refused many commissions, but no one pestered him as relentlessly as I did. The great Giovanni

Bellini and I haggled for years over a commission that he never delivered. I had to threaten to take him to court to get my money back. That became gossip fast enough. How the monstrous Marchesa does behave! Such stories would be welcome doses of reality for those still dazzled by the 'pricelessness' of art.

Inside the State Archive of Mantua.

But all that came later. During those first years, the work was more tedious: every letter sent or received had to be read, dated and catalogued for posterity. I spent more time in the company of the archive's first director, Alessandro Luzio, than I ever did my husband or children. The man grew hunched in my service, dust clogging his lungs and coating the lenses of his spectacles. He made it his life's work to compose the first biography of me. In the end, that first garrulous English woman, Julia Cartwright, beat him to it.

He wrote reams of furious letters threatening to sue her for stealing his research. But he died before anything could come of it.

I think now that his indignation was less from scholastic envy than the fact that she was a woman.

Because that was the other change that I watched happening. Slowly, archives - throughout history founded by men for men - were being invaded by women. Educated, confident, they were starting to ask different questions about the past. The fact that I was so eager to wear the trousers within government (those very same words came from my husband's own pen - I have seen the actual letter myself) made me a heroine. My stubbornness, even my bad behaviour, was now to be celebrated.

It was not long before I was not the only one. Over the years, the pace of change has quickened. Increasing numbers of women, young and old, were now descending on the archives, rooting like truffle pigs in search of lives either forgotten or ignored. Such treasures they found. Well-bred daughters or wives who wrote poetry, sang, played, studied science or even painted. Visionary lay women like Osanna. Convents where abbesses commissioned works of art, nuns wrote plays, choir mistresses composed music. The study of church court records revealed darker riches. Cases of nuns who stuck needles in their hands to fake stigmata. A disgraced convent where, draining the well, they found the bones of half a dozen newborn babies. Lists of Jewish girls who embraced Christ against their parents' wishes. And, most recently of all, the buying and selling of black slaves throughout Italy. A few even had stories attached, others are just dates and names, no faces, no pasts, no futures. It was like watching fishes flip out of dark water, the sun flashing on their scales for a second, before they plunged back into the deep.

Such fishing is all the rage now. Before the recent contagion, I spent a whole day with a scholar who had no interest in me at all save for one or two letters, correspondence around my buying of a young African child for my household. They copied every detail, word for word. Yet I could feel their frustration, almost their disapproval, that I did not say more.

But what reason would there have been for that? Women like myself were trained to be alert to the fashions of court life. The Portuguese had opened a trade route along the coast of Africa and the men, women and children they bought there were sold in the slave market in Venice, alongside Turks, Greeks, Slavs and all manner of other peoples taken prisoner in piracy or war. But there was something about the ebony beauty of these new Africans, most especially the children, that made hearts beat faster. Many of the men, once freed, would go on to become sought-after gondoliers in the city. Others would find their way into nativity scenes: splendid portraits of the third Magus, Balthazar, jewelled robes and turbans vibrant against the majesty of their night-black skin.

It was hardly a surprise, then, that the children became popular in the best courts as servants or train-bearers. My agent in Venice worked tirelessly to find the right little girl - only when he did, he was concerned that she was too small, an orphan barely two years old and plagued by illness. So it was agreed that he would buy her and have her looked after for as long as it took for her to regain her health, before he dispatched her to me.

The stuff of my letters is all that remains of her in history. The fact is, she was not a person of importance in the way she has become now. And I must say, I see no reason why I should find myself judged by the future on this account. Any more than the great Dante judged Virgil for being held in eternal limbo, or we might - I don't know - condemn Socrates for taking his own life, even though he lived in a world before Jesus Christ or the sin of suicide was born.

I could say more about her. If I remember rightly, we named her: Sofina. She became something of a darling of the household, so that when she grew to adulthood, I gave her her freedom and arranged a marriage to a cloth merchant, with a dowry including a chest of old court dresses that, with her nose for fashion honed in my service, went on to secure them both a good living.

A fine story, yes. And no less true because it is not recorded.

Indeed, I offer it as a lesson now to this scholar of mine: that there are times when it becomes acceptable, even necessary, to imagine things that are not written down, as well as interrogating what is.

It is almost three weeks since she first took up her place in the corner of the reading room and the air is noticeably warmer. More of the desks are occupied now - signs of the first influx of summer scholars - and if she is late, someone might take her place. As happens this morning, when an elderly man with a thatch of white hair and thick round black spectacles settles himself there. Even without his style, I know him to be a historian of art (they often have something of the dandy about them, though this one rather resembles an old owl to me), because I have been on his desk before.

Today, it is correspondence between myself and Maestro Mantegna. I would recognise Andrea's script anywhere, for his hand is the worst I ever saw. Every sentence was either a mess of blots where he'd dipped his quill too deep into the well or a line of diminishing scratches as he failed to replenish the ink. It was as if anything and everything that took him away from the business of art was a waste of time.

The exchange here comes from the end of his life, when his son had so emptied the family coffers that he was forced to sell off his house and his own collection of antiquities to fund the debts. As his marchesa, it was my duty to help him, which, of course, I did, buying from him a rather fine head of the Roman matron Faustina. He asked far too much for it, but I did him the honour of taking him seriously as a collector and bargained. Indeed, this is the correspondence that sits now on the art scholar's desk. It is exactly the kind of incident that such men relish, for they can use it as evidence of my bad behaviour as a collector. Which may be true at times, but in this case is sorely misunderstood. The truth is that Maestro Mantegna enjoyed the tussle as much as I did. Indeed, I think in some ways he relished it, for he was always at his most animated when he had a fight on his hands. I still paid over the odds for the bust, though this owl scholar may choose to disagree. Ha! Did he or any of them ever collect a thing?

Either way, this man can find another place to sit. As he turns to my own letters for a reply, a series of sudden cold draughts plays havoc with his notebook. It doesn't take long for him to move. Would it be churlish to admit how I enjoy such moments?

She arrives soon enough and, after a whispered friendly conversation with one of the archivists, settles herself quickly. Eavesdropping. It is one of the few pleasures of this endless afterlife of mine, for gossip was always a necessary adjunct to statecraft and it is important to know something about those who preserve and study me. Love affairs, marriages, ailments, trouble with children, I have heard it all from the women - and more often than not, it *is* women - who work here, though recently it is spiced with frustration over how they are being treated: reduced opening hours, posts left empty when someone retires. If it is a question of money - what else could it be? - it is a criminal saving. Every great state puts its history above a price tag. And though Mantua may be small, it still boasts wonders to attract visitors: the castle with Mantegna's painted chamber, churches designed by the great Leon Alberti, the ducal palace, my own studiolo, the remains of my first grotta, even Osanna's house, they are all still there to be visited.

It seems my scholar has seen them all. I have heard enough of her accent now to know where she is from (English people never seem to open their mouths wide enough, no doubt because of all the rain and fog that would get in). I only ever entertained a few of her countrymen in my lifetime, for it was a rather backward state then with little interest in art. Though I did once receive a gift of a fine horse from the second Henry Tudor when he was in need of noble Italians to intercede with the pope to annul his heirless marriage so he could marry a lady-in-waiting! Such a scandal that would be. Perhaps that is why so many of his kinsmen are so eager to study us now. Certainly, I cannot fault their dedication and appetite.

She is no exception. Most days she arrives early and does not leave until closing. I like how demonstrative she is: the way she blows her breath out noisily when she is struggling over a text, or laughs aloud when she finds my vanity and politicking too obvious or dissembling. She has a capacity for mischief. Yesterday, I caught her surreptitiously refolding one of the smallest pieces of paper along its original creases. Should the archivists spot her doing this they will chastise her, for any extra fingering renders the pages more fragile.

Still, when she held it in her hand it felt like a living thing to me again; its miniature size, closed by a tiny flap of extra paper secured with a dab of wax like a single drop of dried blood, suggests an element of subterfuge, some dark secret information to be concealed under a hat band or inside a rider's cuff. The reality is more mundane, more often than not a scribbled postscript for something forgotten: candied fruits from Naples, or - as in the one in her hand - a request to my father's court for a last-minute music manuscript needed for a concert.

As her confidence grows, so she is also becoming more adventurous in the sources she seeks out. The more colourful, the better.

*The painter has done such a terrible job that it bears no
resemblance to us whatsoever ...*

Not everyone noses out the letter I wrote to a contessa friend
in the days after Mantegna delivered that first execrable portrait
of me.

*... Instead, we have had to commission a foreign artist famous
for his ability to copy from nature.*

Foreign. The very word tells her how our city states viewed each
other then. The man I chose was the court painter of Urbino,
one Giovanni Santi. Alas, the watery air of Mantua proved disastrous for his lungs and he died not long after his visit. I should
have waited for his son, the luminous Raphaello Sanzio, to come
of age. That would have been an image to be treasured.

As for the work Santi completed? It was not so much bad as
unremarkable. A well-dressed young woman, good-looking in a
plumped-up-partridge kind of way - accurate to nature in that,
I suppose, but with a complete absence of character or spirit. I sent
it on not long after to another noble friend eager for a memento of
me, along with some bolts of silk with which to recreate the outfit
I was wearing in it. By then, my reputation as a leader of fashion
was spreading fast.

The power of clothes. Might that be part of the reason I am
so content to sit over her shoulder? Certainly, she continues to
pay attention to what she wears. (Unlike most in this room. These
days, most scholars, men and women alike, look as if they have
just got out of bed.) Before the weather warmed, she favoured
trousers, with bright military-style jackets over sculpted silk tops.

Recently, she has moved into skirts, light velvets and cottons, or brightly patterned dresses that flare out from a belted waist. Her figure is passable. Her chosen colour palette remains flamboyant: blues against fierce yellows, earth reds tempered by sea greens and orange. And always a snaking scarf of a different colour worn casually around her neck: a clever way to conceal what I already know to be a certain crepe quality of her skin, which, along with that thin line of grey on her scalp, marks her out as older than she might wish to appear.

I wonder, do people mock her for it in the same way they mocked me? Though never to my face - they wouldn't dare.

The Monstrous Marchesa, indecently old and dishonourably tarted up.

The man who wrote those words was a hired pen, a known pornographer and scabrous liar, built like an ox with more hair on his chest than on his head, and a penchant for wearing ermine fur and the thickest of gold chains to show up his importance. *Dishonourably tarted up*! He might as well have been looking at himself in a mirror.

It's possible that if I had spent less on clothes, I could have bought more treasures. But no woman of standing could ignore her wardrobe. Apart from illness or confinement there was never a day when I did not 'dress' to enter company, for we were judged by what we wore. Our own shining suits of armour.

Which is why I made it my business always to be informed of what others were wearing.

Her wardrobe would fill more pages than the lives of the
Saints. Last night alone the lady wore a coffer of gold; she has
a cloak, crimson satin lined with ermine and decorated with

jewels: 61 rubies, 55 diamonds, 5 large pearls, 412 medium-sized ones and 114 smaller ones ...

Particularly if both the lady and the meeting were to be of significance.

XVI

Pinturicchio: Lucrezia Borgia at thirteen years old.

I wonder, does Lucrezia Borgia stalk the archives of Ferrara?

> *My dearest sweet sister, I simply cannot thank you enough for your gift ...*

I've never detected the faintest scent of her here, though we've shared the same desk often enough, exchanges of phatic insincerities between women who could barely conceal their dislike under that cordial word, 'sister'.

Reading our letters now is like eating fresh treacle: too thick and sweet to swallow easily. I've considered 'disappearing' some of them - documents get lost, even in the best-run archives. But this parvenu, scandal-soaked daughter of a courtesan and a pope has burned herself too deep into the pages of history to be expunged; and when our family trees became entwined, it was impossible to disentangle them.

The fact is, had Lucrezia Borgia been born with any other family name, I doubt she would be known to anyone now. Yes, I know it is easy to slander women when it comes to matters of the flesh. So I suppose it is possible that she did *not* sleep with her father *or* her brothers. Or give birth secretly to an illegitimate child. Or be party to the murder of her second husband in his bed. Nevertheless, by the time she arrived in Ferrara to marry my brother, Alfonso, she was soiled goods. The union would have been unthinkable if her monster brother Cesare had not been rampaging across Italy with an army financed by their father, the pope.

To sweeten the pill, she brought with her the richest dowry Italy had ever seen, which, I think, placated my father a little. As for Alfonso, I doubt he cared that much. Widowed after the death of his wife, Anna, in childbirth, as duke elect he would have had to marry again soon and I suspect he, like many, was secretly dazzled by Cesare Borgia's military daring.

As the only living female in the Este family, my presence was vital to the festivities. But should I go alone or together? With Francesco and I away at the same time, our borders would be unprotected.

'You know as much as I do, husband. Every dispatch says the same thing. Cesare Borgia himself will not be present at the wedding.'

'And what? You think he'd dare to use my absence to march against us! God damn it, our two families will be related by marriage then!'

'It would be an act of unspeakable treachery ...' I sigh, letting the silence hang.

'... and the most audacious piece of military strategy,' he growls. 'The devil take the man. He has no honour.'

Like every other soldier in Italy, his outrage is spiced with envy. What might he have achieved had he been the son of the pope with the power of French artillery behind him?

'I bow to you in this, my lord. Whether you accompany me or not is your decision.' I let my eyes drop to the floor modestly.

'Ah, it is made already. You must go alone. Still, it's a great shame. I was looking forward to meeting this Borgia siren in the flesh.'

It is amazing to me how scandal can both destroy a woman and make her more enticing at the same time.

'For what it's worth, my reports are that her beauty is much overrated.'

'Nevertheless ...' And he is lost in his own reverie now. 'Your brother will need to be on his mettle in the marriage chamber.'

I shrug my shoulders, as if this is all ordinary court chatter. I have got the decision I need from him and have grown used to letting such things pass. I know well enough where my husband's mind goes when we are not together. For instance, I am aware he has an occasional liking for young men. Despite the gravity of the sin, either because it is man's appetite or at times the only release on offer (usually in battle camps, I hear), sodomy has become almost a commonplace vice these days. I choose not to think about it. My mother was right; in the end, one becomes accustomed to everything and since the birth of Federico we ask less of each other. It is better for both of us that way.

'Be assured you will know every detail, as I will write every day. But don't dare to use my absence to get closer to Federico.'

Vying for his affection – the words and bubbling laughter of a two-year-old – is the fondest part of our relationship.

'Too late! He already lifts his arms more eagerly to me than you. I'll have him riding a horse and wielding a sword by the time you get back.' He laughs. 'You're sure you do not mind going alone, wife?'

'Not at all.'

With our borders defended, I could get on with planning my attack.

*

Intelligence, as my father taught me, is a skill worth spending on …

… crimson satin lined with ermine and decorated with jewels: 61 rubies, 55 diamonds, 5 large pearls, 412 medium-sized ones and 114 smaller ones.

To this day, I wonder which of her wardrobe ladies my clever spy bribed to deliver such accurate counting.

Of course, the bride-to-be was flaunting herself. The entire journey from Rome to Ferrara was orchestrated as a great Borgia lap of triumph. Nevertheless, it was clear I could not outspend her. And she had other advantages. She was younger than me by six years, and my pregnancies – the last barely a few months before (Livia – sweet enough, but she would die too soon to find a place in history) – had left me with a widened girth, while my face was starting to show signs of Uncle Borso's chins.

What was called for was a new hairstyle to distract the eye. In those days, we had an excellent trading relationship with the Sultan of Turkey and his stable of Barbary horses, and a number of small portraits had moved between us as gifts. His were particularly intriguing for the intricacy and beauty of his turbans, which were an excuse for the most elaborate confection of swirling cloth and jewels. If such a headdress could be adapted, perhaps by weaving in swags of fake hair along with silk and precious stones, it would not only be a fashion statement but would add to my height, so that anyone meeting me would find their eye pulled upwards to admire it. It took only a few experiments to perfect it. (I had a group of the best seamstresses from Illyria installed in castle rooms at the time - though it is *not* true, as some have suggested, that I kept them locked in there!) All the new style lacked was a name. Isabella d'Este's *Capigliara.* Descriptions of it would travel round Italy as fast as any postal dispatch. My scholar need only look at any number of fashionable portraits from the years that followed (Venetian women were particularly slavish) to see its success.

*

Awash with Borgia money, Ferrara put on a great show to meet its fate. As to the smouldering beauty of the Borgia siren, all I can say is I didn't see it.

This is not spite, you understand; in such matters, women have to keep a clear head. I can paint her now for anyone who is interested. She was pretty enough in a youthful way, delicate build with a good complexion - rose and cream (it would age fast) and her eyes, greenish, were clear and bright. But a real beauty, such as Cecilia Gallerani in her prime, could have taken her out with a turn of her head. Her voice, light almost to the point of a cooing dove, had the slightest of lisps, which no doubt men found endearing; but in conversation it didn't take long for her absence of breeding to show. She'd grown up amid wealth but little culture, and her taste was painfully superficial. In discussions about poetry or music she was soon outmatched, though she turned the topic easily to one of her own as she had a speed that made up for depth. And – I cannot deny her this – a certain charm when it came to the company of men, for she was most attentive. Even my father, who still had fumes rising off the top of his head at being politically outmanoeuvred, grew placid in her company.

And my brother? Well, he seemed pleased enough. Though he treated the whole event as a distraction from his greatest passion and was soon back smelting iron in his beloved cannon foundry.

As for the battle of our wardrobes, I picked my moment carefully.

Our first public meeting would be in the old castle on the day of her official entry into the city. My intelligence told me she would wear white silk, piped with gold, colours to complement the palomino horse she rode, with an excess of pearls to suit her creamy skin. So I dressed myself and my ladies in deep shades of velvet, the thick nap of the fabric designed to come alive under winter candlelight.

As for my own gown ... echoing the colour of my headdress, it was the richest midnight blue, and its velvet skirts, flowing like a lake around me, were embroidered with gold and silver symbols of musical notations, so clear, so accurate, that any half-trained musician would be able to construct half a melody as I danced. A musical costume for what was known to be a musical city. Worn by the daughter of the duke, herself a renowned player, and, until my father was dead, still the first lady of Ferrara.

*

'*Hah!*' Deep into envoys' reports at her desk, my scholar's laugh catches in her throat.

*

'Sweet Jesus, Isabella! What did she do when she saw you?'

Only the voice I'm hearing now is not hers, but that of my husband.

On my return, all I wanted to do was to hold our son in my arms, though he wriggled free fast enough, eager to show me how he could now thrust a wooden sword like a real soldier.

'Given what I know of women's fashion, I was the equivalent of a gauntlet thrown in a man's face.'

'I don't see why? It was my job to celebrate Ferrara's musical culture.'

He pursed his lips. 'Hmm. I still want to know how the enemy reacted.'

How much of the truth to tell?

To her credit, she had handled it adeptly. But then the whole room was watching to note her reaction. As she entered, every eye upon her, she was all grace and smiles. And when she saw me? Her expression did not change, though the flash in her eyes did. She glided towards me, the smile growing brighter all the time, and warmly embraced me, before holding me at arm's length and announcing loudly - enough to be heard by all: 'Oh, but dear, dear sister. How ... how splendid you look. And how very clever of you to make such a great effort on my behalf.'

And as the room let out a collective release of breath, I could not help but notice a few sly smiles.

*

'Woah!' Francesco's laugh is from his belly rather than his head. 'My God, but I should have been there. Good for her.'

'What? Are you suggesting I behaved badly?'

'Badly? No.' And the laugh is kinder now. 'On the contrary, I would say you behaved, well ... just like Isabella d'Este. Though I can think of a few who would be less generous.'

He was right, of course. The story - a fist fight of fashion - moved across Italy in a dozen saddle bags and there was much comment. Some saw it as an outrageous act of female rivalry, even a gesture of overt snobbery. I have no trouble owning that. Though I would put it another way: that the real outrage was that this upstart illegitimate Spanish nobody, who had been unjustly foisted upon us, was now the future Duchess of Ferrara, inhabiting my mother's rooms and wearing her precious dowry jewels from the royal house of Naples. If the rest of Italy dared not stand up to the Borgias, then at that moment at least I did my best.

'What I did, I did for both our family's names. As I said to you in my letters, it was a most frosty wedding.'

'Well, frosty or hot, wife. It is done. The alliance is formed and we can all sleep safely in our beds now.'

*

At her desk in the archive, my scholar is busy with her notebook. Over her shoulder, I watch as she writes the words.

Just like Isabella d'Este. And I must say, her smile has a certain delight to it.

XVII

Except we were not safe in our beds, because it did not end there.

Less than three months later, the Borgias betrayed a firm alliance with the state of Urbino, and with no warning Cesare's army attacked and took the city by surprise. Its duchess, Elisabetta, Francesco's dear sister, was a guest in our house at the time, while her husband, Duke Montefeltro, was so sure of the alliance that he was dining outside of the city. With his own gates closed against him, next day he was a fugitive on the run, with Borgia troops hunting him down.

The treachery was gross. The attack shameful. The achievement staggering.

Urbino, a treasure house of art and learning, had fallen without a drop of blood being shed. As the shock waves rolled across Italy, we sat comforting Elisabetta and waiting daily for further news. Close on two weeks later, a trio of hungry beggars arrived at our city gates after twilight. Only as the guards started to turn them away, one of them took off a ring and demanded that it be delivered to the palace.

When he finally came into our presence, Guidobaldo di Montefeltro, Duke of Urbino, was gaunt, filthy and dressed in rags. But alive.

That he and my sister-in-law Elisabetta loved each other dearly was well known. She was the sweetest of women, famed for her culture and taste, and unfailingly kind and loving towards me. He was also a most honourable man. But something else was known about them also. Rumours of his impotence were too widespread to be ignored. She and I once skirted around the subject (you might say we both had problems in the bedchamber), but it was never, ever, openly acknowledged. Certainly, there was no sign of resentment in either of them. On the contrary, they moved through life like the closest brother and sister, sharing their love of learning and the creation of a great court with affection and humour, so that there were times, I admit, when I envied their companionship.

The minute he entered they were in each other's arms, tears flowing down both their faces, for they had feared that they would never see each other again. No homecoming Francesco and I shared would ever be so poignant.

Raphael: Duke and Duchess of Urbino, 1506/7.

Meanwhile, Cesare's men were ransacking their great ducal palace of its treasures: Piero della Francesca, Botticelli, Raphaello Sanzio ... The man was a philistine and cared for none of it except its resale value. For those of us who lived for beauty and art, it was unbearable. The only thing worse was the thought that if Urbino could fall, where might he strike next?

Francesco and my father both travelled to Milan to await the arrival of the French king, still in firm alliance with the Borgias. Surely he could now be made to understand that his alliance was empowering a monster? Dispatch riders between us wore out horses as I urged caution. I spent hours in Osanna's stifling little cell, hoping that God might see fit to impart to her wisdom about our threatened future. But her health had deteriorated badly since Federico's birth and her eyes could barely see me, let alone look into the future.

When he did finally arrive, His Majesty was too deep in bed with the pope and his son to heed any warning. At least he had the grace to be generous. To Francesco, he offered the sop of a high commission in his own army. Though even that came at a price (verbal, never written): that we no longer give sanctuary to the Duke and Duchess of Urbino.

There was only one place for them to go: Venice. They had barely settled there when the Borgia 'offer' was delivered, its contents made painfully public. If the duke renounced all future claim on Urbino, the pope would generously 'annul' his marriage on the grounds of non-consummation and - even more generously - offer him refuge in the Church, with the promise of a cardinal's hat. At last, there might be such a thing as a truly chaste cardinal!

The cruelty was perfect. The only dignity to be had was in the duke's refusal.

But when a gale is blowing, it is better not to walk into the centre of it. Francesco accepted the post in the French army, and I in turn took up the reins of government again. For all that I hated Cesare Borgia, our correspondence oozed brother and sisterly courtesy. By then, Mantua had nothing left that the monster wanted. Except the state itself.

*

In the reading room, she has already seen the letter that promised a future marriage between our beloved Federico and the monster's infant daughter. I know some who read it are shocked. But I can see that is not her. She has lived with me long enough to know that children, however young, are as much part of the power game as adults. If, or when, circumstances changed, the agreement would not be worth the paper it was written on. It suited the moment. And the moment, as she must know by now, was everything in Italy.

Until it was not.

I wonder if I might ask you to intercede with the pope and his son, on my behalf for a certain object ...

Ah ... but it seems she is not ready to go there yet.

... for I know his excellency, Cesare Borgia, does not care much for antiques.

I should have foreseen it. Out of the thousands of letters sent out under my seal, the one written to my cardinal brother, Ippolito, in Rome that tumultuous summer of 1502 arrives like a homing pigeon on almost every scholar's desk.

I should never have allowed it to be copied. But how was I to know that my rescue of a treasure from the ransacked Urbino would send such ripples into history, to be cited gleefully as a further example of Isabella d'Este, the collector, behaving badly?

Well, since we are here, let us get the matter of the *Sleeping Cupid* over with once and for all.

Yes, the 'certain object' I wanted was indeed a treasure. Though not as one might expect. From the moment the white marble sculpture of a sleeping Cupid had been unearthed in a building site in Rome ten years earlier, it was clear that it was the work of an ancient master: the way the sculptor had fashioned the child's soft flesh, the abandonment of his body in sleep, his delicate wings tucked up behind him. Yet apart from dirt and superficial damage on the surface, it was perfect. Perfect! There wasn't a collector in the whole of Italy who didn't lust after it.

It was snapped up soon enough by a cardinal with more money than I could ever have raised. So be it. I was new to collecting, but already used to losing to higher bidders.

Except that then a rumour began to spread: this was not an ancient piece at all! Rather, it was a fraud. A brand-new copy, carved in Florence by a gifted student in the Medici sculpture garden, who had then dirtied it up and, in league with a dealer, shipped it to Rome, where it was buried in a suitable place and then – wonder of wonders! – unearthed, with the two of them splitting the profits.

The dealer's disgrace was only matched by the palpable talent of the forger. No one had heard the name of young Michelangelo Buonarroti till then. But they knew it now. It didn't take long before he had his own commission from another cardinal: the miracle of a life-size marble Mary, cradling the body of her dead son in her lap.

In the years that followed, I lost track of the Cupid as it changed hands. Until, at last, it arrived in my brother-in-law's collection in Urbino and, of course, I recognised it immediately. The first time I ran my fingers over the marble flesh, I wept. Yes, wept: not just because it was beautiful, but because, to me, it was proof of how completely we had absorbed the lessons of our ancient masters, so we could equal, even surpass them, in skill and power.

But with Urbino captured, this wondrous piece became a spoil of war. Of course, of course, I had to try and save it.

It would surely be a crime if all this great art were to disappear, never to be seen again and I know his Excellency, Cesare Borgia, does not take much pleasure in antiques

It is true that I wrote this letter while my displaced brother- and sister-in-law were still taking refuge under our roof and that they were unaware of it. Which, I concede, opens me to an accusation of insensitivity. But the poor things were overwhelmed by events and timing was of the essence. If anything was to be saved, it had to be done fast since every day more works of art were being loaded and shipped out to finance the Borgia army.

It didn't take long. The monster was only too happy to offer up such an insignificant gift to a woman who, with our children now affianced, was now his *dearest sister*.

Some time later (I admit she still had other things on her mind), I found occasion to talk to Elisabetta herself about it, suggesting she might see my action as fortuitous, since otherwise it would have ended up in the hands of our enemies. And, as you would expect of my magnanimous sweet sister-in-law, she agreed. Which my critics would no doubt say is the reason I told her.

Unfortunately, the matter did not end there. Once reinstated in Urbino with his court around him again, my brother-in-law let it be known that he would appreciate his treasure back, as *an example to all those others who obtained things that should never have been given*.

My reply - and of course my scholar has ferreted out this too, how clever of her - was, I think, most convincing. Or perhaps it would be more honest to say that I convinced myself, for I have come to understand over these years that that is a necessary element in the art of letter writing. I reminded him, because with so much going on he must surely have forgotten, that the duchess herself had blessed my actions, going so far as to suggest that had she known I was so fond of the statue, she would have given it to me herself. So that rather than an acquisition from a criminal, I saw it more as a gift between two families, who felt nothing but the greatest affection and goodwill towards each other.

I suspect he was not entirely placated by this (I would not have been either), but it was never mentioned between us again. The beloved Cupid stayed with me.

The future rewarded them well enough without it. On their return, the couple were met by the whole city, wild with joy, and musicians, poets, scholars, writers from all over Italy flocked to celebrate victory with them. In the years to come, the court of Urbino would have no equal: renowned for its civility and culture and immortalised – along with my sweet sister-in-law – in Baldassare Castiglione's great *Book of the Courtier*. How often I see it now on scholars' desks, for it has become something of a bible for the virtues of a great court. I've even heard it suggested that I envied Elisabetta such fame. But that is slander yet again. It is true that she and I shared a passion for art and learning, but my tongue was always too sharp for some of my guests, while she had a natural modesty that allowed others to shine at the expense of herself. I could begrudge her nothing.

No, ours was always the most loving relationship and our families grew ever closer, so that soon after their return, when Guido formally adopted his nephew as his heir, they offered the boy's hand in marriage to our own firstborn daughter, Eleonora.

There it is then! The real story of the *Sleeping Cupid*. Further proof, if needed, of how Isabella d'Este's appetite for art made her behave badly; an accusation that, like strong dye slipped into water, has stained the way history has seen me ever since.

But I would say this loud and clear: that all manner of men, kings, princes, dukes, bankers, popes and cardinals behaved much worse in pursuit of objects they wanted. Yet they are never strung up on the scaffold of reputation because of it. Collecting was never a job for the simpering or the timid. And I *was* a collector. And anyone who sets out to resurrect me needs to remember that.

* * *

The Borgia fall, when it came, was as precipitous as their rise.

I am aware that there are some - even in my own time - who delight in eking out the sensational, but I would urge my scholar to get over it fast, since in this way villains will take up less history.

Barely a year after the invasion of Urbino, the pope and his son, closeted and plotting together in Rome, were felled by the same virulent fever. Alexander was dead within the week and the monster might as well have followed, for, as he lay delirious in a room nearby (they say his henchmen half drowned him in a barrel of iced water to bring down the fever), whatever power he had had leaked out of him like a gushing pump. Rumour had it that they were both poisoned at the same dinner party. Rumour also had it that the night the pope died, seven devils were seen dancing around his bed, waiting to drag his body down into hell.

The future is more sceptical on such things than we were, but I admit it gives me a certain satisfaction still to imagine it.

Should my scholar or anyone else want to know more (and it seems that many do), I would urge them to search out a work written by one Niccolò Machiavelli, which circulated in manuscript some years later and was avidly read by those whose job it was to govern. I see it now on all manner of scholars' desks, though when he wrote it he was a lesser-known diplomat from Florence who had the dubious honour of being a first-hand observer on the Borgia final years and had charted the chaos that was Italy at that time with an unblinking eye. Like many, he had a begrudging admiration for the monster's cunning. Though he was even fonder of the goddess Fortuna, who, he claimed,

174

favoured virile young men who enjoyed wrestling with her. But when she turned her back on them, they would find themselves swimming against a river in full spate so that even the strongest might drown.

I found it then, and still do now, a most telling description and one that I think every student of history would do well to remember.

The next morning, she is late to the archive again. I while away the time overlooking the desk of the elderly art scholar who once tried to take her place.

He has finished with Mantegna's letters, and the painter who succeeded him left a light footprint on history. The court artist whose script he has in front of him now will be remembered for all kinds of reasons, his skill with paint being only one of them. The Mantuan correspondence of Giulio Romano is a treasure trove, each and every letter pulsing with energy: ideas for designs of palaces, schedules of construction, costs, craftsmen needed, wages paid, the words decorated with tiny scribbled ink diagrams like lacework in the margins.

If Mantegna found it painful to start writing, Giulio Romano, it seems, could not stop.

How I would have enjoyed receiving such letters from *my* court painter. But alas, they weren't addressed to me. They come from the archive of my son, Federico Gonzaga II. Though you would never recognise him as the Duke of Mantua from the way Romano addresses him. No sign of *Your Lordship* or *Your Excellency* here. No, 'Federico' and his new court painter 'Giulio' were like brothers from the start.

But I don't want to get ahead of myself here. I have learned from a lifetime of commissioning poets and storytellers that the way to hold an audience is to keep the thread of the story tight, holding back rather than giving too much. The name and the scandal of Giulio Romano must wait a while.

When she does arrive, she looks tired. Too much treachery, backstabbing and war, no doubt. She wouldn't be the first to find the contortions of Italian politics indigestible after a while. I might recommend something more anodyne now. Some correspondence in matters of fashion or art, perhaps.

Except, it seems, that is not where she is going. The files she has called up are dated a few years after the fall of the Borgias, and are from my husband's archive, not mine.

On a fresh page of her notebook, I watch as she inscribes the words: *Lucrezia Borgia and ...*

The breath I send makes her shiver, but it doesn't stop her.

... Francesco Gonzaga.

Lucrezia Borgia and Francesco Gonzaga!

Imagine that, if you will. My sister-in-law and my husband. Could an outrage be more perfect? So much so that even if it never happened, some scholar somewhere would have had to invent it.

Lucrezia Borgia and Francesco Gonzaga.

How many ways have I heard this spun? The favourite is surely the cat fight: the slow burning revenge of a woman upstaged at her own wedding. One might say I even deserved it. Though a close second is the dalliance between two heightened sexual appetites, who had little to hold them in either of their marriage beds.

I had been much looking forward to meeting this siren in the flesh ... your brother will need to be on his mettle in the marriage chamber. My husband's voice speaks volumes here, and certainly this version has its attractions: for both parties have equally colourful reputations and a taste for danger.

Except for the fact there is not a shred of evidence for either of these scenarios.

She ignores the wind I send again, and instead under their names writes a series of dates - months as well as years, alongside them are the names of towns on the borders of Mantua and Ferrara, places where both families kept summer lodges or palaces. So, this is what? Ah! A record of where two members of the Gonzaga and Este families met. The meeting of in-laws. What does that prove?

Then there is the correspondence between them. While I didn't read it at the time (well, not all of it), I have seen it often enough now. It's true that it shows a warm connection, treading at times a delicate line between familial courtesy and - usually on her part, but then as we know she had no breeding - a more naked affection. But it never, ever, oversteps the bounds. No. In any court of law, which is not so different from the court of history, all this proves nothing.

What else, then, do you have to convince me?

As soon as she starts rummaging in her bag, I know where we are going.

Yes, here it comes: *Lucrezia Borgia*, a well-worn slab of a book with a most pretty image of a woman (an addition from history, there is no evidence that this is her at all) on the cover. And straightway I am back upstairs in what was once the old panelled reading room. Only in lieu of monks' prayers, the air is thick now with political gossip. Italy is ruled by the son of a blacksmith who has the temerity to call himself il Duce (how quickly the glow of a united country has faded) and talk of war is everywhere. Though the woman scholar, fashionably waved hair and red lip-paint, who has called up my husband's papers, is more concerned with addressing the reputation of the Borgia siren, by then further embellished by history.

Her refashioning of the life of Lucrezia made her famous, winning prizes and selling cartloads of copies. I read it over the shoulders of half a dozen archivists who kept it in their desks for breaks and lunchtime. It told the story of a fun-loving, sweet-natured young woman, a pawn rather than a player, more suited to love than politics and appreciated by men like my husband, well known - and I think I quote directly now, for it made me so laugh to read it - for his *shapely columns of legs*, along with *a solid apparatus of muscle* and *lips full and soft with hungry sensuality*. The only thing that separated this Gonzaga Adonis from greatness, according to Maria Bellonci (for that was the scholar's name), was the existence of a wife whose attributes of being *cold*, *clever* and *politically superior* so wounded his pride that he had to seek relief in the arms of other women. (Years later, this same scholar would return to the archive to write my story, and though her retelling was in its way most discerning, it is one of my lesser faults that I hold grudges, so it was not enough to make me forgive her.)

Still, I bow to her in one thing when it comes to her portrait of this *extramarital affair*: she understood perfectly the motivation behind it. Like everything in our lives, it was politics. In the years following her father's death, and still childless into marriage (two failed pregnancies, one stillborn), Lucrezia Borgia was a most vulnerable figure and desperate to help her brother, who, having fled to Spain, was held prisoner there. Who could she possibly appeal to for help? Except a man, connected by marriage, who was himself a great warrior and susceptible to pretty young women who might need his assistance.

The more you imagine this scenario, the more compelling it becomes: she, pretty face, bright-eyed and trembling, willowy body finely clad, flinging herself down at his feet as a supplicant.

Him, already charmed, bending down and lifting her up: *No, please, dear sister, there is no need to kneel to me ...*

Perfect, both for her cunning and his vanity.

Of course, there is no proof that this is what happened, because no one, bar them, was there. There is certainly nothing in my letters to suggest I knew what was going on. But then, why would there be? I was always my father's daughter in matters of diplomatic sensitivity. If any such 'intelligence' had been communicated to me, it could only ever have been delivered by word of mouth or, if on paper, destroyed immediately after reading.

Yet here I am telling it to you anyway. Well, why not? If you are smart enough to smell smoke where there was fire, then at least let us get it right.

So, yes, a 'liaison' of sorts did take place between them, both in the palaces and places noted and a few others.

I had been much looking forward to meeting this siren in the flesh. The first time they stood in a room together, I could feel it: the pull between the metal and the magnet. When the flame was at its hottest, I suspect they both found what they looking for: affirmation and sexual pleasure heightened by the thrill of danger, for she was his type and he had the kind of appetite that my brother, her husband, lacked.

But even Francesco was not so stupid as to open his arms to political suicide; and whatever took place between them, it did not take long before it fizzled out. And, as a closer reading of those 'innocent' letters between them shows, he began drawing away before she did.

As for my feelings on the matter? Of course, there was anger; any such liaison was stupid, insulting and dangerous to both families. And I never liked her perfume, particularly second-hand on him.

Yet looking back, the process of revisiting it as I have done often enough has softened much of its sting. Because in the end, Lucrezia Borgia did not take anything from me that I wasn't willing to give. Indeed, towards the end of their 'connection', it suited me very well that my husband was in anybody's bed but my own. It is time to move on.

PESTILENCE

XVIII

Of course, we were no strangers to the harvests of death that arrive with plague and pestilence. The great cataclysm when Our Lord saw fit to mow down a third of all mankind may have passed, yet hardly a decade went by when there wasn't some reprise of it, filling cemeteries and bringing panic in its wake: an event every ruler must be prepared for.

If infection was first detected elsewhere, a swift rider might buy you time to set up checks at the city gates, barring entrance to anyone from the stricken area. But when it grew from within - as it did in 1506 - then all one could do was try to contain it, using a battle plan from a war we have fought over and over again. As I know only too well, since that spring I was in charge of the city.

All public gatherings were banned, foreigners and vagrants expelled. Every parish reported the number of infections daily to appointed health officials: too many and the district was blocked off, everyone locked in their houses, vitals and medicine sent in. Others were sent to a quarantine hospital set up on the outskirts of the city. That year, the building held close on a thousand souls, so that in the months that followed there were births mixed in with deaths, and even a marriage celebrated, which brought some joy in the midst of sorrow.

In our country palace outside the gates, burning pomades hung from the ceilings, while my distillery produced lavender and rosemary essence for filigree balls for courtiers to carry at their waist. The sweetness of the air may have helped keep the miasma at bay, but so, I think, did the space between us all, for death was always greediest wherever the poor were crammed together.

Our only other weapon was prayer. Cities were never more pious than when plague stalked the streets. But that year, Mantua prayed harder than ever, for we recently had lost two souls dear to us. The curmudgeonly Mantegna had passed away in his sleep, while our dear living saint Osanna - who would surely have interceded for us - had already been taken by God, passing into His hands at the very hour of the very day that she herself had predicted, Francesco and myself at her side and her tiny cell crammed with bishops and church dignitaries, while outside a man with a bucket stirred the wet clay with which he would make her death mask.

And so we all marvelled at her face, which was as serene and youthful as a young bride.

Death Mask of Osanna Andreasi.

Osanna Andreasi and the Maestro both gone. How could we possibly survive without them?

And yet we did.

Eventually, the contagion subsided, though like the enemy on the battlefield who feigns dead till you turn your back, you dared not open up the city too soon in case it came raging back. At last, when we were certain, I ordered the hospital to be unlocked and we gave thanks to God through public processions, distributing alms to all those who had survived so that they might start their lives again. Acts of charity now, in His eyes, might protect us later.

All this, I think, she will be better acquainted with than many who have sat at this desk, since the recent invisible miasma of bad air that swept across the world was serious enough for even the archive to be closed up for the best part of two years. And when scholars first returned, I could still see fear in their eyes so that, even now, a few of the elderly ones wear ugly white masks, as if they were guests at a poor man's carnival.

At such times it feels to me that the future is less prepared for the scythe of disease and death than we were in the past.

Until, that is, we were assaulted by the great pox.

Where it came from, no one knew. Divine wrath? A malign conjunction of the stars? Whatever it was, it spread like a fire in high wind through Italy and, once over the Alps, throughout Europe. All anyone was sure of was the horror of it: gross pustules erupting on men's faces and genitals, itching and agonising, followed by fever and attacks of red-hot pokers of pain shooting through their limbs. Some died fast, some died slowly, some seemed to recover, only for it to come back again. And again.

My father, keen to show off the erudition of Ferrara's university, called a conference of professors of medicine to study it. It was they who traced it back to a beginning, even gave it a name: *Morbus Gallicus*. The French disease. This plague, they said, did not come from the air, or the stars, but out of the fetid beds of soldiers and whores following the first French invasion when the army lived high on conquest in the brothels of Naples. A contagion of fornication, travelling in common soldiers' loins as they headed north for home, infecting street women along their way, who, in turn, infected others. Another pestilence that fed off poverty. Or so it seemed for a while.

So, when did I know about my husband? Not straightway, that is certain. Yes, soldiers and brothels were as much part of life as flies growing out of a dung heap, but a disease that sprung from them was no concern for women of breeding. Husbands might stray outside the marriage bed - a fresh serving girl, or a courtesan offering high-class service at a high-class price. Even, at times, a liking for boys. But the gutter of common prostitution? Never. How could that have anything to offer courtiers whose manners and taste we celebrated on balmy summer evenings in our palace gardens?

The first shock came from men of the cloth. They began so eagerly, spouting damnation from the pulpit. Until changes in some of their own complexions started to show. Priests, bishops, even up to cardinals in their palaces in Rome! Was there ever a more poetic corruption for the already corrupt?

Yet still there was nothing, *nothing*, to suggest my own husband was infected. On the contrary, from the moment he took my horse's reins on that foggy morning in Ferrara, Francesco Gonzaga seemed to me to be a man on fire with strength and health.

It is true there were times when he was away fighting when he suffered bouts of sickness. But I never thought anything of it. Just as I too still have attacks of ague and stomach pains (*you do not have to eat all the cherries in the basket* - my mother's voice again), so after a rigorous campaign he might succumb to a fever or infection from a wound badly healed, which would delay his coming home. But he always returned in fine spirits, his ugliness and energy unchanged. He had long been a man of swarthy complexion. Over time, his skin grew cracked and mottled from sun and soldier's dirt. But there was never a trace of purple flowers, which is what they called the attack of florid pustules, upon his face.

Our life during those years had developed an accepted pattern. We still shared the marital bed at times, but only for conception. When I became pregnant - I knew the signs early - we led largely separate lives, which suited us both, leaving Francesco to his soldiering and me to the glorification of our court. In this way, the Gonzaga dynasty future was assured even as Mantua enjoyed a certain standing in the world again. Together, we delighted in our children: the ever-dutiful Eleonora, the wistful beauty of her little sister Ippolita, already more prone to prayer than play, and the rude health of her new young brother, Ercole, named in honour of my own father, who had recently died at a ripe old age.

But none of them could eclipse the light of little Federico, whose ebullience and quickness grew with every passing year. Francesco insisted on training the body with riding and jousting, pouring stories of war and glory into his ears, while I was left to nurture his mind. I could only be the loser here, since few little boys willingly choose the school room over the stables, but even his petulance was adorable - the way the corners of his mouth would turn down and his bottom lip stick out, so that it was hard not to laugh when I ought to be stern. In this way, my elder son wound me around his little finger - rather, I suspect, as I had done with my father.

No, in many ways this Gonzaga/Este alliance of husband and wife was something that my mother would surely have applauded.

When, then, did that change?

If my scholar is the kind that needs a date, I would suggest she puts a mark against the year 1507. Not that she will find anything in my archive to tell her. In this, or indeed in any other year. The shame of a husband with a disfiguring pestilence born of devilish copulation could never ever be the stuff of a well-bred woman's correspondence.

No, uncovering this history must be a more cunning business.

*

Francesco's 'little affair' had largely faded and Italy was at war again.

Venice had been busy annexing fallen Borgia territory and to curb their dominance an alliance between France and the new belligerent pope now rose against them. Still in the pay of the French king, Francesco was campaigning while I sat lumberingly pregnant with our third son. It is the final labour worthy of going into the birthing room for, though it calls for a strong stomach.

The court astrologer favoured the due date for around Christmas, but the festivities came and went with no sign. Outside, thick mists rolled through the streets and hovered like a carpet over the water, the frogs silent as the grave, turned to wet stone by the freezing weather.

'Is there nothing you can do?'

I lay on my bed as the midwife's small hands mapped the gross mountain of my stomach. We'd been partners in this ritual for over a decade and it could be that our success had encouraged complacency. Well, it was to be shattered now.

'He still has not turned properly, my lady.' (There was always the assumption of a boy - it helped with the prospect of labour.) 'He offers his rump rather than the head and that will make it harder for both of you.' I watched her fingers playing over my skin, marvelling at how they seemed to have eyes in them. 'I have tried to persuade with my hands, but it would help if you could be vigorous - walk, move, dance, anything to try and shift him.'

I groaned. By this time, I was grown so large my ankles were thicker than my feet, and taking more than a few steps was like standing on the deck of a rolling ship. I did what I was told, but to no avail. I spent a sleepless night, weighed down like Cronus: his stomach was filled with the stones he had been tricked into swallowing instead of his children.

Next day, we tried again, but no sooner was I on my feet than I was standing in my own waters and the contractions were coming in with a ferocity that mangled my breath. At least it had started. Only this time nothing happened. Hours went by, the rhythm of the contractions never changing. I grew tired. And when the squeezing turned to pushing and still nothing happened, the agony was unendurable. It had been years since I had dreamed of my sister with her bloodstained dress, but as day turned to night, I saw her again, felt what must have been her fear.

'I can't do this any more,' I gasped between pushes. They had hoisted me into a birthing chair, with Frassina squatting on her heels on the floor in front of me. 'Where are my snake muscles and ox stamina now?'

'You have them still, my lady, you are just tired!' But I saw her glance at one of the other women hovering in the room.

'He's stuck. I tell you – he cannot come out this way.'

'Don't worry. I can help. I will go in as you push. I shall be fast, but it will hurt more. You must hold the pain without groaning or shouting for you'll need the breath when the next pushes come. Do exactly what I tell you. D'you understand, my lady?' she said calmly, for she always grew calm when I became anxious.

I nodded. 'You've done this before, yes?'

'The streets are full of breech babies,' she said, lifting up her small hands and anointing them with oil. 'That is what God made midwives for.'

And suddenly I was hearing my mother's voice again: the last advice she ever gave me. *Pick a woman with experience and little boasting. And small hands. The smaller the better.*

The smaller the better.

Fear is a fine silencer. I did not scream. I squeezed my eyes tight shut and thought about my Cupid, with its fat stone buttocks. Even goddesses must have given birth.

'Good!' I heard her voice. 'Now – push.'

I pushed.

'Stop.'

I stopped.

'Pant, pant ... hold ... yes, now push again. Push, as hard as you can.'

And I felt myself rip apart.

'Yes, hold. Hold. Now once more, I have him, he is coming. Yes ... yes!'

And so Ferrante Gonzaga was born, rump first and stubborn, out of a bloody struggle. It would suit the soldier that he would become. But I knew then I could not carry on any longer, swelling and expelling like an overweight breeding cow.

Later, when I had slept a little, Benedetto came to take

my dictation - for it would be weeks before I could sit easily at my desk.

'A third healthy boy! You are to be congratulated, my lady. How shall we communicate this wonder to the marquis?'

'As you usually do with good news,' I said, then I stopped. 'No, no, perhaps we should inform him more clearly of how it went. A story for a soldier, yes, since I have suffered in battle too.'

He looked questioning.

'What? You think it's only men that splatter their dispatches with blood?' I said drily.

'No, no, my lady.' But it was clear he was queasy with the idea.

'We shall write two letters then, you and I. For I know that sometimes happens. No, don't bother to deny it. I will give him the good news and you can tell him a little more of the truth. That would satisfy decorum, yes?'

Which is what I believe he did.

Francesco, though, took no notice. I nursed my resentment along with my torn flesh. But there was no time to express it, for it was now that his illness roared in. News came that he was cut down again by fever, this time dangerously high, followed by rashes and vomiting, searing pains throughout his body, all as serious as it was sudden. I offered to send my doctors, who would be more help than the butchers that attended armies, but he would have none of it.

I am better than I was and am sure I will recover with the new moon ...

... he wrote, yet at the same time asked that funds be released so that masses could be said for him in all the churches. Masses! He had never been so ill before.

And now when he returns, there are blotches all over his face, as if the fever - or something worse - has not left him. He is angry and foul tempered to all around. Even the sight of his newborn son brings him no pleasure. Ferrante returns the favour by screaming at the top of his lungs. When young, he was always a child who felt his mother's moods.

'Sweet Jesus, does he never stop crying?'

'His coming into the light was a painful affair,' I say stiffly. 'You perhaps heard how I laboured. There were moments when the midwife feared for both our lives.'

And the pause that follows gives him ample time to ask after me now. Yet there is no such solicitation.

'And you, my lord. Are you still ailing?'

'I told you, I am quite recovered. It was a contagion of the camp. Nothing more. The kind of thing soldiers get all the time. I could not be fitter now.'

Is that when I knew? Certainly, I remember a chill going through me.

Yet, who could I talk to about it? My only real confidante was my sister-in-law Elisabetta. But at that moment she was prostrate in a darkened chamber in Urbino, mourning for her own husband, a man she loved so dearly despite - or perhaps because - he never engaged in coitus. Anyway, what advice could she offer about a disfiguring pestilence contracted through sexual congress with lower-class women? No, my gentle Elisabetta lived on another plane of life.

As for Francesco and me, our paths now diverge. There would be further bouts of reported illness. My letters remain filled with solicitation for his well-being, dispatching new ointments and salves from my herbalists, comforting him, taking his side in setbacks, urging him to take care of himself and not be reckless on or off the battlefield. Publicly, I remain the perfect wife. But we would never live under the same roof again. When he was home, he hid himself away in his new palace of San Sebastiano, trying out all manner of mercury treatments - the only medicine that seemed to do any good at all, though it often caused as much suffering as the disease.

And still nothing was said. Nothing. Or not to me.

'What is wrong with him?' In the end, I asked Benedetto.

'It is ... It seems it is some kind of soldier's wounds, my lady. But he is well looked after and I have no doubt will recover.'

Except, one of the things I liked about Benedetto was how such an able diplomat was not good at lying. Or not to me.

'You would tell me if there was something that he does not want me to know,' I said at last, when I learned that a steam bath was being constructed on the ground floor of his palace where he might receive the mercury treatments.

'Of course,' he said, proving the point again.

'Because it's only a matter of time before he will be called upon to join the king for his campaign against Venice. And ...' I smiled brightly. 'Little Federico is very young still. This is not the time for his dear father and my even dearer husband to die.'

We held each other's eye for a moment.

'My lady,' he said gravely. 'The nature of my Lord Marquis' illness is, I believe, not one that will kill him. Though it may -' He paused - such a master of words ... 'It may, at times, leave him incapacitated.'

XIX

Please tell the king that my illness is probably caused by love.

Incapacitated! by Love!

What a pretty admission! Yet here it is now, on her desk, those very words tucked away in a copy book of my husband's correspondence. Ha! This scholar of mine is turning out to be an archive bloodhound, for this is a letter I have not seen before.

An illness of love.

Men, of course, had licence to discuss things differently. I grew up among brothers who, as soon as they were out of the grip of their tutors, delighted in all talk of pissing and farting and the general grossness of the body. They and others would go on to pass for elegant enough courtiers, full of sweet words when in company with ladies, but I could always spot the smirks or glances that came with some piece of clever innuendo, and, once separated, how the very nature of their laughter changed.

What did Francesco call such conversation? Soldiers' talk. Because in the beginning, this pox was celebrated almost as a battle wound.

... my illness is probably caused by love.

The letter is addressed to our ambassador at the French court. *Please tell the king ...* Such a coy, jovial tone! No doubt Francesco believed that such information, ruler to ruler, soldier to soldier, man to man, would be looked upon indulgently. Another notch on the sword of lust. Who knows, even an 'incapacitation' shared? It was, after all, known as the *French* disease.

But if he thought it would buy him the king's forgiveness, he was wrong. Louis was made of stronger stuff.

How much appetite does this scholar of mine have for yet more bloodletting? It can be done fast. The Battle of Agnadello between the French alliance and the state of Venice was a bloodbath that would be talked about by both sides for decades. Wealthy, stable and unfailingly arrogant, Venice was devastatingly, humiliatingly defeated. She had been a wolf at our borders for over half a century, and her shame should have been our triumph.

Except my husband took no part in the victory. No. While history was being made, the man who had once saved Italy was so incapacitated by 'love' that he could not even move his men into battle position. The letter he received from the French king a few days later referred to him - in what might be seen as a joking fashion - as a poltroon.

Poltroon. Does she know this word? It is one of those that changes shape between French and Italian. But it gives up its meaning fast enough here. A poltroon: a tendency to indolence, a man who lies in bed all day when others are working. In other words, a coward.

Whatever agonies he may have been suffering, the insult slid like a stiletto under Francesco's rib cage. It would have been better if he'd kept it to himself, but in his outrage he roared it out to the world. I held my counsel. Any criticism would have only enraged him further. Instead, I soothed his pride, while showing our undying loyalty to the French cause. In Mantua, I ordered free food and wine to celebrate the victory. My letters to the French court overflowed with detail, even down to the public bonfire where children burned effigies of the captured Venetian general, so the king would know how the whole of Mantua had risen up to salute him. Everything I described was true. The unctuous coating of flattery was my own addition. Excessive but necessary: one of those moments when history and fiction are only too eager to become bedfellows.

Still, nothing I could do or say would be enough to save us.

*

When he recovered enough to lead his men again, he was ordered by the king to go to Verona, newly under French rule. They had barely set up camp when, the first night, they were ambushed by a group of citizens loyal to their old Venetian masters. (What, had he posted no bodyguards or sentries?) The great soldier of Fornovo was captured in his bed and handed over to Venetian troops, along with fifty - fifty! - of our best Barbary war horses and two thousand ducats of tapestries, banners, silver plate, weapons and strongboxes of cash.

Two days later, he was in chains in front of the whole ruling Venetian senate. In my own visits to Venice I had once been a guest of the great Doge Loredan himself. No man projected more power and dignity, and no state palace oozed more beauty or conspicuous wealth. But then there was no state prouder of its reputation than Venice. Or humiliated by the loss of it.

Giovanni Bellini: Doge Loredan.

No. There would be no clemency from Venice towards her enemies now, whatever their status, and her bitter score with Francesco went back many years. The Marquis of Mantua was condemned as a common prisoner of war, to be held indefinitely in a cell with no secretary, no cook, and no recourse to doctors to alleviate his pain.

That was the news that reached me in the summer of 1509.

In the reading room, she and I are back where we began.

XX

I die a thousand deaths ...

As she knows, I did not swoon, though I could name you a number of women who would have collapsed under the shock.

I might say that I was made of stronger stuff, but that would be a lie. I did not swoon, because my fury was greater than my pain. The violence of my howls brought my ladies running, but I barred the door against them. I raged and wept, crushing the image of that faithful Gonzaga hound on the tiles beneath my feet and cursing, cursing my reckless, vain, sick husband. A man so besotted by his own importance - and self-inflicted injury - that he had walked with his eyes half open into a trap.

I die a thousand deaths ...

Fury, yes. Yet my howls were laced with terror.

I think I might have killed myself with my own hands, for I believe this would be far better than to remain alive without my lord.

The words I wrote to the French queen were not just hyperbole. To be a lady without a lord. All my married life, Italy had been a battleground around us, no state invulnerable against an enemy with the money and stomach for the kill. The fate of Ludovico Sforza was proof of that. Years of prison walls and creeping madness; he had been a dead man long before he finally stopped breathing. What difference had it made to him or anyone else that he was once the ruler of a magnificent court? They spoke French in Milan now. Yet all this time, we, the Gonzaga and the Este dynasties, had survived, Mantua keeping her head above rising water thanks to a warrior marquis, albeit one trading off fading glory, and his eminently capable marchesa. But not any more. Now the warrior was in chains, his men and his horses taken, leaving his wife a lady without a lord, and our state a hedgehog on its back, soft flesh open to any wolf or fox with the appetite to take the risk.

The first threats came fast, veiled in faux courtesy. So many 'offers' I received in those first days. Maximilian of Austria, Holy Roman Emperor and French ally, had a large cohort of soldiers close by and was eager to send them *to help the dear marchesa to secure your borders.* The French king himself suggested his own men might provide the same thing. I turned down their 'magnanimous offers' in a suitably simpering way. *Their troops to secure our borders!* Ha! Did they really think me so gullible?

In those early weeks, as we struggled to construct a line of communication, I played every card in the etiquette of defeat. A captured general is an opportunity for his jailors to reap a large ransom. But a large ransom was what Venice had already taken when she confiscated his Barbary horses and baggage train. We had little else to offer in the way of extra funds. My dowry jewels were pawned again and what was left was committed to Eleonora's imminent - and now even more important - wedding to a man who was nephew, no less, to the pope himself. Nothing could come in the way of that.

Venice wasn't interested in wealth, anyway. Francesco's disgrace was a satisfying salve to her wounded pride. No. What she really wanted was her own prisoner general back. A negotiated swap. A common enough practice. But my pleading letters to the French court solicited only the most anodyne, courteous responses. That word *poltroon* was still echoing in the king's ears and he made it clear that the Marquis of Mantua was not a worthwhile bargaining chip when it came to giving up his own prize prisoner. How far my husband's stock had fallen.

Though I strived for normality, the atmosphere in the castle and the court became painfully strained. I would have preferred to keep the children out of it, but young Ippolita's interjection made that impossible. Her infant sister, Paola, and her younger brothers were still children and could be protected. But at fifteen and nine, Eleonora and Federico could not. Eleonora would be married soon enough and my son was the same age I had been when my father fought for our state against the Venetians. Both of them old enough to know what was happening. Ippolita I left to her prayers. I would deal with her excessive religiosity later.

'I know you are worried. But your father will be home soon enough.'

'In time for my marriage?' Dutiful as ever, the tears were already glistening in Eleonora's eyes. She loved her father as much as he loved her.

'Certainly,' I said cheerfully. 'He would be most sorry to miss it.'

'I've written to him twice, as you said we could. But there is no reply.'

'You must be patient. He is busy with negotiations.' Had I made a mistake letting them dispatch letters with no safe line of communication yet open? It had felt the best thing to do at the time.

'How do we know he even got them?' Federico interjected. 'If he's a real prisoner, he will be chained to a wall and not have any food or a pen to write with.'

'Oh, it is not that kind of prison.' I laughed, and for a moment I swear he was disappointed.

'I think we should attack the palace where they are keeping him. I could lead the army. I have the horse Papa gave me and he obeys all my commands.' Like all boys, he is eager for war. He has recently developed the habit of blinking too much too suddenly, as if he had something in his eye. I must see that something is done about that, for it will make him appear shifty in the future.

'That's very brave of you, Federico,' I said. 'But before we unleash your army, we must try diplomacy first.'

Yet diplomacy failed us at every turn. Even with better communication established, Francesco's anger eclipsed his good sense. His letters were noisy with complaint. Did we not realise the constant humiliations he was subjected to? What were we doing to further his release?

*

'It may be that the words are still not his own,' Benedetto urged, as he studied them. 'This is not the hand of his own scribe and it is possible that they have been doctored.'

In which case, they have caught his spirit well enough, I think angrily.

Cold-shouldered by the French, we turn our attention to the pope. As soon as Eleonora's marriage to his nephew in Urbino was celebrated, Julius II had invited the couple to Rome for a ceremony of his own blessing. There would be no better chance for direct intercession. I couldn't leave Mantua. Such an act would be tantamount to opening the gates to our enemies. Instead, I threw myself into preparations for the grooming of my daughter.

My first-born. I know she has played little role in this story. But this is not the moment to address that.

'Of course I will intervene on Father's behalf, Mama. I have already been composing what I might say to His Holiness.'

We are going through her wardrobe dowry. As she models the dresses she will take, I see myself in her place, eagle-eyed for my mother's approval. She has better posture than I did, her figure is plump ripe without excess and she has a mercifully clear skin. Any trace of beauty, though, has eluded her too. And there is little evidence of fire underneath the surface.

'You will need to be careful. Everything we know about Pope Julius confirms that in temperament he is a Della Rovere, and the family is notorious for its temper.' I wonder if I should tell her that this may also be true of her husband to be, for there are already rumours, but it is best not to think of that now. 'Whatever you do, don't press him too far. He has a volcano inside him and it erupts easily.'

'I understand, Mother,' she answers patiently. 'As ever, I will take my lead from you and Aunt Elisabetta on all such things.'

I have already admitted that I might have loved her more. But that does not mean she was neglected. She has had loving nurses and the finest tutors and if she was never fast in her studies, she was thorough and has grown into a competent young woman, accomplished in many courtly things. Though shining in none. Quite unlike me when I was her age.

Indeed, exactly her age. Embracing her on that last morning, it struck me that both of us had left our homes on the cusp of our sixteenth birthdays. But while I felt the sharp loss of my mother, our leave-taking - like everything in our relationship - seemed more an exercise in duty than passion. I've wondered since if my daughter was somehow afraid of me. My sweet sister-in-law Elisabetta, who had always treated her like the child she could never have, came to chaperone her on the journey and even as they stood together on the dock, I could sense the love and solace they would bring to each other.

Do I feel any pang of sorrow for myself in all this? Possibly, though in the end I think I did her a service by not loving her excessively. Like all of us, she would have to stand on her own feet quickly enough.

Back in the firestorm of negotiations, summer has turned to winter. Francesco's cell will be colder now, though at least he is allowed a doctor to visit and a chance to exercise outside. I've heard it said that prisoners kept too long on their own come to depend on the kindness - or not - of their jailors, so that they start to see them as more important than the world outside. Certainly, he was listening to someone other than me. And whoever they were, they were clever. Every overture we made was fed back to us - and him - as wanting. Could it be that the formidable Marchesa of Mantua, whom everyone knew was always happy to step into her husband's shoes, was prevaricating deliberately? It was outrageous, but Venice more than most states prided herself in producing invisible, obedient wives. Should men want something more flamboyant, there was always an ample pick of courtesans. Such was the depth of her hypocrisy.

'Is this just their way of punishing us further? Or is there something else behind it?'

Benedetto purses his lips. It is a question that needs no answer. We both know that however vengeful Venice is, she is not stupid.

Yet when it comes, my breath is still knocked out of me.

He is seven months into his imprisonment when a clear offer is made. Not to me. I knew nothing of it. Rather, it was hammered out directly between Francesco and his jailors, and arrives with us, through a scribe's hand, as a fait accompli.

It is insupportable that this go any longer, my husband writes. So, having negotiated matters for himself, an agreement has been reached that allows his release. We are to send young Federico to Venice, where his presence will act as a guarantee for his father's future good relationship with the state. Of course, he will be excellently cared for - treated as an honoured guest - and on his arrival Francesco himself will immediately be freed.

Federico, not yet ten years old and heir to the house of Gonzaga, to be used as a hostage to free his father. To be removed from his home and my tutelage into the custody - and no doubt the indoctrination - of the Venetian state! A plan that his own father has agreed to, even gone so far as to suggest this is his own idea!

The lava of my fury held me back from replying immediately. Hot tears do not make for cool diplomacy. Benedetto, whose loyalty to Francesco remained unshakeable, counselled me to stand in his shoes for a moment: a great soldier, ill, isolated, angry at his political impotence, lashing out even at those who had his best interests at heart.

Your Lordship, you know I want nothing in the world more than to free you. But ...

In the archive, she has my letter in front of her now. I can feel the concentration on her face as I hear again Benedetto's goose quill scratching the words on to paper.

... it pains and torments me to say that I cannot do this, because I see the danger – in fact the certainty – of ruin for our state, our children and your own person.

The words still burn off the page now, yet when I spoke them I was as calm and determined as I had ever been in my life.

You see, if Federico were to go to Venice, we would still not be sure of your freedom.
  On the contrary, there would be both motive and opportunity to keep you longer in prison, as they would have both of you there.

Years later, I watched a man walk a rope strung across a gorge over a river for people's entertainment, and it struck me that the skill with which he placed each foot was not unlike the choosing of my words that night.

For this reason, though you may disdain me and deny me your love, I will be more content to be disobedient and preserve your state, then to reside in your grace and see you, together with your children, deprived of it.

At her desk, she sits quietly rereading the letter, while in my studiolo I watch Benedetto's dry smile as he reads it back to me. But the silence that follows is filled with more painful words.

'My lady?' he says at last.

I shake my head angrily.

'I understand your distress, but if we are to move forward from this stalemate ...'

'– a stalemate that is not of my making. I have put forward offers enough.'

'Yes, yes.' He waits for me to compose myself. 'However, in such a situation we must accept it is not unusual –' He hesitates.

'– for the enemy to ask for a child as hostage? Is that it? You do not have to teach me history, Benedetto. I know it as well as you. But I will not send my son to Venice. And that is an end to it.'

He was right, of course. Once the idea was in the air it took no time at all for the French king to make a similar offer, albeit dressed in frillier clothes. He would exert pressure on the Venetians to release Francesco and give young Federico a place at his own court, where he would be handsomely cared for as the heir of a valued ally (in other words, a hostage, without the use of the word). At the same time, the queen made a similar overture to welcome Ippolita as a lady-in-waiting. A wonderful offer for a noble young woman! Blackmail masquerading as privilege. Vipers every one of them. I thanked them with a river of pretty words but held off from a decision. And still we waited for the pope to make his move.

When it finally came, as with everything else in politics, it was double edged. With his accustomed eloquence, Benedetto spelt it out for me.

While Julius II had chosen to ally the papacy to France, he was too shrewd not to see the danger of a foreign power holding too much sway in Italy. And as he nudged nearer to death, he saw his path to heaven made smoother by a crusade against the Turks. For which he would need Venice and her ships. He was ready to make peace.

And Venice - for no one can defy the pope for too long - was ready to accept.

Built inside the treaty was the release of Francesco, with the cunning proviso that to ensure his future loyalty, the Marquis of Mantua would join this 'new alliance' as a commander of the papal troops. A perfect solution. In this way, Francesco would be rehabilitated through his appointment. And to further show his great love for the Gonzaga family, the pope would 'host' Mantua's heir, his own nephew-in-law, Federico, for a while in Rome.

Benedetto did not rush me. He knew the agony I was in. There was no arguing with it. If Federico was to become hostage to anyone, then an uncle who was also the pope was the right guardian. There would be no better offer.

Yet I could not let him go.

He sat silent waiting for my response. He was always more patient than me.

'Ah! We both know what the other is thinking, Benedetto. We might as well use words. You begin. I must give up my son because ...?'

'Because although he is your son, Your Ladyship, he is first and foremost Mantua's heir. He is now almost ten years old. Young, yes, but no longer a child. When your husband, the marquis, was his age, his mother died and though he missed her, he became used to it soon enough. It is no bad thing for a ruler to grow up fast, for they are often the ones that survive best. He would learn much from being in Rome: make connections, lay the foundations for alliances into the future. He will also know that he played his part in saving the state, and this too will be an education, allowing him to return a more worthy heir. Your feelings, which every mother would understand, are less important at this moment than his journey, which in the end he must make alone.'

'Bravo,' I said bitterly. 'So - I must leave the decision to a ten-year-old.'

He smiled. 'Not any ten-year-old.'

I had tried to keep the worst from him. He had continued his studies, playing with his younger brothers (winning every game), and living his life as normally as possible. But he had missed his father, for Francesco spoiled him in ways I did not.

Their greatest shared passion has always been horses. I was no longer such a confident horsewoman. Since Ferrante's birth, I suffered a certain giddiness if I rode too fast, but that day I chose to go riding with him. The stables were to the south of the city, on the small island of Te; a handsome set of buildings, constructed soon after our marriage, and Francesco had paid great attention to their design, decorating one or two of the external walls with portraits of his best horses. How much he loved them!

Once mounted, we moved out into the forest. I watched my son go through his paces, his face breaking into a proud smile as the horse recognised his seat and responded to his touch. We found a place to sit by the river bank and I dismissed the servants, leaving the horses to forage in the grass.

'You're a fine horseman, Federico,' I say proudly.

He shrugs. 'When I am marquis, I am going to build a palace on this island, so that I can get up every morning and walk to the stables. I will bring my bride here to ride with me and I will have paintings of my favourite horses on the walls inside, with their names inscribed underneath.'

'Horse portraits? Inside as well?'

'Yes. Papa thinks they are more trustworthy than people.'

I laugh. 'You don't think we already have palaces enough?'

'No,' he says in all seriousness. 'Papa says there is always room for another. Of course, I shan't do it until he dies. Venice will set him free soon, yes?'

'Very soon.' *Papa says, Papa thinks* ... It warms and pains me at the same time. 'He speaks of you all the time in his letters, of how eager he is to see you.'

'So, will he come here? Or will I meet him in Rome?'

'Rome? What do you know of Rome?'

He pushes at a mound of earth with a stick and does not look at me.

'Federico?'

He shrugs. 'You always say it is important to listen to what is being said, even if it is not said directly to you. I heard that someone might be going to Rome. To help with Father's release.'

The drip-drip of gossip, even inside a wax seal. At another time I might have pursued the leak, but now is not the moment to appear angry. 'And how would you feel about that?'

Except I know already. Rome! He can't keep the excitement out of his eyes. Rome. Who does not want to see what lies behind that word?

'I wouldn't mind. I would be the guest of the pope, yes? Like Eleonora?'

'Certainly. You would live in the palace near to him. He is your uncle, after all.'

'They say he is a really good horseman. And a soldier too!'

Ah. My son already has a sword in his hand. I thought of the stories of Julius leading the papal troops to take back the Borgias' cities. The irascible Warrior Pope. That is how he will go down in history.

'Will you come with me?'

'Not at first,' I say gently.

He pushes the stick further, tossing earth into the air. 'How long would I stay?'

I hesitate. 'For a while. It's a long journey and there is much to see and do. You would have a place there, at the pope's court.'

'And Father would be free?'

'Yes,' I say lightly. 'Your father would be free. In fact, he would be a commander again in the pope's army.'

He waits. But not for very long. 'I would not want to leave you,' he adds slyly. 'But I think it would be good for me. If I was in the company of the pope, I would get better at Latin.'

I laugh. And so, my heart is broken. For I let my son go, to bring back my husband.

*

I have already said that when I left Ferrara for my marriage, my mother had my rooms closed up and only she held the key. I wonder – when she entered them, did she feel my younger self there? And if she did, did it bring her pleasure or pain? – for I think sometimes the two intertwine in unexpected ways.

I chose art as my way into memory. Ten-year-old Federico captured in paint. I picked the painter (Francesco Francia, I doubt anyone has heard of him now) because he was fast and reliable and in thrall to the fashionable grace of Raphael, though, alas, with little of his substance. But substance was not what I wanted. I needed comfort and this it gave me, a portrait of my son's innocence: peach skin and rosebud mouth, the sweet mischief of a boy caught in the moment every mother yearns to preserve, before the beard and the pull of women's breasts banish them for ever from childhood.

Francesco Francia: Federico Gonzaga.

Once in the hothouse of Rome, I knew such a journey would not take long. He would be surrounded by dazzling wealth and privilege, and though his letters to me over the coming years would be loving enough, the gossip was of an ageing pope so besotted with the freshness of his young charge that he indulged him in every way. No, whenever I found myself worrying about the young man who would eventually return, it was Francia's portrait that I returned to for reassurance.

As for my husband, he was summoned immediately to wait on the pope, and take over his command of the papal troops. After which, he fell ill again. By the time he finally returned to Mantua, it was almost two years since we had seen each other and it felt as if nothing - and everything - had changed.

XXI

He entered the city like a conquering hero, in full armour, with his men behind him, and the people erupted in joy to welcome him. I may have done a good job, but I was a woman and Mantuan only by marriage. With their lord returned, the state was safe again. At the banquet that night, he made an effort with his appearance. Without his armour, his brush-thick hair was newly cut, his beard trimmed and his wardrobe fine enough. Yet there the similarities to my husband ended.

Prolonged imprisonment, they say, ages any man. It felt as if his very frame had shrunk. That bull muscle torso, as agile as it was solid, was collapsing in upon itself and the more he tried to hold himself erect the more noticeable it was. It did not help that he moved with a slight gait, one leg straighter than the other, the discomfort written on his face.

What is the phrase used by those afflicted by the French disease? Like red-hot pokers running through the bones. Soldiers can be unexpected poets of pain, for they make every wound a badge of honour, and once he was in the saddle perhaps all this would disappear and his troops would see only resilience and indomitability. Except he had not been on a battlefield once since his release - and, looking at him now, nor was he likely to be.

Close to, his face was gaunt and yellow, his skin above his beard painfully pitted with the remains of the last bout of pustules. My husband was forty-five years old, yet he felt like a man in the throes of old age. Prison or pestilence? Either way, the fire that had once blazed out of him was gone.

If those around me saw the same thing, they chose not to show it. Gaiety flowed as liberally as the wine. I watched him trying to find his way back. One of my newer ladies - her beauty will make her a formidable diplomat - caught his eye and for a moment I saw a flash of his old energy. He'd been a free man long enough to make other conquests, if that's what he desired. Yet he seemed to lose interest soon enough, turning his attention back to the wine flask.

I had had the banqueting table placed in front of the fresco of the Battle of Fornovo, so that everyone could relive the dash and brilliance of his soldiering. Halfway through the evening, I saw him staring up at it.

'We should have got Mantegna to do it.'

Up until then we had been like strangers to each other.

'He would never have finished it,' I said. 'Or given you such pride of place.'

'The man didn't know what he was doing. Look at the backside of my horse. It's like I'm riding on a fat whore's arse.'

A titter of laughter went round the table. He was right: the perspective was crude. Mantegna would have caught rider and horse in a frozen image of majesty. If he had ever finished them.

'Still, I seem to remember you got it cheap, right?' he said, raising his voice further to include others. 'You have a reputation, you know. Some people out there say you are a wife who really wants to be the husband.'

I smiled, as if this was a joke meant to be funny. I had made an effort with my own appearance for his homecoming. Anxiety had shaved some weight off me and I complemented it with a new scent and a new dress. In the right light, I would say I was quite agreeable to look at.

'Don't worry. I defend you stoically.'

'I am sure you do. What do you say?'

'That you have always been a fishwife in the way you bargain.' He laughed too loudly. 'But that you have a good eye.'

He reached for the wine again. No, I think. He is not out to fight, or not deliberately. He has just been too long in men's company.

'It is good to have you home, my lord.'

'Hmm. Yes.' He stretched out his leg under the table, pushing his hands hard up and down his thigh as if to massage away some pain.

'So ... do you remember when we first sat here, wife?'

'Of course. The day of our wedding.'

'My God, how those ceremonies went on and on. You were such a fat little pigeon in your white and blue wedding flounces - your breasts poking up like fresh watermelons. I couldn't wait till it was all over.'

He was wrong about the colours of my wedding dress, but I said nothing.

'And you smelt delicious. But then you always do.'

He leaned towards me for a moment, taking an exaggerated sniff, then threw himself back into his chair. I caught a stronger scent off him too now, something exceedingly sour under the sweet. Breath or body? I would prefer not to find out.

'And how long ago was that, Isabella d'Este?'

'Twenty-one years, I think.'

'Twenty-one years!' The wine was moving fast in him now. 'And how many children have we given the house of Gonzaga in that time?'

'Six. Eight if you count the dead ones, God rest their souls.'

'God rest their souls,' he repeated, staring at the tablecloth. 'Still, six living children. Not bad, eh? The three boys healthy as young stallions. And in that time, what have we survived? Two invasions, the fall of Naples, Urbino, Milan, the Borgia rampage. And victory in the greatest battle on Italian soil. A triumph for the house of Gonzaga. My God, you married the right man, eh?'

But he was not really talking to me any more. He muttered some further things under his breath, the words slurring. He was tired already. Much quicker than his younger self. And more susceptible to the wine. After a while, he put his head down on the table and sighed deeply. I looked up to try and catch the eye of one of his gentlemen, but two of them were already on their feet, moving in quietly. They knew this new Francesco better than I. They came up behind him and spoke gently in his ear and he raised himself up obediently. For a moment he lurched forward as if he was going to embrace me, then seemed to think better of it and moved away, allowing himself to be guided out.

His steps, I noticed, were uncertain. He had grown used to being looked after. I think I found that almost the most painful thing of all.

XXII

My husband has returned, yet he is not here. He stays in his palace of San Sebastiano for so long that it is soon clear this will be his permanent home, a place where there is no provision for me. He sees the children once or twice, but never for long. Ippolita, radiant with childish excitement for it seems her vow to save her father has been heard, speaks constantly about entering the convent, but he shows little interest in her either. As for the younger ones, they barely remember him and are withdrawn and awkward in his presence.

Some of the administration of state - scribes, a few record-keepers - still remain with me in the castle, but with their master back there is little of urgency to do. His chief companion is now his secretary, Tolomeo Spagnoli, a man I despise for I know he has procured more than just information for my husband in his time. Surrounded by such men and his doctors, Francesco leaves his palace only to see his dogs and horses stabled on the island of Te, nearby. He rides daily, but infrequently to the hunt - and there are whispers that he sometimes lets others take the kill. If that is true it would be a first, for no man has bested my husband when his hunt blood is up.

Having been at the knife edge of government, I am now an idle wife again. I do my best to distract myself. A collector in

Venice, with whom I have had excellent connections, is close to death. I am not the only one sending him good wishes while I study his inventory. Except my budget is severely reduced now, and I am shaken by the prices I must pay for beauty.

We have lived this way for the best part of two months before the call comes for a meeting between Francesco, myself and Benedetto, to take place in the painted chamber in the castle: a suitable setting for Gonzaga business.

Francesco (left) and Sigismondo, Camera Picta.

The hour is midday but when I arrive - and I am never late - he and Benedetto are already there and it is clear they have been talking for a while.

Francesco has had a high chair brought in for him, placed in front of the wall where he is framed by an image of himself and his younger brother Sigismondo as children.

But if he is aware of it, he pays it no attention. Instead, he sits with his back rigid stiff against the wood, his legs planted unmoving on the floor, at times leaning over with both arms on his knees, his gaze fixed firmly on the floor.

He interrogates me with a number of questions about trivial matters, but shows no interest in my replies, then signals for Benedetto to leave. I have been careful during this time not to make direct eye contact with him, but as he rises I send him a questioning look. His face, of course, is impenetrable. As I turn back, I see Francesco following my glance.

'So! It seems that you and Capilupi have been getting on splendidly in my absence, yes?' he says as the door closes quietly behind us.

'My lord, without him I fear you would still be in prison.'

'Hmm. He says the same thing about you. The man can't stop singing your praises as a proxy ruler. You know, I believe the old trout is half in love with you. Did you slip him some kind of love potion from your distillery?'

I laugh. 'There was no need. His love for the Gonzaga family is unshakeable. Your incarceration was an open wound for both of us. Every day you were still there was a day too long.'

He grunts. 'On that we can agree.'

In the light coming through the one window of the room, it's hard to gauge his expression. I am not used to having to judge him just by what he says, for his humours usually communicate themselves through his whole body, his magnetic energy charming or cuffing the world into submission. Now even his prominent eyes are sunken. A year in a Venetian jail for a man as proud as him. I need to tread carefully.

'I still remember when you picked Capilupi out for me, when I first arrived,' I say brightly. 'I think you must have known that he would be my teacher as much as my secretary.'

'Yes, yes ...' He frowns, shaking his head, as if suddenly all this bores him. 'You both did well. I must come up with some reward for him.'

'His son is looking for a benefice in Rome. If Federico continues to enjoy the pope's favour, as he does, we must do our best to help him.'

Federico. His name is out now. It has to come at some point.

'Oh yes, yes! The boy is having the time of his life.' He guffaws loudly. 'Every letter is juicier than the last. The pope worships him. He tells me they eat dinner together every night, you know that? Then play backgammon or cards! And if Federico loses, Julius slips him the money to pay up. My God, what would I have given to be so favoured at his age? It was a brilliant strategy to send him.'

Games and gambling. I was right. My son tells different stories to different parents.

'And the ladies are already lining up for his favours. Ha! I can give him advice on that.' He hesitates, as if he has at last noticed my lack of enthusiasm. 'Oh, I know you didn't want him to go, but he needed to get away. It's not the right place for a soldier, coddled like one of your lap dogs under his mother's skirts. How are your precious dogs, by the way? My God, a lovesick secretary, eh?' He moves on without a pause, so that it takes time for me to catch up with him. 'Benedetto Capilupi, of all people. What did you do? Make him an offer he couldn't refuse ... He is such a thin old stick. I hope you did not crush him.'

And before I could respond he is roaring with laughter, saliva spitting from his mouth. 'Ah - you should see your face! You're going to have to make allowances for a coarsened husband. The dirt of the prison cell gets into places even holy water can't reach.'

He pushes his hands down deeply into his knees, as if to stop them trembling, his eyes on the floor. I watch him carefully.

'Francesco?'

'What? Don't tell me. You are happy to have me home!' he snarls. 'Because I have been much missed.'

'Of course you have. You said it yourself. We have survived terrible things. But the house of Gonzaga is triumphant.'

'When did I say that?'

'Ah - at the banquet, that first night.'

He looks at me blankly. And I feel myself go slightly cold. 'You probably don't remember. You were tired. Tell me, how are your horses?

'My horses? Oh - it's a fuck feast. We'll have the fifty stallions that those bastards took off us back soon enough.'

'That is wonderful news! Really. I dare say you will be joining the troops again soon.'

'What? You want rid of me already?'

'No. No - I just ...' I trail off.

We sit in silence for a moment, his right leg juddering every now and then. He leans his head back and stares at the ceiling where the majestic trompe l'oeil parapet stands open to the sky. There is so much to see, but he is not looking. His eyes are closed and his breathing is heavy. For a moment, he seems to be sleeping. Is this how it is going to be between us - tiptoeing around a damaged man, holding any other feelings at bay? I think of Elisabetta welcoming her husband in her arms after he was shown into this very room, broken from ten days and nights on the run. It is a gift to love one's husband so much. But it has not been given to me and I cannot start pretending now.

'You know they took me in chains,' he says at last, eyes still closed. 'After those filthy Verona peasants sold me to Venice for a few pieces of copper, their poxy soldiers put me in chains. Me! The man who led their troops to victory at the greatest battle of the century at Fornovo. And after they had paraded me in front of their dandified senators, they threw me in a cell the size of a nun's snatch. The place was infected with vermin. No doctor, no scribe, the stench of sewage and a pauper's diet. Francesco Gonzaga, treated worse than a common criminal. If I had been a lesser man ... Do you know what they say about Ludovico Sforza?' And he is looking at me directly now. 'That by the time he died in a French gaol, he weighed no more than his bones.'

'I cannot imagine ...'

'Of course you can't,' he sneers. 'It would kill you just to try.' And his voice is rising now. I wonder if he has been drinking, a way to cope with the pain, but there's no smell of it on him. 'Not even to see more than a chink of sky for four months. Four months. Eaten alive by lice the size of butterflies. You could crush two dozen in your fingers one night and they'd be crawling back out of the damp again within an hour. Jailors who at first wouldn't even change the slop - claiming they didn't understand my foreign dialect. My dialect! Venetian mother fuckers!'

He's right ... I couldn't imagine. I had never let myself go far into that cell for fear it might damage me too. Maybe it was his anger that had got him through, a wall of rage meeting each and every humiliation. Men enter hell more often than women; we all deal with our nightmares differently. I pull my chair closer and my hand hovers over his arm. His face is covered in sweat and there is something putrid again in his smell. He has dosed himself liberally in his old scent - a concoction of ambergris and musk, which always came well salted with horse and leather. But this is different, thicker, more sickly. The perfume of decay? It's all I can do not to pull away.

'It is all right, my lord,' I say quietly. 'You are safe now.'

But he's not listening. 'And then ... and then they come to me and say no one is interested in negotiating my freedom. Because my wife ... my fucking wife, no less, is doing well enough without me. Busy with her art and her court, entertaining her poets and her simpering hangers-on. And her clever besotted secretary. Oh, yes, they knew all about my wife. Everybody does, apparently. How she loves having her hands on the reins. Gets a thrill from the way the horse's flanks move under her. Don't look at me like that! That was more or less what they said. Told me I would have done better with a Venetian wife, because they do as they are told. Not that I ever got close to one. No chance of getting a hand up those skirts. Hah! You have to go to courtesans in Venice. They offered me a couple of them, you know, as part of the negotiations.'

'My lord, this was just the poison of diplomacy. Benedetto and I always knew you were too clever –' I catch myself too late.

'Oh! Benedetto is it now? And what else did "Benedetto" say about their deal?'

The bile in his tone takes me aback. I no longer know where my husband is more damaged, his body or his mind.

'Francesco! For pity's sake, stop this. Benedetto Capilupi worships you, you know that. His loyalty is beyond reproach. Whatever they said to you, not a word of it was true. It's what enemies always say to try and break a prisoner.'

'Of course I knew that,' he shouts. 'What? Do you take me for an even bigger fool? I went along with them to catch them off their guard. Get myself a larger cell, more freedom ... I was always one step ahead of them. My God, a lesser man would never have stood out against their demands.'

Stood out against their demands! I see his hand on the letter instructing me to send Federico to Venice as hostage in his place. Was this what it took for his pride to survive? That he must rewrite history? Well, I wouldn't do it.

'As you say, my lord. A lesser man ...' I reply flatly.

He retreats into a morose silence. Should I be feeling pity? Yes, he has suffered more than me. But our union never thrived on pity. It smacks too much of contempt.

'Still, you needn't cry for me, Isabella,' he says, at last looking up into my dry eyes. 'I'm not dead yet. Far from it. I still have what it takes to crush any army they send against me. Oh yes. The Marquis of Mantua is finally home and his wife ...' He paused, '... his wife can now return to her wifely duties.'

Wifely duties. The words send a chill through me. Wifely duties. I knew that at some point it must come to this.

'Praise be to God,' I say brightly. Where to step next? 'And praise also to Him that you are recovered from your malady.'

'My *malady*?' He stops, his eyes narrowing. What? Does he really think I didn't know? That we women understand nothing of the world? 'Oh, my "malady". Yes, I was struck low for a while, but thanks to good doctoring it is gone now.'

I don't even need to contradict him; the lie is written on his mottled face. The ice is so thin between us I can hear it cracking.

'I am delighted to hear it, my lord.'

Except I too know something of this 'good doctoring'. The way, for instance, a physician's language depends on who is paying the bills. How what used to be called a 'cure' has been replaced by the less ambitious offer of 'relieving treatment'. What had begun as God's thundering judgement on sex between soldiers and prostitutes is now, for those of higher birth, simply a way of life.

Yet, should a noblewoman dare ask the same doctor what happens when an infected man gets into bed with his wife, there is only huffing and puffing and mumbled talk of women's virtue as defence against all ills. Gossip, however, tells it differently: how a few 'virtuous women' have been beset by strange fevers, noxious juices leaking from their wombs - even, God forbid, giving birth to dead children. Such whispers rise up and are lost in the air. In years to come, perhaps some painter will uncover them lodged in a dusty cornice and wonder if he should be putting another kind of love on the walls. But not us, not then. We were too wedded to the perfect body of Venus taming the perfect body of Mars. There was no beauty to be had in pustules and cankers. And no gods ever got ill from a surfeit of love.

I feel the smile stretched across my lips. 'However, I myself am experiencing certain symptoms at this time ...'

And for that second, his eyes grow dark with panic. What? Does he fear he has already infected me? Would it be so wrong of me to admit to enjoying this moment?

'It seems they are connected to the time of life I am going through, so that I am in almost constant flux from the erratic rhythm of my menses.'

I watch the panic shift to distaste. Strange how men who glory in blood on the battlefield are less inclined to release their seed into it. Husband and wife playing with the truth in different ways. If I do not believe him, then he does not believe me entirely either. But neither of us will pick up the challenge.

'I see,' he says abruptly, giving a little snort. 'Very well, I shall make other arrangements then. Until you are better. I shall, of course, relieve you of the business of government.'

He pulls himself heavily up from his chair.

'Tolomeo Spagnoli, my secretary, will become my chief advisor, and the administration will move to the palace of San Sebastiano, leaving you the castle for your "entertainments". I had intended to ask Capilupi to join me for, as you say, he is devoted to the Gonzaga family, but since he is so *devoted* to you, you may keep him - to help you with your shopping and matters of fashion.'

The smile he attempts doesn't reach his eyes, for there is a kind of deadness in them. It could be pain, or the concoctions his doctors are giving him to ease it. Or just a man for whom life offers nothing to smile about any more. Fury clogs my chest. Here is my punishment: I exclude him from my bed and he excludes me from government. It is a cruel thing, cruelly done, and he knows it.

'You must do as you see fit, my lord.' And not even a sick man could not mistake my icy courtesy for affection. 'We are all rejoicing to have you home.'

As he limps to the door, I am left in the company of the rest of the Gonzaga family: as cold and imperious as the day they emerged from Andrea's brush.

But I was bred from another dynasty, a family where women had straight backs and did not suffer being made fools of gladly. If Francesco Gonzaga had a state to return to, it was because I had worked tirelessly to preserve it and I would not now be reduced to the status of exile in my own home.

I wonder, does this scholar of mine relish the idea of a little travelling? As I was about to discover, there was a great deal to see in this marvellous land of ours.

XXIII

It is the closest I would come, I think, to running my own campaign of warfare, for the movement of a household of sixty or so people, even with a major domo, takes a great deal of planning and organising. Together, my ladies and I would travel the length and breath of Italy - from Naples to Milan, Bologna to Florence and on to Rome.

Wifely duties. They come in many colours.

Any ruler so sick that he cannot leave his own palace runs the risk of becoming an expendable player on the chess board of power. Whereas my - what shall we call it? - reputation (there is much to be said for such a thing, even when it is disapproved of) opened all manner of doors. Everyone, it seemed, wanted to meet the redoubtable Isabella d'Este and her 'ladies'. Like any good ambassador, I reported back to my lord on everything: the quality of hospitality, the official entertainments, details of my hosts and fellow guests and, most of all, the conversations that we had, including - of course - comments on the glory of Mantua and its great marquis, with suitable praise for his consort wife.

So many places. So many letters. So many, in fact, that it can be daunting to any but the most committed scholars.

But when she walks in today, I know she is ready to be on display with me. Such an effort she had made: a fine new outfit to match the warming weather, a sea-green silk dress that floats around her calves, with a row of small pearl buttons down the front. The material has a softness and sheen of age about it and its cut, on the bias, is particularly cunning in the way it encourages the flowing movement of the silk. An old style, I think, for I remember a few women wearing such things in the past. But she complements it with a completely new hairstyle. That swirl of curls is now swept up inside a cream and yellow turban - a cunning plaiting together of two of her bright scarves. Oh, but I could almost include her in my entourage, for this is a clear homage to my own headdress, the capigliara - how could it be anything else?

With her face exposed, I can study her more closely. If we are to travel together, she would do well to stay out of the sun. The lines around her eyes and mouth are more pronounced than I first noticed. Too much laughter for a woman is a pleasure that comes with a price. Though she has good teeth, not something I could say about many. We were taught early to keep our mouths closed, as any portrait will show. Scholars read it now as a sign of female decorum - a virtuous woman does not flirt for any male viewer - but believe me, it was also about teeth. While poets might rhapsodise over 'shining pearls', most of us soon developed a few stumps or gaps.

She also has a new pair of spectacles, with - impossibly - the pattern of leopard skin on their frames. I suspect they are there to help with magnification, which she will certainly need now as my new scribe (Benedetto Capilupi was an old man by this time, in the grip of gall stones, and the rigours of travelling would have caused him agony) has a hand as small as it is fast, which suited me perfectly, for my letters went on for pages and pages.

As I have said, there was a lot to tell. And since Francesco could never have read such a volume himself, it meant his toad secretary, Spagnoli, would be forced to spend time in my company reading them to him, digesting the ways in which I was now Mantua's most effective ambassador in the world at large. Oh, yes, I found things to entertain me during those years.

Where shall we go to first then? A pilgrimage to my childhood, perhaps.

*

Aside from my grandfather's bad breath, I had no memory of Naples. But Naples, it seemed, remembered me. I was welcomed into palaces where my mother had grown up, regaled with stories of her goodness by women now so ancient they could hardly see my hand as they stroked it and told me how very like her I looked. The city around them, alas, was painfully poor, the result of decades of invasion, warfare and the attrition of the French disease born from brothels that continue to sprout out of labyrinthine streets like fresh crops of mushrooms after rain. But inside their slowly mouldering palaces, the surviving dowager queens of the house of Aragon stayed true to a more elegant era when they ruled unchallenged over the whole of southern Italy. And since my appetite for all Neapolitan cuisine was now a culinary legend, every banquet or meal ended with a cornucopia of marzipan fruits and sugar statues.

And then there was Rome. Rome! Such pictures I had painted in my mind, yet none of them prepared me for both its squalor and the grandeur of its history. Trees sprouting from broken pediments, sheep and goats pasturing in the ruins of fallen temples, while fifty yards away another new palace was using pilfered stones and ancient pillars to house a cardinal or banker, many of whom were as eager to meet me as I was them, for we were all fellow collectors. In this way I was shown every wonder there was to see, from the excavated Roman statue of the giant Laocoön – sculpted soon after the death of Christ – to the newest creation of God's world on the ceiling of the Sistine by Michelangelo's brush.

The only thing I missed was my beloved son, for he had been freed from his bond by the irascible old Julius just before his death and had taken up a gracious invitation to the French court, where his manners and good looks would benefit both our alliance and his education.

Though he was far from forgotten. The Vatican palace had been his playground for years and he had made fine friends in Raphael, as he is now known, at work on the pope's private apartments alongside his black-eyed boy prodigy, Giulio Pippi (the name Romano would come later, after the city that made him famous).

Together, the two of them guided me through the fresco masterpiece of the great *School of Athens*. I wonder, do people still recognise Leonardo's grizzled features in the face of Plato? Or the peasant stock of Michelangelo as Heraclitus? Raphael had even put himself into the painting, a small sly figure on the margins next to the astronomer Ptolemy, though obvious to all who knew him from his black cap and un-bearded chin.

Raphael: Self-portrait (detail), School of Athens.

No one but Raphael could have trod a finer line between scholarship, wit and beauty. As the papal artist, he had earned the title of Maestro, but the elevation did nothing to dent his affability and enjoyment of life. I made him promise that he would come and work for us in Mantua. And, of course, he agreed, though we both knew it would never happen because this new pope would surely keep him for ever.

This new pope. Oh yes, I was his honoured guest too, for Giovanni de' Medici, now Leo X, was an infinitely more genial man than his predecessor and so beguiled by my company – by his own admission, he was a man addicted to pleasure – that he wrote personally to my husband, asking that his 'sweet cultured' wife be allowed to remain longer. Which was helpful, because by this time Francesco was chaffing at my absence, asking with every second letter for details of my homecoming.

Except I had no intention of returning. The truth is, I loved every minute of those travels. I had regained my seat in recent years and was a competent horsewoman again. Between cities, my ladies and I would rent houses along the way or, when the day's distances were too great, sleep under tents, like real soldiers, telling each other ghost stories as we sat around dying fires. Of course, we were at the mercy of the weather and the state of the roads. There were times when we found ourselves masked like infidels against storms of dust, or when the rain so soaked the route that our horses strained to lift their hooves from rivers of mud.

There were disasters: the drawbridge into a fortress near Terni, where a rotten plank of wood gave way at the edge and a young page and his horse fell into the moat. If I hadn't looked back at that very moment, the boy would have perished, for he couldn't swim.

He was my faithful shadow after that. But there was laughter too. The day that one of my ladies didn't pay enough attention to the stony road so that her horse lost its footing, tipping her out of the saddle with one foot still in the stirrup. She travelled a good many yards half upside down before she was rescued, and the sight of her squealing, with her petticoats over her head, had us laughing so hard we could barely stay upright on our own horses.

'You should be grateful, Livia,' I shouted as she brushed herself down. 'At least today you're wearing undergarments.' Because everyone knew there were times when she didn't bother and I was never so prim that I couldn't enjoy a little bawdy (though, in this, others might say different). Certainly, it made a most delectable story for Francesco. As I knew it would. For I was a most dutiful wife, pouring colour and energy into every letter, doing my best to open a window on to the world outside his increasingly rank bedroom.

Was this a cruel or loving thing to do? I leave that for others to decide.

My concern was the status and reputation of Mantua, and in lieu of a warrior husband, I employed my army of sparkling ladies to keep the flame alive.

It was not my fault if he did not see it the same way.

*

It was deepest winter when I took up an invitation to go to Milan to enhance the new court of my Sforza nephew, Beatrice's older son, who as the wheel of fortune turned was now reinstated as a puppet duke. (Alas, the boy was a most unprepossessing creature, with none of his father's power or his mother's spirit, and his reign would not last long.)

There were many places I would prefer to have been. The old palazzo of Pavia was a sad relic of Lodovico's great days: Leonardo's frescoes, even his luminous Last Supper in the church of Santa Maria delle Grazie, were flaking off the walls. The assembled court was a bunch of hastily gathered itinerant nobles, the cuisine dismal and the entertainment worse. (During one evening, some light-fingered villain even sliced a dozen gold droplets off the back of my skirts!) But I was duty bound to support my nephew and promote the cause of Mantua and the Gonzagas with the latest power broker in Italy, the Holy Roman Emperor, Maximilian.

And to achieve that, I had to woo his chief envoy, an uncouth German cardinal.

I gave the task to my most practised warrior, the sweet-tongued, golden-haired Brognina, now at the height of her powers. It took her no time at all. The man was soon following her around like a lap dog, lying at her feet during the evening's entertainment, loudly mangling Italian compliments to her beauty in a way that sent ripples of shocked laughter through the assembled guests (some public decorum was expected, even in the most worldly of cardinals). She shone so brightly under this attention that the Swiss ambassador soon became similarly smitten.

Two powerful men vying publicly for favours of the same lovely woman is destined to bring any court to life, providing that most powerful of lubricants: gossip. It was bound to get back to Francesco. For some time, his letters had been arguing that the place of a dutiful wife was by her husband's side. Now, in his ill temper, and no doubt encouraged by the poisonous toad Spagnoli, he chose to read such gossip as a direct blot on the dignity of the Gonzaga name, and put direct pressure on me to come home. I had a marital war on my hands.

My scholar is not at her best today either. As she settles at her desk I notice she is coughing, swallowing noisily every now and then as if to clear her throat. When we criss-crossed Italy, I would minister to my own ladies whenever they were ill, but this is not an ailment of travelling. Rather, it is an irritation of the nose and throat coming from an extended inhaling of the dust of disintegrating ink and paper. I've seen it often enough before. Indeed, they even have a name for it now. Archive fever, they call it - the penalty to be paid for breathing in the past, though scholars tend to wear it as a badge of pride. She swallows again and takes something out of her pencil case. I smell ginger and honey, perhaps a crush of thyme as she unwraps a pastille. Excellent. I would have prescribed something of the same mix for her myself. Suck deeply on it now, for we have much to get through today.

The archive folder containing the warring words that passed between Francesco and I during this discord is in a most sorry state, its old cardboard wrappings tattered and torn. So much so that when my scholar retrieves it from the trolley, the front cover tears apart in her hands, sending a blizzard of fragile pages over the floor. The archivist on duty rushes to help gather them up, but there are far too many to attempt any chronological order then and there.

Once at her desk, my scholar tries again to bring some kind of order to the dates. Only after a while, I notice, she becomes distracted. I watch her stop, then return, once, twice, to a certain single page. What is it she has found? Of course, all manner of documents get misfiled or lost over time, slipped stiches in the tapestry of the past, but this seems different. The paper is damaged, the ink has disintegrated and while I recognise Benedetto's hand fast enough, his once perfect script has grown shaky with age and pain.

> *Your Esteemed Ladyship ...*
>   *Yesterday I went to vespers at the church of Our Lady of San Pietro*

Sweet Mary, but I know this letter. I have not seen it since ... since when? Could it really be that dull February morning in the mouldering palace of Pavia? Certainly, I have never read it over a scholar's shoulder.

Until now.

'You will be honest with me, Signor Capilupi, yes?' I had said as we parted company. 'Always tell me what you think I need to hear. We have a pact on that from many years ago, remember?'

*

The opening sentences are innocent enough: an invitation to hear Vespers at the cathedral with Francesco. Only, then it jumps to a conversation that had taken place between them afterwards. A conversation that my husband himself initiated ...

> *... His Lordship's words – and I have never heard him speak like this before – were that if there is to be love and harmony inside your marriage, you will surely do his bidding ...*

And immediately I am back again in that cold, drab room, my ladies watching carefully as my face darkens.

Because, if you do not, he can show you no further favours, as it would be proof that you had no interest in his love.

... Do his bidding ... show me no further favours! Me, who has stood by and supported him through every trial. His complaints grow louder: he finds me too proud and cruel in attitude. And then ...

His Lordship showed me how the marks of his affliction have healed. He told me that he is returning to strength and virility with every passing day, and he gave me to understand ...

The wind of my rage rolls through time, lifting the pages of her notebook and shivering the letter under her fingers. She looks up, disconcerted by the turbulence. She closes her eyes and shakes her head as if to stop me, then, frowning, doggedly returns to the page. But the syntax is hard going and I have to wait until she catches up with me ...

And he gave me to understand that he would like to consummate marriage with you again, because he still sees you as a fresh young girl.

'*Haaah!*' The sound explodes out of her, half cough, half exultation.

Therefore, my lady, I advise you to come home and satisfy your lord and make up for lost time.

'*Oh, my God!*'

Shock? Delight? Disbelief? There is no hint of fatigue or illness in her now. Here, on paper, is the proof that this sexual pestilence was common knowledge even in the most noble of households. Every head in the room snaps up in response. I have witnessed a few such moments before, when after weeks/ months buried in the past, someone, somewhere finds a treasure, forgotten or mis-archived, like pulling a diamond ring from a bucket of mud.

> *His Lordship showed me how the marks of his affliction have healed … he would like to consummate marriage with you again … a fresh young girl …*

She whips a hand to her mouth as if to apologise. But there is no disapproval here. Far from it, this is a joy to be shared. Someone laughs, others smile or shake their heads. If she can hit gold – and gold this clearly is – then it could happen to any of them. At his desk at the far side of the room, the ageing owl art historian with the black spectacles lifts a questioning hand in her direction, moving his thumb up and then down, like an emperor at gladiatorial games. What? Do the two of them know each other? Ha! If so, this is the first time I have seen any sign of it.

She raises her thumb in answered triumph.

> *Come home and satisfy your lord and make up for lost time.*

I feel again the crush of paper as my fingers close over the page.

My diseased husband is demanding sexual congress with his wife and using her old secretary as his procurer. It has been so long since I read those words that she is not the only one taken aback.

*

In time, I would forgive Benedetto. He was duty bound to tell me the truth, and the outright wishes of his lord could never be ignored. Of course! That was why Francesco singled him out for such a 'confession'. He knew the depth of our relationship, knew that Benedetto would be compelled to pass on any conversation, even, or especially, one of such intimacy. Marquis to secretary. Man to man. I've long known that my husband used those around him as his procurers. The Spagnoli toad, for instance, had found him boys in the past. But Spagnoli would have been of no use when it came to getting this message back to his wife. For that, he needed Benedetto Capilupi.

I was being ordered home to my husband's bed, for the marks of his affliction had healed. Of course. That is what the doctors were for. Yet healed did not mean cured. Or if it did, he had found better physicians than I had ever come across. How often had he been 'healed' before? Sitting next to me that first night at dinner, he was a man on a journey towards death. I'd seen it in his eyes, smelt it on his skin. Yet when he had assured me weeks later there was nothing wrong with him, he had smelled even worse.

We both knew I could no longer bear children. Though I might not have been drowning in blood when I had used the excuse, I was beyond fertility now. Eight births. Six living children. Three boys. All healthy. *Come home and satisfy your lord ...* No. I had done everything that was asked of me in the marriage chamber. And I would not return to be bedded by a rotting husband, especially one who used such subterfuge to get what he wanted.

*

She can look in vain for any reply to Benedetto, for I never wrote one.

Francesco's own letter to me arrived ten days later. Long enough for him to know that I was not obeying him. Written in the hand of the toad, there was, of course, no mention here of sexual congress. Instead, using the 'scandal of my ladies' behaviour' as his excuse, he now demanded my immediate return. *Demanded!* To capitulate would mean the end of my independence, and I would be for ever at his beck and call.

I kept my temper - just.

> *Your Lordship has little cause to complain of me.*
> *Thanks be to God, I have never required supervision or advice as to how to govern my person ...*

But no one, certainly not him, could be in any doubt as to the depths of my indignation. My very hand vibrated with fury: fashioning words so direct they have found their way into a dozen studies of Renaissance marriages, a woman's voice singing out over the centuries confronting the demands of courtesy and wifely submission.

> *Indeed, even if you loved me as much as any person has ever loved another, you could never repay my loyalty ...*

I would receive no further criticism of my behaviour. And any suggestion of renewed marital conjugality would never be referred to again.

*

Letter from Isabella to Francesco, March 1513.

In the reading room, she sits back in her chair, eyes shining, a smile playing on her lips. She clears her throat again, but there is nothing to complain of now. Archive dust has rewarded her well today. Even the driest of scholars squeeze pleasure from eavesdropping on such a marital spat. But they do not know the journey that preceded it. That is something that she and I now share.

In my sojourns with Osanna in her cell, I would wonder sometimes how it was that she could enter my mind to know what I was thinking before I could tell her. God never granted me such a skill. Or if he did, it was only in politics, and I used it to manipulate rather than give comfort. But stillness has been thrust upon me in this eternity in which I now exist and, in the same way I sometimes hear the voices of the monks resonating around the archive stacks in the old church, I have got used to being in others' presence inside the dust clouds of the past.

So that at times it feels as if their minds may be in some ways becoming porous to me.

I watch her smile broaden. Or could it be the other way round?

XXIV

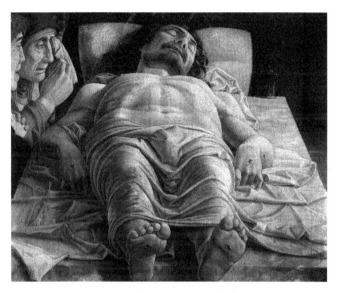

Mantegna: The Lamentation of Christ.

Alas, in the end, it was a pyrrhic victory. For the longer I stayed away, the more painful the news from home became.

Far from being healed, Francesco was seriously ill again, the disease burying itself ever deeper and faster into his body, until at last it became clear that it would indeed be a dereliction of my duty not to return.

Mantua, as well as my husband, needed me.

It was the saddest of homecomings. The stench of decaying flesh pervaded his palace of San Sebastiano. The mercury baths and salves still recommended by his doctors often caused more suffering than the sores they were designed to help. There were times when his mouth was so full of ulcerating wounds that he could neither speak nor eat solid food, or when his limbs became so raw with sores that he had to be bandaged all over, yet when they were removed, they ripped another layer of skin with them. Sometimes, it was impossible not to cry just looking at him.

There would be no more riding to hunt, and finally no riding at all, not even visiting the stables to mount his beloved Gonzaga horses. He surrounded himself only with his closest courtiers, his jester dwarf, his falcons and dogs, so that his room often stank as much of animal excrement as it did of his disintegrating body.

Having doused myself in my strongest perfumes, I and the children would visit him. Alas, his temper had got no better - he fell easily into bouts of crying and shouting, as if he could not decide which he felt more, self-pity or fury; and then there were other times when the pain was such that he could not bear anyone to touch him. Whatever his sins, this was too cruel a punishment. Still, there were a few brief moments when the old Francesco emerged and, for a while at least, we were once again a union of husband and wife.

And here, I would have her witness one last encounter that took place between us. It came not long before his death, when he summoned me to meet him. He had had himself moved from his bedroom into the main salon of San Sebastiano palace and was seated in a grand chair, dressed in fine velvet over bandages, the banners and insignia of his army set up all around him, and, blazing off the walls, Mantegna's nine epic paintings of the *Triumphs of Caesar*.

I have not spoken of them properly until now. As this scholar of mine knows, war and its celebrations were never my passion, and as soon as they were finished Francesco had taken them for his own palace, so that I never lived with them, never experienced the way their epic size and composition made you feel as if you were somehow thrust into the middle of the victory parade, soldiers, banners, carts, weapons, captured men and animals all around you, jostling for your attention as they marched across each of the nine great canvases.

'So? What do you think?' He is following my gaze. 'Magnificent, aren't they?'

'Yes,' I say meekly, because it is true. I am humbled in their presence.

'His painted chamber is one thing, but for me these will always be his masterpiece. And a great deal better than all that Arcadian nonsense you made him produce for your walls. His heart was never in dancing nymphs and sunsets. My God, how you bullied him, eh, Isabella? He used to complain about you, you know.'

Except, rather than rising to the bait, I find myself nodding; what point is there in us crossing swords now? Had I really bullied Mantegna? Was that the right word? All I can say is that if there was another way to command his brush, I never found it. In his eyes, I think I was always the spoilt sixteen-year-old. He would eventually do what I asked (and possibly, yes, my instructions were too specific), though never without a certain resentment. But then most artists I have known - apart, perhaps, from the divine Raphael - seem more at home with complaint than charm.

'D'you remember that painting of his ... Ah! Damn it ... Aaah ...' He lets out a strangled cry as he tries to move his leg. 'The one that was in his workshop when he died.'

'Of course.'

Who could forget it? We had gone together, the Marquis and Marchesa of Mantua paying our respects to the widow of a great servant of the state. It had been propped up against a wall, no date, nor any commission that anyone knew of. Even his wife didn't know when he painted it, only that it had been there, covered up, for many years.

Neither of us had ever seen anything like it.

In front of us, the body of the dead Christ was laid out full length on a slab. It took up the entire painting, but the composition was executed with such astonishing foreshortening that you read his whole beautiful tortured torso - and yes, beauty was the right word - from the feet backwards, the colour palette of his skin so bleached that it felt as if the paints themselves were in mourning. Humility, dignity, sorrow, pity, it was all there.

An image of a mutilated dead man. It would not be long before my husband's diseased body will itself be on a marble slab. But who will want to look at him? Is that what is going through his mind? What, I wonder, will my tears be like?

'My mother always told me I would bow before Mantegna's brilliance.' I have to say something to take both our minds off the thought.

'Ha! Your mother. Excellent woman! I always liked her. She never gave your father any trouble.' And now he laughs and, for a second, he is once again the old ebullient Francesco. But it costs him and he doubles up with a sudden fit of coughing that shakes his whole body as his face contorts with pain. It takes a long time for him to find his way back. I make a move towards him, but he puts up his hand to stop me.

'No, stay where you are!'

'Shall I call for someone?'

'God, no. They would only cause me more pain. Aaagh. Don't worry, I suffered much worse on the battlefield.'

Though we both know that is not true. He takes a few more breaths and steadies himself.

'So how is it? Waiting for me to die?'

I shake my head. 'I would give anything to help with your pain.'

'Hmm. Yes, well, you are not the only one. Still, we have done well enough, wouldn't you say, you and I? What? Six living issue and three boys. There have been a good many worse unions in both our houses.' He nods, stretching his leg again and cursing slightly. 'Though you were always more the warrior goddess than Venus. I should have known from that first game we played together. You cheated, you know.'

'I did not.' The words are out of my mouth before I give them permission.

'Ha! Yes, you did. And you never liked the bedchamber, even at the start. Oh, don't look so surprised. What? You think a man can't tell? Who knows how it would have been if you'd been more inviting ...'

He is a dying man and this is just more cruel humour. I should let it go. But it is too late for me now to become someone else. 'I think we would both of us still be in this room together now, even if I had,' I say quietly. 'If there is one thing life has taught me, it is that men and women have different appetites.'

His laugh is more like a growl. 'You're right there. Still, I did not ask you here to quarrel. We need to talk about Federico.'

'He will make a fine marquis.'

'Maybe so. But not yet. His time in Rome spoiled him, made

him too much the courtier and not enough soldier. He's still too green to rule. You need to stand behind him when I go. Govern in his stead till he is ready.'

'Don't speak of such a moment, my lord.'

'Don't be stupid, Isabella. Such courtesies never suited you. I am already dead. The rest is simply suffering.' He cries out as he shifts in his seat. Again I watch the agony move across his face and again I move forward.

'No, no,' he shouts. 'No touching. I cannot bear to be touched. It's as if there is a pack of rats living in my body, gorging my innards and bones.' He throws his head back against the chair rest. 'I tell you, I am Prometheus bound to the rock now.'

He gulps for air, holding my eyes for a few seconds. 'And for God's sake, don't cry. There is nothing to cry about.'

'I am not,' I say, as the tears flow.

'There you go. Always the contradiction. I could never govern you, Isabella. You always thought you could do better. Well, after I am gone you will have your chance. Just make sure the boy marries fast and produces sons even faster. With two brothers at his heels, there'll be trouble if he doesn't.' He leans his head back. 'You should go now. They'll be coming to change my dressings soon and I will make an awful racket.'

I would see him only once more. Towards the very end, his servants brought two of his favourite stallions from his stables over the bridge to the palace of San Sebastiano, and together they mounted the low tread stairs to the upper floor into his bedroom. The horses stood by his bed and he lifted himself up so that he could reach and touch their skin, and they in turn bowed their heads so he could stroke their necks and twine his fingers in their manes. I think he gained more pleasure from this than any visit from his children, for his animals had always loved him unconditionally, and they at least did not seem to notice his smell. Or if they did, they were still able to recognise the man beneath it.

*

He died in the spring of 1519, his family gathered around him. His last words, clear and strong for all to hear, were that he had always been aware of my marvellous wisdom and capacity, so that he now put the welfare of all our children into my care.

> *Nothing was to be seen on the faces of all present but tears, nothing was to be heard but the sobbing of the women, while the children stood by, stunned and silent.*

She sits frowning at her desk, her chin propped on her clasped fists. Sometimes it is the simplest words that carry the most feeling. Around his bed, I see Ippolita's face, ghostly pale against the white of her nun's headdress (there was never any stopping of her will and she has made a fine nun), her brothers Ercole and Ferrante, not quite old enough yet to shed adult tears, while in the background the keening of my ladies' voices as they rise and fall over the intoned prayers of the Franciscan friars. Tears, sobbing and silence. A dignified description for what was, in the end, a dignified death.

The man who wrote those words, Mario Equicola, was the new secretary of government. New, because I had already issued a warrant for the arrest of the old one, Tolomeo Spagnoli. Those who accuse me of holding grudges would do well to study the charges: fraud and embezzlement, using my husband's seal on land deals and financial payments when he was too ill to know better. The soldiers I sent would find his house empty - like the rat he was, he had deserted the ship as soon as he realised his master's death was imminent. Still, it gave me pleasure to put my name to the arrest form.

*

In the reading room, our long breaths mingle in the air. Another day filled with the tumult of years. Except the deaths did not end there, and it is best if we get through them fast, for I am tired of crying in the future for things that happened so far in the past. Precious old Benedetto Capilupi, still wracked by gall stones, made the decision to go under the knife. 'My father's pain has been unbearable for all to see', his son wrote to me, though it was hard to know if he was speaking of the surgery or the failed recovery. His passing, just before Francesco's, was an equal mercy of sorts.

Meanwhile, in Ferrara, Lucrezia Borgia, like so many before her, died soaked in her own blood, a shrivelled newborn in her arms. Her letter to me after Francesco's death was an expression of such naked grief that I found myself almost sorry for both of them. I'm not so hard-hearted that I cannot see a kind of love story when it passes before my eyes, and in the end, as I said, she had taken nothing from me that I wasn't happy to give. While I have nightmares of hell, and aspire to glimpses of heaven, I could never do much with the long grind of purgatory. Should they find themselves together there, perhaps they might bring each other a little sustenance. I wonder, might Dante approve?

And finally, there was Raphaello Sanzio. Thirty-seven years old and overflowing with laughter and talent. He died as he had lived - in love with love and life: coming home early after a night with his mistress through the streets of Rome, he caught a chill, which turned to a virulent fever, and was dead within two days. He made everything he did look easy, as if the creation of beauty was as natural as breathing. I would have given much to have wooed him away from Rome; but it could never have been, for he was not only the pope's favoured painter but also the city's foremost architect, responsible for the preservation of antiquities as well as the Sisyphean project of the new St Peter's.

It was as well then that I did not have the luxury of time for further grief. There was too much in Mantua demanding my attention. With Francesco buried, nineteen-year-old Federico would ride his white horse out from the castle to the cathedral, where he would be crowned the new marquis. Though not yet the bone fide ruler of the state.

Because Francesco's last will and testament, dictated the day before he died, made me executor and advisor until our eldest son reached the age of his majority at twenty-two. My husband had finally awarded me the honour I so deserved. The gift of government. And a poisoned chalice.

THE DOWAGER MARCHESA

XXV

'I know that your father's wishes were not to your liking. I see myself only standing in the background. You understand that?'

'Yes, Mother.'

Of course he wasn't pleased. How could he be? But I was too busy to pay much heed to his hurt pride.

Francesco had picked a bad moment in history to die. The accession of a new young King of Spain with the title of Holy Roman Emperor inherited from his uncle was sending shock waves through Italy. What he lacked in looks (rumour was that he was exceedingly ugly, with a chin that stuck out like a jetty), Charles V made up for in ambition, his every whim backed by up eye-watering amounts of wealth now pouring into Spanish coffers from the New World. Where France had once been the undisputed powerbroker in Italy, states like ours now had to walk the tightrope of flattering both would-be conquerors.

Then there was the rest of the Gonzaga brood to care for. My second-born son, Ercole (if he features less in this mad story, it is only because he caused me the least trouble), was already destined for the Church, and in need of an experienced ecclesiastical tutor to start his ascent towards a cardinal's hat. While Ferrante, that puppy who had torn himself out of me all those years ago, was mad for a military career and a training he could not get in Mantua. Caught between the armies of France and Spain, my political instinct favoured Spain. But I was not the only one with sons to settle and it would take diplomatic stealth to place his suit above others. My new secretary was already hollow-eyed from writing more than he was sleeping. There was just so much to be done.

'I shall deal with only the most mundane, time-consuming matters - court judgements, the overseeing of city affairs.'

'Yes, Mother.'

Since his father's death, I have watched his scowl get darker by the day. How I mourn the passing of that rosy-cheeked little boy I had seen off to Rome so long ago - the fond letters, the sweet little oriental cat he once sent me as a present, the verses he wrote after my beloved dog Aura died. But, as Benedetto reminded me, first-born boys must grow up quickly and a sense of entitlement was part of his education.

With each passing day, he grows ever more like Francesco. Jet-black hair, thick as glue, and a rough complexion. He takes after him in other ways too. He has a passion for dogs, horses and the hunt. And women. Or rather, one woman in particular. Perhaps had he come into his patrimony earlier, the daily grind of administration might have taken his mind off this dalliance. Perhaps ...

'My handling of the everyday administration frees you to spend more time with the army. And to travel. Predicting how allies - or enemies - might think or behave is vital, and there is nothing like first-hand experience to -'

'I know all this, Mother. You forget that after Rome, I spent two years at the French court learning such things.'

'Of course you did!' Those who complain about the cost of girls' dowries have no idea the damage a boy at a foreign court can do to a well-run treasury. 'But you were younger then.'

'I was old enough to be sent away.'

I laugh. 'Eloquently put. Nevertheless, it is your father's decision and we must respect it. There is also the business of your marriage, which was foremost in his mind. This is the perfect time to get to know your bride better. The court at Monferrato is eager to host you. How is your correspondence with Maria Paleologa?' I ask sweetly, though I already know the answer.

'She's still a child. She writes about dolls!'

'Surely not! She's probably referring to the mannequin I sent to her to show off the latest Mantuan fashions. She'll need to keep abreast of such things if she is to shine here. She has an excellent education in all such things and will grow up quickly now, you will see.'

The marriage negotiations had been one of the last acts Francesco and I shared. The state of Monferrato was rich and stable and a most effective buffer between us and Milan. The perfect union. In retrospect, perhaps the ten-year age gap had been something of a risk, but I wasn't to know Federico would become besotted with someone else.

'Her age didn't bother you when you first met. Such a pretty girl! I remember you were quite smitten, even insisted on going through the ceremony and exchanging rings then and there.'

His scowl knits his eyebrows so fast together that for a moment I'm looking into his father's face. 'I was younger then,' he mutters.

'The same age as when you went to France,' I say cheerfully, pretending not to notice how he had just ceded me the argument. Surely I had fenced more cleverly at his age?

'Listen to me, my son. I understand your frustration ...'

But his look tells me clearly that I do not. What he wants is to be the ruler of his own state with his mistress by his side, without his mother's eye looking down on him.

*

I had accepted the infatuation when it first began two years earlier. It was only natural that a young prince enjoy a few amorous diversions. No man should meet his virginal wife unprepared. Some mothers would have taken a hand in such things, employed professional women to do a professional job. But the bushfire of pestilence made that a risky prospect, so I didn't mind - at first - when his eye alighted on a young woman in my own sitting room.

Isabella Boschetti.

The fact that I had chosen her would haunt me for years, for she was the rotten apple in the barrel. She came with the finest credentials. Her father had fought in the Battle of Fornovo alongside Francesco and her mother was the sister of the poet and writer Castiglione. Isabella! Even her name was an insult, for she had been christened in my honour. She was married early to a twig off a branch off a bigger branch of the Gonzaga tree, and when I enquired - a husband can be an embarrassment in some circumstances - I was assured he was a pretty, foppish creature, words that suggested a marriage of convenience, thus guaranteeing her first loyalty would be to me. I didn't even need to factor in the price of an eventual dowry. Did my parsimony affect my judgement? If it did, I was suitably punished for it.

She had a pretty face, a good singing voice (though in speech, even then, there was a tendency to squeakiness), and what felt like a fetching modesty. How did I not see the sly under the shy, I who had such experience of ladies-in-waiting?

The strange thing is that until my son walked into the room, she had shown no interest in men. Indeed, she had remained so much in the background that by the end of her first year I wondered if I had made a mistake.

They were close to the same age. Federico was back from his sojourn at the French court, sporting a suitable veneer of sophistication and no doubt a few fumbling notches on his belt. But I suspected he was still unsure of himself with women and so I brought him into our company because I knew my ladies would encourage him with their good-natured playfulness. I look back on that first encounter with a kind of horror. Because I, who am alert to everything, did not see it. She didn't immediately join in the teasing. Instead, she asked a few questions - I can't recall what - and seemed, well, rather timid. I remember thinking she had a most affecting smile and that she should use it more often.

Which, clearly, she did. Before I knew it, he was seeking her out. He invited her and a few others riding, then asked her back a second time to visit the stables - she was an excellent horsewoman, and I do not know what else, for neither of them told me. He chose to visit me more often when he knew she would be in my company and now I became aware of a kind of fire in the room: looks exchanged, secret smiles, nervous laughter.

Though I would come to hate her for what she did to my son, when I look back to those early days a question remains in my mind. Who seduced whom? For along with the heat, there was also - and it pains me to say this - a certain giddiness to them both. The world is full of stories of romance. The French in particular are to blame for this: how Cupid's dart moves from the eye into the heart, introducing a slow infection of the blood, which moves around the body until it lodges in the entrails, where love and lust fuse. They say it is the most delicious of all diseases and the fact that I never felt it does not mean I am immune to recognising its effects on others.

If they had been anyone else, I might have allowed myself to be charmed, for it was clear that my son was happy.

But it could not be ignored. After a while, she began to take on airs, paying more attention to her looks than to her loyalty to me. My other ladies became uncomfortable in her presence. They knew, of course, but no one dared admit it for fear of my reaction. Then there were the gifts, subtle at first: the rubied net with which she decorated that waterfall of chestnut hair (my own was growing thinner now, augmented daily by fake pieces), or the way that, in conversation, she casually started to raise her right hand, on whose little finger now sat a small gold and sapphire ring, an object she could never have afforded herself.

When I finally asked her about it, the encounter was short and unsatisfactory. She looked at me directly - what did I object to most, the lisp or the squeakiness - and told me it was a present from her uncle. With not a hint of her lying.

'How very good of him,' I said. 'When I see him next, I must congratulate him on his taste. And generosity.'

And she had smiled, seemingly unconcerned at being unmasked as a liar. It was not a response that any of my other ladies would have dared.

No. By then, Isabella Boschetti knew exactly what she was doing.

Not long after, I dismissed her from my services, suggesting that she join her husband. I shan't share the conversation. There is no trace in history of any meeting between us. Just as there is scarcely a mention of her in my letters, and bringing her to life too often now would award her a greater prominence than I can bear. Or allow. That, if you like, is my revenge for the damage she did.

I knew that whatever I said, or did, Federico would house her somewhere else and their liaison would continue. He was, by this time, sexually besotted. I say again, I did not begrudge him pleasure. He had to watch his father's manhood rot away and his younger brothers would soon be snapping at his heels. He needed to show his virility. I tolerated the situation, assuming that he would tire of her.

But with his father's death, the rules changed. Federico's most pressing duty as marquis now was to secure the state by producing legitimate heirs. She might manage to hold on to his favour - she would not be the first clever woman to fish-hook her way into a man's heart through his loins - but the sooner Maria Paleologa was in his bed, the better. A sacrifice was needed to accelerate the process.

XXVI

Mantegna: The Court of Gonzaga, the Camera Picta.

Once again, the court of Lodovico Gonzaga stares out at me from above the fireplace, frozen in action as if a spell had been cast and at any moment they might all be released.

I'm not so far removed now from the age that the pancake-faced Barbara Brandenburg was when he painted her. With each passing year, I have more admiration for her. She was ten years old when she came from Germany to become a Gonzaga. A young scholar, she could already speak four languages, but she didn't let it get in the way of her duty and the fourteen children she brought into the world. Fourteen! No doubt always in search of the perfect spine.

'You asked to see me, Mother.'

I turn to greet him. 'Ah, Federico, yes! It seems some work is needed on the chamber. It's fifty years since Andrea started on it and layers of soot from the fire have darkened the colours, while stains of saltpetre have leaked through in places. See the painted curtains and the dog under Ludovico's chair?'

'Hmm.' But he is not that interested. 'What needs to be done?'

'Lorenzo Costa is in favour of using soft bread to clean away the dirt and an application of linseed oil.'

'Then he should do it.'

I had toyed with asking Costa himself to repaint it, but Mantua's present court artist has little of his predecessor's poetry.

'Personally, I find this scene rather joyless.'

'Nevertheless,' I say carefully, 'there was a purpose to such formal presentation. Your great-grandfather met his most important guests here, sitting himself directly under his own portrait, so that ambassadors found themselves having to address two marquises at the same time. The chamber was made for the conduct of government. You should use it more.'

'Perhaps when I am allowed to govern!' He shrugs. 'You know the thing I like most here?'

I laugh. 'The horse?'

'Not any horse! It's a portrait of Xanthus, grandfather's favourite, named after one of Achilles' stallions. He sent Mantegna to do studies of him so he could put him faithfully on to the wall.'

'How do you know that?'

'Father used to bring me here when I was learning to ride. Though we had to keep it our secret because you said I was too young. "Imagine mounting that beauty," he would say. "You'd step off the wall and the hunting dogs would follow you down the stairs, across the moat to the stables and into the forest. Then, when the kill was finished, the grooms could lead them back up and on to the wall as if they had never left."'

How old would he have been then? Six or seven. I remember thinking then that I would never, ever forget his plump sweetness. Now I see only what was once my husband's face.

'You told me many years ago that you would build a palace on the site of your father's stables.'

'Oh, and I will. I have ideas for it already! I know who will do it. I've written to him.'

'I see. Might I know his name?'

'Giulio Romano.'

'Ah, Raphael's black-eyed pupil.'

'He is his own man now. Already drowning in commissions. But he's not appreciated properly in Rome.'

'Yes, I have heard.'

My expression does not change a whit. What? Am I supposed to not know? It is not every day that the pope's own painter shows his dissatisfaction over late payment by drawing scenes of naked carnal intercourse on the walls of the pontiff's summer palace! The gossip is that models for the women were all courtesans and that the positions they engaged in were ... well, athletic, to say the least. No, for all his youthful talent, Giulio Romano, born Pippi, already has a fine reputation for trouble.

'Well, I am sure once he gets more experience he will be splendid. And will you have portraits of your own horses on the walls? Remember when you spoke to me about them, that day on the bank of the river so long ago?'

'Oh yes. I intend for there to be a whole salon devoted to them, with each of their names written underneath to ensure they have a place in history.'

His excitement now is unguarded. It is something we have shared from early on - a love of art. Even if we do not approve of the same artists.

'Your father, I know, would have given it his blessing. He and I used to ride to the hunt from those stables often. I remember you also telling me that day by the river that you and your wife would do the same thing every morning. The Marquis and Marchesa of Mantua meeting the new day.'

You and your wife. It is quite an achievement, guiding us back from the brink to safe ground. His scowl tells me I have overstepped the mark. Still, it was worth the try. It didn't always work with his father either.

'Either way, the frescoes here must be preserved,' I said brightly. 'The real pity is that all these rooms were so neglected during your father's last years.' And my sigh, I think, is very credible. 'You know, Federico, this castle has been the official home of the Gonzaga family for close on a century. No one could have a finer home. Restoring it to its greatness would take work. I have to say, only you, out of all my children, have the taste and the incentive to do it.'

It's a little crude, yes. But like his father, he is susceptible to flattery, as long as it is well disguised.

'But ... I don't see how. I mean, this is your home.'

'My home? Ah, you are kind, but I am simply the dowager marchesa now, and though I might hope to be of some use to you for a while, it's only right and proper that I move my apartments elsewhere and leave the castle to you and ...'

... your wife. Only of course, this time I don't say the word out loud.

XXVII

Digital reproduction of Isabella's final studiolo.

In reality, it was no great sacrifice.

My collection had long outgrown the space allotted. As had I. I could no longer comfortably mount the small staircase connecting my grotta and studiolo. It was never wide and no woman survives eight pregnancies without some toll on her body. Then there was the attrition of hospitality: every prince, duke or cardinal I ever visited vying to produce the richest banquet to impress me. I've never concealed my love of food. It would be pointless anyway; my letters are full of demands for the purchase of the marzipan and sweet cakes that I yearned for. And how can I possibly regret something that gave me so much pleasure?

Not long ago, there was a fashion among those who studied me to suggest that my appetite was a substitute for love or the

satisfaction of sexual congress. I would urge my present scholar
to ignore that idea, for it seems to me entirely misguided. I may
have relished eating too much, but, apart from the saints, who
doesn't have a weakness towards one of the deadly sins? There's
not an inch of sloth in me, nor - as discussed - any trace of lust.
She's seen my anger blow furnace hot, but it passes soon enough
and whatever envy I have felt I have been open about. As for
avarice, she knows by now that my only interest in money was
for the things of beauty it could buy. But greed, sliding towards
gluttony ... well, what are confessors for if not to give us penance
to start afresh? And then forgive us once more when we fall
again. When that constipated monster Martin Luther started
tearing down the walls of the Church, he was merciless towards
so many of the sins that made life bearable. I knew a few nobles
who at times were swayed towards his purity, for he also called
out corruption, but that road was always too harsh for me. No.
I was never one to fight battles that I couldn't win.

I threw myself into the work of relocating. Carpenters prised
the wooden marquetry panels off the walls; workmen disman-
tled, then reassembled, the marble doorframe from the entrance
to my studiolo. I took everything with me, even down to the
floor tiles. All that was left was the ceilings, which I have heard
remain to this day, their peeling gold and stucco a sad memory
of Gonzaga grandeur.

I already knew where I would go: a suite of rooms on the
ground floor of the adjoining palace with not one but two larger
chambers to display my treasures, and next to them an exact
replica of my studiolo.

I even had my own private garden. What bliss to open
windows on to bird song, to sit amid the scent of orange blossom,

as I had done with my mother in that other palace so long ago. It is still there today, I know, for I've seen pictures of it on scholars' desks - both intimate and grand, with its carved frieze still legible on the walls: *'Isabella d'Este, granddaughter and niece of Aragon's kings, daughter and sister of dukes of Ferrara, wife and mother of Gonzaga marquises.'*

Meanwhile, I was in contact with Federico's betrothed family, making light of the rumours, assuring them that he would call for his young bride soon. I admit I was naïve. I assumed Boschetti's hold over him would gradually weaken, that another woman would catch his eye, as had always been the way with his father.

But that didn't happen. She was now his constant companion and the functions of the court began to revolve around her. When our paths crossed, I behaved with perfect courtesy - rumour had it that she likened my smile to be being bitten by a viper. Still, I couldn't dent her growing influence, right down to her accompanying him on diplomatic visits to Venice, as if *she* was the official Marchesa of Mantua herself. How those Venetians senators must have sneered behind their backs! One might despise their hypocrisy, but they were careful enough to keep their courtesans behind closed doors.

And, in the end, a courtesan was what Isabella Boschetti was.

But she was one step ahead of me. I didn't notice her pregnancy immediately, and no one had the courage to tell me until the tell-tale added extra pleats in her skirts gave it away. They say she danced almost until the end, like the whore she was. When at mass, I somehow forgot to pray for her safe delivery.

She did not need my prayers. She gave birth to a boy. My spies informed me it was not an easy labour, but that mother and child were doing well. I decided to see for myself. And this encounter I will share.

She was not expecting me. Of that, I am sure. Had she been, I suspect her servants might have tried to deny me entrance with some fake concerns about her health.

The swaddled baby was asleep on the breast of a large wet nurse sitting by the fire, while Boschetti was sitting up in bed, cleaned and dressed in new lawn and lace, her hair combed and flowing like a Madonna. She was lovely enough, though a little fragile, I thought. There is something affecting in the face of a woman who has newly given birth, as if the elemental nature of the journey is still written on her countenance. But I was determined not to be deterred by it.

'I have come to meet my grandchild,' I said, and moved to take the baby.

The wet nurse shot her an anxious glance, but she nodded and the bundle was given to me.

'You may leave us now,' I said. Another glance and the woman was gone.

Once one is far enough removed from the childbearing years, every baby looks the same: squashed and unformed. Or so it has been with me. He half opened his eyes and began to cry, a thin mewling sound that got louder as he realised he had been pulled from the teat. I hooked my little finger into his mouth and hushed him (certain habits one does not lose), and waited till he started to suckle before placing him carefully back in the cradle, which I saw to my horror was the same one I had reserved for his father so long ago. How dare she, how dare they both ...

All this time, she was watching me intently. What was she thinking? That I had come to dash his head against the walls, like some usurped Greek heroine? Such a monster she must think me. Good.

'He has a fine colour,' I said, as I adjusted the swaddling even tighter around him. 'He will be dark, I think. The Gonzagas invariably are.'

She said nothing. 'So, tell me, my dear.' I settled myself near the bed. 'How are you?'

'I ... I am well, thank you.' And I was pleased to hear that her voice - how can he bear that edge of squeakiness? - was a little shaky.

'Still, I gather it was a long labour. Such a shock, don't you agree? One cannot be prepared. Some women, they say, curse, even blaspheme at the worst of it, regretting the pleasure that brought them to so much pain.' I paused. 'But perhaps that was not you,' I added cheerfully.

She pulled herself up against the pillow, wincing slightly. Oh, but it was such a delight to have her at a disadvantage.

I gestured to the servant who had entered with me and she handed over a basket, then left as I waved her away.

'See. I brought you some cherries. The sweetest of the crop. I used to love them when I was lying in.'

I offered her the basket, but she shook her head. I selected one or two and put them in my mouth, blood red and juicy.

'So,' I said after a while. 'I think it's time you and I talked, don't you? My son is most fond of you. How could he not be? You are quite lovely. And I am sure you are fond of him too. But you know this cannot go on. He is close to gaining his majority now.'

'I don't see what that has to do with me,' she said at last, her voice growing stronger.

'Oh, I think you do. As the official ruler of Mantua, his life must change. I am not asking you to give him up, you understand - well, not entirely.'

'Dowager Marchesa –'

'I think it best if you call me Your Ladyship, as you once did.'

'Your Ladyship.' She hesitated. *Go on*, I think - *you have started now, you had better finish.* 'The fact is - I love your son. And he loves me.'

I felt a shiver, as if a little devil had just popped his head out from underneath the bed.

'If that is true, then of course you will want what is best for him. Which, as we both know, is to fulfil his duty as the ruler of this great state. And for that he must marry and have legitimate children to secure the line. The birth of this ... this little ... boy', (the word bastard was close on my tongue) 'makes that even more imperative.'

'I am not stopping him from doing that.'

'Yes, you are. You have power. I will not deny that. That is the reason I am here. To tell you that this is the moment for you to use it wisely. Whatever happens, you will be well looked after, both of you.' I glanced at the child. 'You have my solemn word on that.'

She frowned, but she was not cowed. Despite myself, I felt a memory of this moment flooding in: the sense of elation, the triumph of having risked death and brought forth a miracle. Even if she didn't have courage, this would give it to her now.

'And if I do not?'

'Do not what?'

'Do as you say.'

'Then when it ends ...' I sighed. 'Which it will, for it always does, it will not go well for you.'

She nodded slightly, as if she was taking my words in. Then suddenly she let out a cry, cradling her hands over her stomach as if she was experiencing severe pain. I watched her in admiration. It was exactly what I would have done, had our positions been reversed.

'You are in distress?'

'Ah, no. I ... oh. Yes, perhaps ... perhaps. I am in need of the midwife.'

'Of course you are.' I got up. 'I shall call her immediately. You must be careful with yourself. Your dear uncle, remember? The one who gave that lovely ring so long ago ...? You know his young wife caught a chill after the birth and both she and the baby were dead within a few days. He was beside himself with grief for weeks to come.'

But she was not listening. 'Ah!'

And now I was finally calling for help. As I reached the door, I met my son coming in.

*

'How are you, Mother?

His voice was ice cold.

Barely an hour had passed before he arrived in my rooms. I was standing arranging a set of ancient coins in a velvet display case, my dogs playful around my skirts. 'Oh, do not ask about me! How is your ... Madonna Boschetti? It was most distressing to see her in pain.'

'She is better.'

'Good. I simply called to give her my regards and suddenly ...'

'– it is best if we do not pretend, Mother.' His complexion was high and there was a scent to his sweat. 'You threatened her.'

'Oh, nonsense! What did she tell you? You know women after birth are notoriously emotional and get easily confused.'

'You ordered her to give me up.'

'I did not.'

'Yes, you did.'

I lift up my hands as if I cannot deal with the argument. 'Do not raise your voice to me, Federico. I can hear you well enough.'

At my feet my troupe of dogs, including two of Aura's own children, start yapping and growling. For a moment, his fury is such that I think he might kick one of them. I watch him struggle to control himself as I busy myself with settling them.

'I understand this is not easy for you, Mother,' he says carefully after a while, as if he were talking to a child. 'But the baby is a Gonzaga.'

'Not a legitimate one.'

He sighed. 'We both know Father had children before you were his wife.'

'Two, and only girls,' I retort coldly. 'By women of no accord. By the time he was your age, he was about to marry me.'

'Don't you understand? Maria Paleologa is still too young.'

'She will be twelve next birthday. That is old enough to be brought to court to familiarise her with her new home. If you like, I can take charge of her, so that she will not "bother" you too much. But she is your bride and her place is here.'

How unhappy would she be? I have asked myself that question. At her age, my own mother had refused to let me go, for fear my budding youth might prove too much of a temptation to a lusty young man. But that was exactly why I needed this girl here now. Each mother must do what is right for her child. In the eyes of the Paleologa family, there could be no greater humiliation for a daughter than to be formally betrothed and then discarded.

He gave a bitter little laugh. 'How foolish of me. I thought the news of a grandchild might in some way please you.'

'Then you are wrong. And the reason you thought it is that you are surrounded by courtiers who say only what you want to hear. It is a common disease among rulers.'

'Whereas you can say what you want.'

'Not only can I, it is my duty to do so. That is what your father's last wishes made clear. Your infatuation with this ... this woman is making Mantua a laughing stock. And we can ill afford to lose what little influence is left us.'

'And whose fault is that, Mother? Which other ruler suffers the humiliation of sharing power with his mother?'

'Oh, you exaggerate.'

'No, I do not. You should hear what people say about you. Even when Father was alive ...'

'– And what did they say then, pray?'

'How you were a law unto yourself. How when Father would ask for you to come home, you took no notice. I was there once, you know, when Tolomeo Spagnoli told him that he should order you back.'

'Spagnoli!'

He ignored me. 'And do you know what Father said in reply?'

I waved my hand in fury.

'That once when he did, you simply refused and would do so again, which would only add to his humiliation. Those were his very words. If anyone has undermined the state of Mantua, Mother, it is you. I should have taken over three years ago. Spagnoli said –'

'Spagnoli! Spagnoli! How dare you speak that name in my presence. The man was a snake and a criminal. And I am sure he poured a thick vial of poison into your ear about how you could rule perfectly well with his help.'

'It would be better than being hidden behind your skirts.'

'My skirts! And what do you think people say about how you hide behind hers?'

He lifted his hand, and for a second I feared he might even strike me, but instead he brought it down hard on the velvet display, jumping the coins off and scattering them to the ground. The violence of the gesture, met by the mad chorus of yelping dogs, stopped us both.

I raised myself up and took a few breaths. Sweet Mary, how could I let this happen? How often do I have to learn that no argument with a man is won by challenging them directly? I have been living without a husband for too long.

I put my hands together and brought them to my lips as if in prayer. 'Federico - if I have angered you, I am sorry.'

He said nothing. But the pout was still there.

'I want nothing but the best for you and for Mantua. I accept that I am outspoken at times. But it is only in your interest.'

And now I let the tears flow. It is a ploy that works miracles for some women. I was too old and fat to gain much from it now. Still, sons do not like to see their mother cry.

'Mother ... please!'

'You do not need to give her up. That was never what I was asking. But I beg you, do not offend the Paleologa family further. The letters from their court talk of their mounting worry. Her mother hints that there were other offers -'

'Then she should take them.'

'How can she? Rings were exchanged. You and she are bound formally together.'

'I shall ask the new pope to annul it. I can do better than her.'

A cold sword of terror went through me. *Think, Isabella, think.*

I shrugged. 'You can ask, but I guarantee you he will not listen. He has inherited a disastrous debt from Leo's profligate spending, while every day the noises made by that belligerent German monk grow louder. He has no time for adjudicating marriage contracts. Unless you have a fortune to offer him in return. Which, I would remind you, you don't.'

He stared at me and then laughed. Oh, but the sound is just like his father's. 'My God. You never stop, do you?

'What?'

'Your politicking.'

'I am simply ...'

'You are simply predicting what an ally or an enemy will do before they do it. Yes, yes, I know. Ha! All right, Mother. We will make a truce here. You will leave my mistress alone and I will govern from this moment on. In return, I will write to Maria's mother and tell her I shall request for her daughter to come when the new castle apartments are finally ready. Now, does that satisfy you?'

I wiped my tears, though they were already dry.

'Oh, Federico. I have always known you would make a fine ruler.'

He stared at me coldly. 'I already am.'

Such a triumph it was.

Until it wasn't.

*

It was not long after this that the notorious Giulio Romano arrived from Rome.

There had been a further chapter to those licentious drawings of his: before they could be erased from the walls, Giulio had copied them - no living draughtsman could match his speed - and, using Raphael's old printer and engraver, had turned them into a series of 'secret engravings', which once they were released travelled faster than the plague through the houses of 'artistic connoisseurs', including a number of cardinals and senior clerics. Such blatant scandal fed directly into the heretics' attacks on the corruption of the Church. What could Pope Clement do but send in the papal censor with troops to destroy the printing plates and throw the engraver himself into prison. Giulio, not surprisingly, had decided this might be a good time to leave Rome, and had become available to attractive offers from other patrons. My son's being the most insistent.

In a matter of weeks, the man was holding the title of Mantua's court artist and he and Federico were inseparable, engrossed in grandiose plans for a glorified palace for that 'other' Isabella on the site of his father's stables on the island of Te.

And still no letter of invitation had gone out to his bride.

It was clear that his dowager mother had no place in Mantua now. Such was the open antagonism between myself and his mistress that we could no longer be in the same room together. Hunting parties, dances, balls - I attended none of them, while every soiree I hosted myself saw fewer courtiers taking up my invitation. Foreign guests who once would have spent the day admiring my collection now had pressing appointments with the marquis rather than his mother. Even Mario Equicola, my own secretary, *my own secretary*, found excuses to be elsewhere.

Something Benedetto would never have done. Or that was what I told myself.

For the second time in my life, I was an exile in my own home.

Except now I had somewhere to go: the city from which Giulio Romano had fled, the place where my 'reputation' had opened all manner of doors ten years before, where every palace shone with new art and each day the ground threw up ancient treasures, a few of which I might now even be able to afford.

Had the great Osanna still been alive, she would surely have counselled me otherwise.

Raimondi: The Massacre of the Innocents engraving.

In the archive, the text she is engrossed in today does not come from any archive shelf I know and I am impressed that she has found it.

The book itself is new, though the black-and-white engraving on its cover I recognise as old. Set against the background of Rome's Sixtus IV bridge, an orgy of violence is unfolding: naked soldiers, thick with muscle, slaughtering a group of women and babies, one of them a cunningly foreshortened figure of a mother with a child in her arms running full tilt towards you as if she is trying to burst out of the frame to save herself from the carnage around her. The art of composition. Aways the signature of a great artist.

There are some, I suspect, who might not recognise the hand of Raphael Sanzio, but those who followed him as I did knew only too well that he could conjure up the heroic male body as forcefully as his rival Michelangelo when he chose. Herod's Massacre of the Innocents, though, grew out of his imagination. Raphael himself, God rest his soul, would never live to hear the real screams of slaughtered women and children, or see the streets of Rome flowing with blood.

Nevertheless, the engraving feels painfully prophetic to the book's subject and title.

The Sack of Rome.

Written barely six months after the event itself, this work is by one Luigi Guicciardini, a Florentine diplomat, and the fact that he composed it so fast and so accurately stands as proof that we, like the ancients we revered, took the recording of our history seriously, for not only does it seek to understand the madness of the politics of the time, it also incorporates dozens of first-hand witness accounts.

She will need a strong stomach to get through it. But since all copies of my letters from that time are lost and the originals never reached their destination, it will allow her to enter into the belly of the beast, for it tells of things that even I did not see.

Though, God knows, I saw enough.

XXVIII

How to explain the sack of Rome? Tragedy? Farce? God's judgement on the Church? The devil in heretic's clothing? Or simply the endless bloody business of politics? Having lived through it, I know it to be all of those. Once the killing starts, the holiest city of Christendom will be stained black for generations to come. All the more reason then to offer up a few memories of its beauty to put against the loss.

I arrived in the spring of 1525, renting a house on the edge of the Quirinale, one of the seven hills that made up the ancient city.

Maerten van Heemskerck: the Colonna Palace, 1530s.

To make one's home in the Colonna palace was to live inside an architectural palimpsest. Named after the family that built it, its newest rooms had been frescoed by Pinturicchio, the man Mantegna so despised all those years ago (wrongly, I would say now, having lived with his sparkling colours), while an older wing housed a library, thick with the scent of disintegrating leather. But it was the earth itself that held the greatest treasures. The palace, like so many others, had been constructed out of the ruins of imperial Rome. It had once been the site of a great temple. Generation after generation had plundered its stones, yet a memory of its grandeur remained in a few towering segments of wall, one with a slab of broken entablature precariously on top, where in the early mornings a single bald-headed Roman eagle would perch, looking down on centuries of change beneath him.

I settled my household quickly, making contact with dealers and collectors. On my last visit, my purse had been empty from war and while my dowager's allowance was no fortune, I had time on my hands and was always at my best nosing out bargains.

Except when I look back now, Rome was changed even then. The invitations from bankers and cardinals still flowed, but the banquets and entertainments were less flamboyant than I remembered. Death had scythed down some of the richest of the old hosts. We still ate off silver plates, but once collected from the tables they were returned to the kitchen, rather than being tossed into the Tiber as had happened under the hospitality of the mad banker Agostino Chigi (though everyone knew he had nets sunk under the water so they could be dredged out later). Ostentation had gone out of fashion. In art, too. Michelangelo had long left for Florence, Raphael had been dead close on five years, and with his protégé Giulio Romano now disgraced and in exile, there was no anointed successor to take his place.

The most glaring example was the progress of the new St Peter's. Or rather the lack of it. It had been all the talk on my last visit: how Pope Julius had torn down the crumbling old basilica to lay a foundation stone for a church that would be a testament to the magnificence of modern Rome. Yet barely a column or wall had been added since I was last there. Every ruler knows great churches grow at a different pace to men, consuming money faster than a gutter guzzles water in a rain, but the financing of St Peter's had a darker side, for it had been the selling of indulgences to raise the next tranche of money that had lit the fire of rebellion in Germany.

It may seem strange, but in those days we did not speak much of the great heretic, Martin Luther. It was not that we were blind to his attack on the corruption of the Church. Rather, I think now, we were almost too familiar with it. And between us and violent foreign heresy there was always the great barrier of the Alps, so that Rome - the home of the head of Christ's true church on earth, led by the pope - remained, as ever, inviolate.

The new pope, Clement VII, was another Medici. I had known him when he was an adviser to his cousin, Leo, and the two of us met again with great fondness. He offered me gracious hospitality and went so far as to assure me he would look favourably on a cardinal's hat for my second son, Ercole. It would not be long before he was both a laughing stock and a tragic hero. Yet he was not a bad man. He had none of the sclerotic temperament of Julius, nor the appetite for excess of his cousin. Rather, he was a cautious politician who did not take decisions lightly. What in another era might have been a virtue was now a dreadful flaw, for a ruler who cannot make up his mind at a time of crisis ends up alienating both sides. Particularly if he finally chooses the wrong one.

It's easy now to say what he should or should not have done. Yet even I, a more practised political weathervane, failed to gauge the force of the gathering storm until it was too late.

When I was a child in Ferrara and the city suffered from earthquakes, my mother would reassure me by telling me how you could always tell if there was real danger because before the earth cracked open, the dogs of the town would start barking madly, as if their ears had already picked up the splintering under the ground before it reached the surface. The barking of dogs. If we had had sharper ears, would we have detected something going on under the ground to warn us? The answer is yes: the vibration of a thousand soldiers' feet moving slowly towards us. My only excuse is that, like so many others, I had become used to Italy being a battleground for foreign troops and had grown hard of hearing when it came to detecting disaster.

*

Like everything in these wild years of Italian history, the politics are dense enough to be indigestible even for some of us who lived through them. I must hope my scholar has a firm enough footing by now to follow the main arc of the drama.

It starts - as it had so many times before - with who rules Milan.

Such a rogue state it had become since my pretty little sister had been its duchess, fought continually over by the powers of France and Spain. But the final clash that took place in 1526 between two new young kings would seal its fate. Both were swollen with ambition, but only one, Spanish Charles, had the title of Holy Roman Emperor and the bottomless wealth of the

New World behind him. With such odds, one might think a pope with any political acumen would throw in his lot with the greater power. But Clement was a Medici, and his family and the state of Florence had been in bed with the French for decades. It was this loyalty that would be his - and Rome's - undoing.

The battle for Milan saw the French routed, their best generals killed or captured. As the rest of Europe slowly acknowledged the unstoppable rise of Spanish power, Charles's army ran riot, his soldiers plundering everywhere they went, not simply because that is what armies do, but because their pockets were empty for lack of pay. (The richest men, I have come to realise, are often the meanest.)

The sound of dogs barking ...

Finally, in the late winter of 1526, an alliance of sorts was formed to resist him, and after a prolonged period of prevarication, Clement joined it.

Charles's response was swift: he ordered his commander to march the army south, towards Rome. But not before he had enlarged it with cohorts of Europe's most feared mercenaries, German Landsknechts, Lutherans with a violent hatred of the pope.

My intelligence in all this was impressive. The power of family again. The commander and professional soldier, the Duke of Bourbon, was my nephew by marriage, while my own war-mad son Ferrante, now nineteen years old, had risen high enough in the ranks of the Spanish command to have charge of his own cohort, with a dedicated rider to carry dispatches.

The vibration of soldiers' feet grew closer, yet still the pope did nothing. Spring came late that year, I remember, and in every garden and out of every patch of scrubland and ruins, trees and bushes were sprouting and flowering. The air was heavy with the promise of growth. How could anything bad happen here? I hosted dinners and attended others, where we sipped wine and talked of how negotiations would go between the pope and the Duke of Bourbon. For negotiate they must. The idea that a Catholic monarch, certainly not one carrying the title of Holy Roman Emperor, would sanction an attack on the Holy City was inconceivable. It could not, would not, happen.

The army was a few days' march away from the walls when confidence collapsed into panic. People started digging trenches and holes in gardens to bury strongboxes of treasure and Pope Clement - too little too late - ordered a defence force to man the barricades. What they saw as they lifted their heads above the battlements was thousands of men flooding in from all sides: cavalry, infantry, carts and horses pulling cannons, lightweight artillery and huge siege weapons into range under the walls.

No one can be on both sides of a battle at the same time, so before the cannons start firing, I would have my scholar walk through the camp with my soldier son, Ferrante, as a guide. Because what he saw that night told a different story: not so much a great army as a rabble of half-starving men, unpaid for months, whose only hope of survival was to take by force what no one else would give them.

'I swear, Mother, they were so exhausted they would gladly have just lay down and slept for two days if it hadn't been for the speech the Duke of Bourbon delivered. Sweet Jesus, he was a true Caesar or a Sulla that night, riding through the camp, spurring them on. *"I know you're tired. I know you are unrewarded for your efforts, that you long for food in your belly and money in your purse and a safe passage home. But there's only one way forward. The walls might look forbidding, but inside is a city grown soft on corruption, and corruption breeds cowardice. Once the walls are breached we will meet no opposition. Tomorrow with the taking of Rome, you will surge into history and all the sacrifices of these long dark months will be rewarded. You'll sleep on soft straw, drink good wine and feast like Romans and, in time, a share of the wealth will be yours. As your commander you have my word on that. The alternative? To lie down and die in the barren land right here, because there is nowhere else to go but over the walls."*

'You should have heard the way they cheered him, Mother! He could have ordered them over the edge of the world and they would have followed. Because he never asked them to do what he didn't do himself. At dawn, he put on his silver armour with a plume in his helmet so everyone could see him and he was one of the first to scale the ladders placed against the walls.'

Told like that, it is almost a heroic story.

Perhaps if things had gone differently at that moment. If the duke's glinting armour had not been so conspicuous through the cover of an early fog. If he survived that first assault to lead them as they reached the streets, then perhaps they would have behaved differently once the soft inside of Rome was at their mercy.

Perhaps ... If ... Such potent, yet useless words when it comes to the writing of history.

Instead, the duke took an arquebus shot at close quarters into his groin, falling like a giant silver bird to the ground. He was dead within half an hour, and his last words, spat out through his agony - 'To Rome! To Rome!' - moved like a line of ignited gunpowder through the men he had promised to reward as they swarmed over the walls into the city set on revenge, butchering anyone who stood in their way.

And so began the sack of God's Holy City of Rome.

God. His name would rise into the air over and over again in the hours that followed. God in heaven, sweet God, dear God, please God, have mercy God! Who else could the Romans call upon to save themselves? But on that day, God was not listening. The pope himself barely survived, fleeing through the overhead corridor that connected the papal palace with the fortress of St Angelo, while cohorts of German heretics rampaged through the city's palaces, churches and convents. They trampled Raphael's great Vatican tapestries into the mud, smashed statues of the Virgin and saints, destroyed holy relics, raping nuns on the altars of their chapels, while out on the streets, the Spanish occupied every house that looked rich enough, murdering its inhabitants or torturing them to reveal the hiding places of their wealth.

My scholar knows me not to be a woman of faint heart. In my time I have signed warrants for men to be executed, and yes, submitted some to torture. I still remember the thief whose left hand I spared from amputation all those years ago when I was new to government and wonder how he fared afterwards. I have buried dead children, watched my husband rot in front of my eyes and suffered attacks of gout where it felt as if a hungry wolf was feasting on my hands and feet. We all of us lived with pain. And death. But not as it happened in Rome then.

What other atrocities does she need to hear? How they cut the throats of wives and children in front of men's eyes to make them give up their wealth. Sliced off their fingers, branded them with hot irons, until some of them threw themselves out of windows rather than suffer more. It all happened. And I am ashamed to say that if the heretics were barbarous in their plunder of Church property, then the Spanish matched them in everything and more. Greed is a deadly sin in any religion.

Matthäus Merian: Soldiers dressed as the pope parade through Rome, engraving, 1674.

But this is my life and my story. And though I might rage and shed tears for others, I can only speak for myself. I didn't suffer these things, nor see them at first hand. Yes, I watched from the roof of my palace as the soldiers roared through the streets. I heard the swearing and the screams - the weather was warm and they opened windows on the hard work of torture. But I lost no fingers, or teeth, or treasure. Because I was protected. Not by God - no, I think He was nowhere to be found in Rome that day - but by my son, Ferrante. An order had been sent out through the army that no one, on pain of instant death, was to attack or occupy the Colonna palace until he himself arrived there.

Twenty years ago, my stamina and snake muscles had saved his life, as he was pulled, buttocks first, from my womb. Now he would save mine. And a great number of others. Because though I'd been told not to open the doors, how could I refuse, when all those who knew me started flocking to the palace?

I have no great reputation for charity. The first time I met Sister Osanna, I fell on my knees for I knew I would never be as good as her. I felt the same inadequacy in the presence of my own sister-in-law Elisabetta, whose generosity often put me to shame. Yet that day in Rome, I did not hesitate when droves of men, women and children arrived begging for sanctuary, so that when we finally bolted the doors and windows, there was close on a thousand souls crammed inside, praying, moaning, sobbing, with whatever wealth they could carry sewn into their clothes.

The violence ran all that day and into the next, but our palace remained secure, until finally, on the edge of evening, a great banging on the gates took place and I heard Ferrante's voice outside. We lifted up the heavy slats of wood jammed against the doors, enough to make out him and a group of soldiers holding torches. I had not seen him for the best part of two years and I had feared he was dead. I wanted to put my arms around him, but the blood and the stench stopped me - that and the feverish energy coming off him.

'You're safe, Mother?'

'Yes, yes - I -'

'Listen to me. There is something I must say. In a few moments other soldiers will arrive. With another - Spanish - commander. You must allow them entrance. They will not harm you, but ...' He stopped, trying to find the words. '- but I have had to come to an agreement with them about the others in the house. It's their right to take hostages to extract payment, and I can't save everyone. So, ransom money must be raised if they're to be left unmolested. You will need to explain that to them.'

'But I have given them my -'

'There is no but, Mother, this is how it is.'

I did what I was told, but when the Spanish commander arrived, I was repulsed by his arrogance and greed. How dare he?

I put myself forward as the negotiator. If there is one thing I have learned in life, it's how to bargain. He demanded ten thousand ducats. Ten thousand! Divided even between hundreds, it was a crippling amount. I told him it was impossible. That my 'guests' had come with only what they could carry and unless he adjusted his demands he would end the day with a heap of corpses on his hands and still no money.

I countered with another offer. We haggled - haggled, as if we negotiating over the annual harvest of olive oil. But I did not step back. To this day, I cannot tell you how I did it. It wasn't bravery. At no point was I afraid. On the contrary, I was overflowing with rage. Rage against their cruelty, their greed, their avarice, and their betrayal of their own faith. German heretics at least had an excuse of waging war on what they saw as the followers of the Antichrist. But in this house, we all prayed to the same God under the same head of the Church. How dare they?

Finally, when it was decided - I gave a little, but he gave much more - the soldiers went in and took what was needed from everyone. There were painful scenes, anger and tears. Suggestions that I was favoured, even that I was in on the deal, making profit from their ill fortune. But their fear was greater than their outrage and they did as they were told. Not everyone had brought enough to pay their share. To those, I lent the money needed. By the end of the day, every last gold ducat or piece of jewellery and precious stone had been weighed, valued and counted - and from then on, the commander and his troops, along with those of Ferrante, became an army at our door, defending us against the next round of bloodsuckers roaming the streets looking to break in and repeat the extortion. We had survived.

When the worst was passed and another night made the streets a little quieter, Ferrante took me aside.

'I can't stay longer. It will take days to impose order and I'm needed elsewhere. I have provided a signed safe conduct for you to leave,' he said. 'But you are not to tell anyone, *anyone* - do you hear? You must go alone and take only your own servants.'

'And my belongings?'

It will seem callous to some that I should ask the question, but I had parted with large sums of money for a number of precious objects and was in no mood to let them fall into the hands of barbarians.

'Oh, Mother! As long as they can fit on to the carts, you may take them. I will come with men and escort you through the streets to the western gate. There will be soldiers to accompany you as far as Ostia, from where you can go to Civitavecchia and send your belongings by ship to Mantua before carrying on home.'

'And everyone else?'

'Must stay where they are. But they will continue to be protected. You have my word on that.'

'What will happen to Rome now?'

He shook his head. 'I have no idea.' He sounded weary. 'And, Mother - cover yourself well and wear nothing that distinguishes you. I cannot guarantee your safety once outside the city walls.'

A few days later, we left secretly under cover of night, foot soldiers carrying a few torches in front of us to guide our way. When we were through the city gates, Ferrante made his good-byes and this time he let me take him in my arms, though his body remained rigid.

'Don't allow this to poison you,' I said. 'You are a good soldier and you do not need to be like the others.'

He shook his head. 'There is no other kind but this, Mother,' he said softly. 'It's how soldiering is. Tell my new cardinal brother, Ercole, to pray for me. I shall see you all in Mantua when this is over.'

'Don't die,' I shouted after him. 'You hear me. I will forgive you many things but not that.'

'You always expect to be obeyed, Mother,' he said as he turned away. 'I shall do my best.'

The city we left was already an open-air morgue. Decay and heat would bring contagion soon enough and because plague does not differentiate between the innocent and the guilty, huge numbers of Romans as well as soldiers would perish in the weeks ahead. Pope Clement, who had paid a great ransom to the emperor to stay locked in his own fortress, would finally flee, disguised as a beggar, to the city of Bologna, his humiliation complete. Compared to which, the loss of my treasures en route by boat would be small, though I would rail about it anyway.

At her desk, she is sitting, pencil in hand, the book still open in front of her. It all happened so long ago. But man's inhumanity to man casts a deep shadow. I knew it would affect her. I read Guicciardini's account myself when it circulated in manuscript from only a few years afterwards. But no one wanted to be reminded of such abject terror and humiliation, and it wasn't long before the pamphlet fell into obscurity.

I am both pleased and horrified to see that the text is resurrected now.

'Devastating, isn't it? I thought you'd find it useful.'

The voice is that of the spectacled old art scholar, who has now placed himself on a seat at a desk opposite her.

So, it seems that they are acquainted after all. And to the degree that he is suggesting materials pertinent to my life! I should have been paying closer attention. My tussles with Mantegna, the letters of Giulio Romano ... I wonder, could it be that the two of them have discussed my taste in art behind my back?

'I had no idea.' She shakes her head as if to dislodge the images that have taken root there. *'I mean, of course, I knew it happened. But not the depth of barbarity and cruelty.'* And once again I find her voice fittingly melodic. Which is just as well, as I do so hate squeaky-voiced women. She lets out a breath. *'Blood and Beauty. There are times in her life when the two seem almost welded together.'*

'True enough. Still, your Isabella has to have been one of the luckiest women in Rome.'

And I must say, I like his tone even less than I like his presence.

He gives a violent shiver, turning sharply to look around him. I wait till he settles, then send another icy blast.

'You didn't feel that?' He meets her questioning look. *'The cold draught?'*

'Ah!' she says softly. *'That'll be her. Isabella. You probably offended her. It's not hard to do.'* She shakes her head. *'It sounds mad, I know, but sometimes I have this sense ... well, that she is sitting over me as I read her letters.'* She stops herself, then laughs. *'Maybe it's just a hangover from archive fever. You've never felt anything like that, right?'*

And his look tells me that no artist worth his salt has ever bothered to communicate directly with him.

'Sadly, no. Though, when I sat here a few days ago there was a draught at times.'

'Ah, it must be the desk then.'

Behind them, someone looks up disapprovingly. While the archive does not demand silence, there is always someone willing to take offence.

'Should you need a break ...' he says, glancing at the further set of folders, unopened on her desk. *'My offer to show you Giulio Romano's Palazzo Te still stands. It is most impressive.'*

'Thank you.' She smiles and I already know what she is going to say. *'- but, er ... we are still on our way back from Rome and the Te won't be finished for years.'*

As he shambles back to his desk, I consider following him with a few arctic blasts, but think better of it. The truth is, I have never fared well at the hands of art historians. They find me - and 'they' are almost always men - capricious and ill-tempered as a collector, as if being a woman somehow makes me lacking in taste. Instead, they like to pontificate about my studiolo or, more likely, concentrate on those artists who turned me down. I could recruit a small army from those who come solely for my correspondence with Leonardo!

What else has he *shared* with her, I wonder?

Across the room, she is already on to another folder, this one from Federico's personal archive. A pencil is perched on the edge of the desk. I let out a fast wind, pushing it on to the floor and scattering it across the tiles. The noise makes her jump. A few heads look up and she turns quickly behind her, as if she might surprise me there. Oh yes, you feel the force of my wings now. She does nothing for a moment, just stares at the floor, frowning, as if waiting to see what I might do next. Finally, she gets up from her seat, retrieves the pencil, and puts it back precisely in the same place again.

We both watch it for a moment or two.

'*What?*' she says under her breath. '*He is just a retired art scholar who misses teaching, that's all.*'

The pencil remains still. I am not entirely placated, but there is so much still to tell.

She shakes her head and that same small smile with which I have grown familiar lights up her face. She waits a little longer before picking up the pencil and taking a letter from a folder of my son's correspondence. She starts to read.

My dear esteemed mother,
   Ever since I learned that the soldiers had entered Rome ...

XXIX

... and having not received even the smallest communication from you ... I have been in a state of deepest anxiety and grief, fearing that some disaster has happened to you.

I never received the letter that Federico dispatched in panic in the days following the sack. Still, looking back, I think it no bad thing for a son to have had to imagine the horrors that might have befallen his mother, partly thanks to his own less than cordial behaviour.

As it was, my journey back to Mantua was the worst of my life. Everywhere we went, we moved in the footsteps of a marauding army: deserted villages, lines of desperate families on the move, a countryside so devastated that however much we were willing to pay, there were nights when we went hungry too.

Yet when we finally came inside the borders of the state and approached the city, a great crowd flowed out across the bridge to greet us, cheering and led by my handsome second son Ercole, resplendent in new red robes and scarlet hat. Not only had their dowager marchesa escaped the sack of Rome, but she had also delivered them a new Gonzaga cardinal.

The whole court came to pay their respects, hungry for tales of violence and bloodletting. Even *she* - I shall not bother with her name again; there is really only one Isabella in this story – managed a few graceless attempts at concern. I, who had hosted so many poets in my time, now honed my own talent for storytelling. It came at a cost; the more vividly I conjured up devastation, the more nights I woke, clammy with sweat, as blood-soaked Spanish thugs blasphemed and threatened me. Sometimes, I think it was worse in my dreams than it had been in real life.

In a matter of months, the world had changed. Charles V, the twenty-seven-year-old King of Spain and Holy Roman Emperor, was now de facto ruler of swathes of Italy.

Bernard Van Orley: Charles V, King of Spain, Holy Roman Empror.

In Mantua, we would be as obsequious to him as we had once been to the King of France. Such were the rules of diplomacy. But I would never lose my hatred for his cruel, thieving soldiers who had gorged themselves on other men's agony.

I let loose some of my fury on to other opportunistic criminals. The boat that carried my belongings never reached Mantua. The merchant who took my money claimed it had been 'hijacked by pirates'. First, he said it was the Genoese, then changed his mind in favour of the Turks. Another rumour - they swarmed like twilight mosquitoes in those first months after the sack - was that he cold-bloodedly sold my possessions for profit. And how that served me right, because I'd used my secure position to take treasures from the sack for myself.

Isabella d'Este. What were the words her art scholar used to describe me? *'One of the luckiest women alive.'* How slander slimes its way through the centuries! The truth is all there in my letters. Yes, I bought one of Raphael's precious plundered tapestries from that cockroach Spanish commander who we paid to protect us. How else could I get it out of their thieving hands so that I could return it later to the pope? Yet because my palace was not sacked, that made it easy to damn me as a kind of collaborator.

And return it I did, even though I had to pay a further ransom to the 'pirates' to get it back. I swear if I had been any other collector, history would be singing my praises, for it was not easy to part with such an exquisite work of art.

It didn't help my case that Charles now showered further favour on the house of Gonzaga. I was an honoured guest at his coronation as Holy Roman Emperor, sitting close enough to see the tears that rolled down the pope's face as he blessed the arrogant young soldier who had so humiliated and imprisoned him.

Mantua, meanwhile, was in a state of frantic preparation following the announcement that Charles would grace us with a visit for a ceremony over which he himself would preside, bestowing on Federico the title of duke.

A dukedom for Mantua and the Gonzagas! An honour given in perpetuity and an elevation that only the Holy Roman Emperor could sanction! And with it came a further compliment: the offer of a bride for the newly created duke, a woman with connections to the imperial family.

*

The fact that Federico was already betrothed was conveniently ignored. But there was a viper in the basket of fruit. Charles may have been young, but he was totally devoid of sentiment, and like many clever rulers what he gave with one hand he took away with the other. The bride had status, certainly – she was part of the royal family of Naples. His own aunt by marriage, no less. But there was a drawback. A serious one for the future of the house of Gonzaga.

I knew Federico would come to me. Who else could he go on such matters?

'There's no way I can decline the offer, Mother.'

'Of course not. A dukedom for a wife. I am sure she is an admirable woman.'

He let out a noisy sigh. 'But ...' The word hung in the air.

'But you are worried about "issue", yes? You're right, it's a concern.'

Oh, but there is a cruel poetry to this moment. For years my son has rejected a wife because she is too young, and now he must take one who is too old. Thirty-eight, to be exact. Though she'd be even older by the time any bedding took place. Mantua would get no legitimate heir this way.

'I'd dearly like to reassure you. Women have been known to give birth in their forties.'

'They have?' he says, his inflection suggesting a question rather than a statement.

'Not without risk, of course. Your aunt, Lucrezia, Duchess of Ferrara, was thirty-nine when she conceived her last child. Both she and the baby died in childbirth. Also – well, you understand that any such fertility will depend largely on you.'

'What d'you mean?' he bristles. How easily men take offence in such matters. It is almost worth provoking them to see it.

'Only that if you are to secure the lineage with more than one son, you will have to devote considerable attention to your wife for a good many years.'

Of course, I'd made it my business to know how his mistress felt about it. In the time I've been away, though her influence has not waned, it has taken on a certain hectoring quality, more suited to a wife than a whore. Stories of her tantrums have me caught between outrage and delight. Still, I mustn't allow myself to be distracted by revenge. The sooner he is married to a reliably fertile woman, the greater Mantua's chances of surviving whatever history might throw at us next.

'*He is too much the courtier, and not enough the soldier. He needs you.*' The ghost of Francesco stands firm at my shoulder.

'If I may suggest?' I lean over and pat his hand. 'This is not the time to question the "generosity" of the emperor. Graciously accept and when the title of duke is yours – for once given, it can't be taken away – some other ... possibility will, I am sure, throw itself our way.'

He stares at me, his frown knitting his eyebrows together so they hang like a cliff over his eyes. There are times when he reminds me so much of his father that I have to stop myself from laughing.

'I ... I would not want to cross the emperor.'

'You will not need to. Welcome him in all sincerity and leave the matter with me. Be assured, I have only Mantua's best interests at heart.'

'Thank you, Mother.' How much he wants to believe me. 'It is a relief to have you back.'

'And to be back. Now, let's discuss preparations for this visit. These magnificent decorations that your "great" court artist is supposed to be conjuring up. They will be ready in time, yes?'

XXX

Raphael: Raphael and Giulio Romano, 1519-20.

History - and the long march of art scholars - will cast Giulio Romano and myself as artistic enemies. At one level it is understandable enough. I've never hidden the fact that my celebration of the human body was more about beauty than carnal activity. As artists fell ever more in love with the joys of painted flesh, I found myself increasingly out of fashion in this regard. Yet I could still appreciate brilliance when I saw it. And despite the outrages of his youth, Giulio had it.

Indeed, I think of him as a kind of love child of a moment of change. (I may not have had the greatest collection of my time, but I was as fervent about art as any jumped-up scholar now.) He was barely thirteen when Raphael took him to work on the pope's apartments. Yet even as he drank in his master's grace and fluidity, he was also exposed to the thunder of Michelangelo's battle of body and soul.

Every great artist was entranced by the past then. In Rome, they crawled through tunnels to half-excavated palaces to see paintings on the walls, witnessed the unearthing of great heroic sculptures, naked muscle and sinew pulsing through marble and stone. Through all of this, a new kind of human body was born. Most powerfully on the ceiling of the Sistine. Michelangelo kept his work jealously guarded, but the gossip - and in this case I know it to be true - was that towards the end, Raphael himself broke in to see what his arch rival was doing. And with him, he took his young apprentice.

Giulio then, like soft clay, bore the marks of both great painters. In a perfect world he would have had his own master for longer, for his talent was still raw when Raphael died. But with no one else to take over, he was given his head, working on half-finished commissions with such flair that they brought ever more in their wake. Which in turn encouraged his outrageous behaviour, so that by the time he arrived in Mantua, his fame was soaring like a comet.

No, he would never have been my first choice as a court artist. But there was no faulting the speed of his execution. Or the power of his brush. And anyone who studies me should know that I knew that.

Out of all the artists I ever met, Raphael alone had a physical beauty to match his talent. Mantegna looked like crumbling stone, Leonardo was a dandified streak of frayed rope, and Titian had a face like a hunting hawk. Giulio, though, had presence. He was tall with an abundance of black curls, and those black eyes, which I remembered from the boy in Rome, had arresting pin-pricks of light at their centre, almost as if he had painted himself in a portrait and then come to life. As to his personality? Well, after a lifetime of Mantegna's bad temper, I admit his youthful charm came as a relief.

From the minute he walked in, he emanated a confidence, almost an ebullience, that was impossible to ignore. And there was no mistaking his passion for art. We'd barely exchanged greetings before he begged me - *begged* me - to show him my collection, a request I've never been able to refuse, though over the years I've grown used to a certain slippage of concentration in even the most unctuous of guests. Not Giulio Romano. He was interested in everything. He stood for an age in front of each of Mantegna's paintings in my studiolo, went through every drawer of my medallions and Roman coins. But he was most taken of all by my statues. Michelangelo's Cupid, of course. And the bronze miniature copies of the Roman works that I had commissioned over the years because I could never afford the originals. He held each one of them in his hands, studying it from every angle, drinking in the warm perfection of the cold metal.

Piero Jacopo Bonacolsi: Boy with splinter.

'This was your idea, yes, I think? To have Jacopo Bonacolsi copy them in miniature?'

'Of course. Why not? There's no better craftsman in the whole of Italy when it comes to sculpting bronze.'

Or allowing a collector to enjoy the perfection of ancients at a fragment of the price, I think, but do not add. 'Though I also have a few originals.'

'Ah yes,' he said as he turned his attention to Homer with his chipped nose, and then the bust of Faustina. 'Oh, oh, but she is splendid. I'd forgotten you had her.' And his eyes shone with appreciation. 'Is it true that she once belonged to Mantegna?'

I nodded.

'How much did she cost you?'

And I was so taken aback by the directness of the question that I told him the truth.

'You got her cheap! She'd command at least four times that now.'

'You follow the market then?' I said, for I had no wish to enter into further debate about my haggling.

He gave an immodest shrug. 'I have gathered a small collection of antiquities, yes. Of course, they are nothing compared to your ...' He waved an extravagant hand. '... your cornucopia.'

A collector? Either I had forgotten or had never known. 'So what would you consider your most prized work?'

'Ah, that's easy. I have a Roman Venus. She is leaning against a tree trunk.' He lifted himself up to mimic her graceful, coy stance. 'She both knows and does not know we are looking at her. But the wonder is that the marble drapery is so fine that every contour of her body shines through it.' I had a sudden image of him in the company of laughing men, an audience that would surely include both my son and my husband. 'She's been my model of womanhood ever since I bought her. You might have seen her in my decorations of Cardinal Dovizi's apartments.'

Dovizi. Of course. Another rich cleric whose love of antiquities barely veiled his fondness for more living flesh. 'If I did, I have no memory of her,' I said coolly.

'You disapprove?'

Again, his directness takes me by surprise.

'I ... I haven't given it much thought. Though I admit I am growing a little tired of Venus, with or without clothes.'

'You prefer your goddesses armed?' He grinned, his eyes flicking to Mantegna's painting of Minerva, swooping in full regalia to chase out demons from the Garden of Virtue. Even on the greyest of days, the blazing rays of sunrise that surround her bring a glow to the room. With or without my 'bullying', Mantegna would surely have given her the same luminosity. An armed goddess bathed in the light of virtue. I think of Isabella Boschetti with her dark cunning smile and fleshy charms and how she has hooked her way into my son's soul.

'I wonder, was he as difficult as everyone says?'

'Who? Maestro Mantegna? Oh, no. Not for me,' I said primly, to counteract what was beginning to feel like premature informality in our conversation. Though I admit I was enjoying myself. 'Though he stretched one's patience when it came to delivering on time. Something I gather you excel at.'

He shrugged. 'I was trained by a master who had too many commissions.'

'I know. I met you with him once. You seemed more interested in making trouble than art.'

'We've met before?' And for a second his confidence is shaken. It's clear he has no memory of it. Which, if he is to profit from his charm, he should at least pretend he does. 'When?'

'Oh, you were still a boy, new to Rome. Still, he had enough faith in you to let you work on the *School of Athens* in the Apostolic palace.'

'The *School of Athens*?' He nodded and looked away. Words that used to be laden with glory now reek of death and destruction.

We had arrived at the sack of Rome and his easy manner deserted him, which was as it should be, for there are those who think that the public scandal of his erotica further fuelled the fury of the German heretics.

'I wonder, Your Ladyship? If I might ask you about what took place there. In the Vatican I mean, during the catastrophe.'

'I know no more than you,' I said flatly. I had had my fill of providing others with vicarious excitement. 'The story is that the army used the pope's chambers to stable their horses. There and inside the Sistine.'

I watched him wince. 'And Raphael's tapestries? I heard they were trodden into the mud and that you managed to buy one from the hands of the Spaniard who'd plundered it.'

'Not everything one hears is true.' Though I swear there is no mischief in his tone. 'But, yes, the tapestry was saved.'

'The act of a great collector, thank the Lord. And thank the Lord also that Your Ladyship was safe.'

'As safe as one can be when heretics roam the streets in murdered cardinals' robes drinking from golden chalices filled with communion wine.'

He was silent for a moment. 'I wanted to ask something else. About an artist you might have met there, named Marcantonio Raimondi.'

'You mean the engraver who was imprisoned for your - your scandalous drawings.'

He frowned. 'He wasn't held for long. Many championed the pope on his behalf.'

'I know. I dined once with a cardinal who spoke for him,' I said. 'I am afraid I know nothing of what happened to him in the sack. Why?'

'I've heard it went badly for him. They broke into his house, destroyed his workshop and took everything. There's been no news of him since.' He shook his head. 'The man was the greatest engraver and printmaker in the whole of Italy,' he said angrily.

I think of the prophetic image of Raphael's engraving of *The Massacre of the Innocents* set against the backdrop of Rome. Yes, Raimondi was a most superior craftsman. 'Then when he is found, I am sure my son would offer him a home too. Or failing that, Venice. I hear a great many artists have already gone there.'

He nodded and for a moment neither of us spoke. 'It is all over for Rome now,' he added quietly.

'Yes,' I replied. 'I think you are right. It is all over.' And as I said it, I remember thinking that I did not want to discuss these things again, for it could only bring more pain. If my dreams were calmer, there were still images lurking behind my closed eyelids. Yet I couldn't let it rest there. 'Which makes it even more clever of you to have left when you did.'

'I didn't flee,' he said fiercely, hearing the word though I did not use it. 'I had done myself damage, yes. But I did not run away. On the contrary, I made the decision to come to Mantua because of what this city offers any painter and architect. Because of what has already been achieved here. Not least, what you, as its marchesa, have done through your patronage and exquisite collecting.'

Oh, do not try and charm me, I thought. *I was buying great art when you were spitting out milk from a wet nurse's breast, if, that is, your family had enough money to employ one.*

'You think I flatter? Believe me, Your Ladyship, I have more respect for you than to dare to try. Your reputation goes before you. "The marchesa is a bloodhound when she gets the scent of beauty in her nostrils."'

'Ha! And which mouth might that "compliment" have come from?'

'Any painter you commissioned or dealer you bought from. Raphael once said that if you had been a cardinal, the *School of Athens* would have been on your walls first.'

I fear my laugh now gave me away. Compliments are always most successful when they contain a grain of truth. And it was a long time since I had shown my collection to a man who appreciated it so much.

'You have my solemn word', he said, and those black eyes shone brightly, 'that I will dedicate the rest of my life to making Mantua the glory of Italy. For you and for the generations of the Gonzaga family to come.'

'I'll bear that in mind if I need your services. For now, all that is required is some theatre to dazzle the emperor.'

And the smile that lit up his face reminded me of that dark-eyed imp dancing around Raphael's feet so long ago.

*

I only wish my father had been alive to see it, for he, more than many, had a passion for the artifice of stage sets.

On the morning of the feast of the Assumption, Charles's route from the city gates to the palace took him under dozens of specially constructed triumphal arches, wood painted to look like stone, festooned with garlands, and each one hiding a figure of a god and or a goddess, who 'came alive' as he passed, reciting Virgil's verses of praise for Caesar and offering him laurel crowns to place on his (already) crowned head. The city, fortified by the promise of protection that came with imperial favour, cheered his every step. By the time he dismounted at what could now be called the *ducal* palace, he had had an extended lesson in classical hyperbole and I think it might have been a relief for him to stop smiling, for even abject adoration can be wearing if it goes on too long.

So much flamboyance. So much wealth. As a woman renowned for demanding value for money, all I can say is that we got a dukedom out of it, even if my son still had no heir to secure it.

Two further events I must pick out for her now.

The first, a short ceremony of betrothal between Federico and Giulia d'Aragona, the bride herself represented by a portrait, which, if it was to be believed (which my scholar already knows they never should be), showed a woman still in the first flush of youth, the only concession to reality being that her eyes were too close together.

The second, an accident that would change the course of Gonzaga history. During a hunt in the forest of Montferrat, the eighteen-year-old marquis of the Paleologa family took a series of ill-advised jumps that sent his horse and him crashing to earth, the one on top of the other. They shot the beast then and there. The marquis survived long enough to be given last rites. A tragedy for the state of Montferrat. But a triumph for Mantua, since the title would now pass to his sister Maria Paleologa, betrothed as a child to my son.

Giulia d'Aragona might have a powerful uncle, but that was nothing compared to the heiress of Montferrat, whose status and lands it would take an army to win any other way.

Federico's courtesan was about to get angrier still.

XXXI

Titian: Federico II Gonzaga, Duke of Mantua.

'I agree, it calls for decisive action. But the obstacles are not as great as they first appear.'

I pride myself on being a woman capable of disguising her feelings when the political moment demands, so there is no hint of gloating in my response when an agitated Federico arrives in my quarters, determined to swap a new bride for an old one, but with no idea how to do it. I let him talk for a while before joining in.

'First, your betrothal contract with Montferrat is long standing, and has never been formally terminated. The emperor knew that, but chose to overlook it. As did we. Then there is the issue of the family ties. Traced back through my lineage, you and

Giulia d'Aragona are in fact second cousins, a union that demands special permission from the Church before it can go ahead.'

'That won't do.' He growls. 'If we were going to object on those grounds, we should have done so earlier!'

'Which, of course, we couldn't, because you had yet to be elevated to the position of duke. However, it is something that remains a worry for us all. How could it not? The way to resolve it is to convene a conference of Church lawyers, here in Mantua, to "help you" with the matter. You don't have to do anything. Leave the ruling to them.'

'And the emperor? When they do rule in my favour, he'll take offence.'

'A risk we must take.' I've never been fond of chess. The game always called for more patience than I could muster. But I have cultivated an ability to read most political opponents' moves before they make them. 'Charles will soon find himself with more pressing matters than being a marriage broker for an ageing aunt. He has the leftovers of a Holy Empire to oversee, parts of which are turning heretic very fast indeed.'

I am not telling him anything he could not have arrived at himself. Not for the first time, I would like my eldest son to show more speed.

'And Montferrat? Maria and her dowager mother?'

'Certainly, there is work to be done there. A betrothal that lasts fourteen years without ever visiting or summoning the bride results in resentment and complaint.'

His face takes on an angry pout. The world is full of men who do not like to be reminded they are in the wrong, but this petulance is particularly unattractive. Among the many reasons I dislike Boschetti so much is the way she has diminished any dignity in him.

'Throughout this whole time, I have kept in touch with both Maria and her mother and our connection will count for something as you renew your courtship. Remember, you have a formidable new weapon at your disposal. Maria was betrothed to a marquis-in-waiting. Now she will be marrying a duke.' I allow a smile into my voice. 'And, I must say, a singularly eligible one at that.'

He twists his mouth a little to show he is coming round.

'What I would suggest ...' I pause, but not for long. 'Is that you dispatch a copy of the recent portrait Tiziano Vecellio made of you. He is the best portraitist alive and he caught you so brilliantly: your intelligence, your style, your power. Such a gift would double as a fine love token and a reminder of your ...' I wandered around in my mind, looking for the right word. '... potency.'

'Ha! You are right, Mother. It's a fine portrait and would make an excellent "calling card".'

Oh, my dear husband! I swear there are times when it seems as if you hadn't died at all. 'Good. I guarantee it won't take long for them to embrace the marriage again. Ah, but there is one other matter. Where your new bride will live.'

'She will have your quarters in the castle, no?' Clearly, he has given it no thought.

'Suitable for a marchesa perhaps, but not, I think, a *duchess*. No. I would say this new status demands that you and your wife share - a new palazzo. Perhaps something from Mantua's own court artist -'

And now, just for a second, I have the joy of seeing him thoroughly alarmed.

'Oh, I am not suggesting the Palazzo Te! No, no, that ... glorified edifice is for your own amusement.' How reasonable I sound - all my old resentment towards another woman washed away. 'No, I was thinking that we might do something here.' I wave an arm around me. 'A whole new wing, perhaps. A suite of rooms with a hanging balcony and garden, even a new courtyard inside the "ducal palace" itself, for that is how it will be known from now on.'

How could the idea not appeal to him? He pulls at his beard, which is not as full as his father's, though Titian had done wonders with his brush. 'Giulio has yet to finish the decoration of the Te.'

'True. But your beloved horse portraits are done and Madonna Boschetti must be *entranced* with the lushness of your domestic quarters.' (A whole salon devoted to the explicit sexual adventures of Cupid and Psyche. The emperor had spent a good deal of time there on his 'guided' tour.) 'As you've said yourself more than once, no one works faster, and I would be only too happy to add part of my dowager's income to the project.'

'Yes,' he murmurs, confused now to hear me so positive in my feelings towards his trollop. 'Yes. He and I have already discussed similar plans for the future. I'll speak to him about it.'

'When you do, make sure to tell him the commission comes also from me. *For the glory of the Gonzaga family for generations to come.* I wager that will mean something to him.'

*

Everything about the next few years of my life would be most satisfying. And I would like for her to celebrate them with me, for it is the last time I will feel that way.

The ducal palace now came alive with the music of a hundred stonemasons, carpenters and labourers, while I danced the daily tightrope of diplomacy. A state and Church conference was convened in Mantua and, after much deliberation (such things always take an age, for there are so many 'experts' who need to show they know what they are doing, even when the outcome is a foregone conclusion), found in favour of Duke Federico's first betrothal. By the time the decision reached the emperor, he was too occupied elsewhere to take serious offence.

In Montferrat, the bait of a dukedom - and the chance to redress the shame of the protracted courtship - won over Maria and, more importantly, her mother.

Things could not have been going better when Lady Fortuna let loose a thunderbolt: news of the bride's death from a sudden and virulent fever. Fourteen years of correspondence, flattery, gifts, diplomatic reassurances and Maria Paleologa picked this particular moment to expire! One might think the marriage had been doomed from the start. I concede to a moment of panic when I found out, but it was replaced with a surge of energy the like of which I had not experienced since the soldiers poured into Rome.

The dowager marchesa of Montferrat, like my own mother sixty years before, had given birth early to two healthy daughters within two years of each other. But unlike Beatrice and myself, only one of them had found a husband. Maria's younger sister, Margarita, suddenly become heiress to her state, was twenty years old and, according to my intelligence, robust in health, no worse looking than her dead sister and exceptionally dutiful.

Federico himself now went into battle. The Duke of Mantua, it seemed, was suddenly on fire for a bride. Daughter and mother were showered with promises and gifts. By day, he played the courteous suitor, by night he gave his attention to an increasingly spitting cat mistress. Of course, she was not the kind of woman to go meekly into defeat. But he was busy, and such tantrums are tiring for a ruler taking charge of his own destiny. The more stories I heard, the more triumphant I felt. When his suit prevailed, he announced that he would leave for Montferrat immediately so the marriage could be celebrated with all speed. It would almost have been worth visiting her to experience her fury. But I had far too much else to do. It was my job to take over the running of the state till he returned.

We joined in a somewhat awkward embrace. I have had some perfumes hastily made up in my distillery for himself and as gifts for his wife-to-be and mother-in-law, but I could tell he was not using his yet. For some years, he has carried her smell on him. Before the worst of the decay set in, I could always tell when Francesco had been skin to skin with another woman. Just as I never mentioned it then, neither would I do so now. Those who like to see me as too outspoken have no idea how disciplined I am.

'I shall keep you abreast of business at every stage of the work and all government matters, just as I did when your dear father was away.'

I was as good as my word.

It was now a race against time to get the new palace apartments finished. As I read my letters over her shoulder, I am back in the chaos and creation of a building site. I visited almost daily, marvelling as carpenters built spiral staircases into empty air, or teams of plasterers turned stone walls into silk-smooth surfaces.

I had long envied the bond between Giulio Romano and my son. They'd been young together in Rome and the friendship of adolescence had transferred itself to the role of artist and patron. Patron and artist. It is a relationship I always loved. What greater pleasure could there be than to be allowed inside the creative mind, to watch an imagination leap and shimmer, be it in the writing of words, the composition of music, or the creation of an image? I, who had so much taste, never had such talent. But with Federico gone, I became Giulio's sounding board.

And the man knew how to work! He was there each day, his fine clothes and mass of black hair coated with perpetual stone dust, his attention everywhere at once, cajoling, ordering, praising, questioning. It was high summer and the heat was relentless. Sweat ran from men's faces and bodies, mixing with the scent of freshly sawn wood and the tang of blacksmith's fire. He had a portable desk, carried by a servant, which could be set up at any moment, so that he would sit with his sharpened charcoal darting over the page, redrawing a section to show how two sides of a cornice might meet, or the way a detail could be changed to turn a problem into a solution. Each time I visited, a chair was set out for me to join him and he would make the time to explain or elucidate.

The first time I walked into the central courtyard of the Palazzo Te, I knew he was an architectural master. But it was how he used his knowledge that marked him out, changing or playing with classical details, so that his façades seemed both old and outrageously new at the same time. I think the same sense of mischief that made him put copulating couples on to paper, or a fresco of a chariot driven across a ceiling by a god with his balls hanging out for all to see (I don't exaggerate - Apollo's genitals are still there for anyone who cares to look up), was behind his bending and breaking of the rules. History will see Michelangelo as the great revolutionary in this regard, but I am here to tell you that in many ways Mantua's court architect was there before him.

With less than three weeks to go before the couple was due home, the hanging terrace garden on the new wing was almost ready for inspection. The staircase between the ground and upper floor was only half complete, and while workmen scrambled up and down ladders like squirrels, I was the size of an old boar and too proud to humiliate myself by stumbling or, worse, falling. So he fashioned a special handrail that I could cling to.

'There is not a lot to see yet, and it will be secure enough for you within a few days.'

'Good,' I muttered ungraciously as I watched two of my ladies make the journey unaided, their faces shining with excitement. How galling to have a mind that could still parry and play and a body that moved like an overloaded hay wagon.

'You're sure it will all be finished in time?'

'No. But somehow it always is. Once the stairs are done, the gardeners will arrive with potted trees and sculptures and a small miracle will take place. You will see.'

'And the interior?'

'I have written to the duke. If we work through the nights, we will get the coats of arms finished in the grand salon and then paintings may be hung. But there is no time for more. The rest of the walls must stay white for now, with tapestries of leather hangings.'

'Oh! I could not agree more!' I said emphatically.

He glanced at me. 'Could it be, Your most illustrious Ladyship,' - his tone one of exaggerated courtesy - '... that you fear my compulsion to cover every space with nudity and copulation?'

'On the contrary, I assumed you had grown out of such childish games.'

He shrugged. 'In my defence, I paint only what the

ancients painted before me. The ruins of Nero's golden palace testify to that.'

'I am sure they do,' I countered. 'Alas, being lowered down on ropes and crawling through tunnels was not an experience open to women like myself.' And now we are both laughing, for we have grown to like each other more than either of us expected. 'Still, whatever it was you saw there, there are limits to how slavishly we Christians should copy our pagan ancestors.'

No, whatever his faults, Mantua had a court artist worthy to take up the mantle of Mantegna.

'If these had been my quarters as a young bride, I would never have chosen others. The sooner you start work on a whole new courtyard for the ducal palace, the better.'

'I am still committed to the decoration of the last rooms in the Te. One of which I think would amuse you. Perhaps I could show you around it when I am further on in its execution. No hint of copulation there.'

'Just as long as you don't lower me down on ropes or expect me to climb too many stairs.'

Ten days later, news arrived that the wedding ceremony had taken place and the marriage had been consummated. As ever with a great victory, I ordered the ringing of every church bell, the distribution of wine and food and a display of fireworks from the castle battlements. From the Palazzo Te, Isabella Boschetti would have had an excellent view.

XXXII

Margarita Paleologa turned out to be a thoroughly sensible girl. She was well educated without being overbearing, regular featured (her teeth left something to be desired), with a soft voice, charming in its way. She also had the most cheerful disposition, which led me to suspect that the work of the bedroom did not prove too arduous for her. She and her ladies *adored* their new apartments and settled fast. Margarita welcomed Federico with open arms when he was there, and accepted his absences when he was gone. Which made him much more likely to return.

In short, she was bred for duty.

Children dropped out of her: one or two dead within the first few years, but eventually a healthy-lunged Francesco, heir apparent to the dukedom of Mantua. As the court celebrated, the Boschetti cat arched her back and stretched her claws and for a while Federico responded when she yowled. (I had invested in a few younger ladies-in-waiting and they brought me back the most delicious gossip.) Yet however much noise she made, she couldn't fight history. The Duke of Mantua was no longer a callow youth. He had a family and a military and artistic legacy to consider, with a much-expanded budget for the latter thanks to his wife's generous dowry. I had won. I was on one of my last visits to Venice when the news came that *she* was no longer a permanent guest in their love-nest palazzo, but instead had been given a more modest dwelling, further out of town.

My work was done. I deserved some artistic reward.

A visit to the Palazzo Te now became most attractive.

*

It is an accident of history that while so many of the great Este and Gonzaga residences have been turned to rubble or ash, Palazzo Te has survived more or less intact. And to judge from the number of scholars who request Giulio's correspondence from the archive, its reputation has proved equally durable.

Its setting, however, as my colourful acolyte will see soon enough, has lost most of its beauty. The island of Te was once an idyllic spot, reached by a small bridge spanning a dyke of the river outside the city walls. Such memories I have of hunting there with Francesco in the first years of our marriage. Riding through town in the early mornings, out through the southern city gate, there was often a mist coming off the lake so that the stable block he had built there seemed to rise out of a bed of cloud. Alas, later images I've seen in the archive show no trace of city walls or even water any more: the canal has been drained and replaced by a wide road with blocks of heavy grey buildings spewing up and out on either side. An ugly, crowded landscape, entirely bereft of atmosphere.

Best, then, for me to try and recreate it for her as it was in that spring of 1532, when I took up Giulio Romano's invitation to see him at work.

I went by carriage - my days on horseback were long over - and as we left the city the mist had already burned off, so the view to the island was clear. And what a view it was: what had once been a modest stud farm for horses was now a palace, built on the same single-storey scale, but made up of four elegant wings, so that when you entered its inner courtyard there was this wondrous sense of space everywhere, with a vista through an open loggia on to fish ponds and gardens beyond. Should I bore her further with Giulio's architectural cunning? When she comes with her owl expert, he will no doubt point out its mischief and originality. The way the stone exterior is really stucco over bricks and mortar. How each façade plays games with different rhythms of classical columns, keystones and rustication, so despite the weight, your eye reads lightness and movement. Even I, who was disposed to find it too arch in its cleverness, cannot help but be charmed.

Giulio's favoured apprentice meets me at the entrance, with copious apologies for his master's absence.

'... *called away, but will return as soon as he can!*'

He guides me through the more offending rooms, with their sexually explicit frescoes, with tasteful speed, speaking all the time about the challenge his master had given himself with this final project, a chamber tucked away at the end of the east wing.

What are my expectations as I enter?

The bar is high. I have been bred on artistic illusions of reality. As a child, I relived the seasons of the year in the Palazzo Schifanoia. In the duke's studiolo in Urbino, craftsmen manipulated a thousand slivers of different coloured woods into images so real you felt you could pick up the lute from a shelf, or close the door of a half-open cupboard. From the epic story of creation on the Sistine ceiling to Mantegna's trompe l'oeil ceiling, I was accustomed to being transported into different worlds.

Yet the room I walk into that day affects me in a singularly unfamiliar way.

To begin with, it doesn't feel like a room at all. It's impossible to judge its size, for the walls and ceiling, entirely covered in paint, all seem to merge together, with no corners or edges to mark the ground. It's dark: there is a small single window, I later realise, but it has been shuttered and painted over, so the only light comes from candles lapping upwards from the floor. Except this isn't even a proper floor. The ground under my feet is a mass of undulating pebbles, dipping deep in the middle then rising up with bigger stones as it curves to meet the walls. The immediate sensation is of losing one's balance. Then, as my eye grows more accustomed, I

Giulio Romano: the Fall of the Giants, Palazzo Te, Mantua.

am assaulted by magnified devastation. Wherever I look, all around me are tumbling rock faces, punctuated by vast broken columns of stone, collapsing at vertiginous angles. And everywhere, bodies of gigantic, half-naked men crushed and trapped underneath, limbs sticking out from rubble at distorted angles, great gaping mouths in agony as a rain of boulders hit them from above.

Turning, I see a slab of rock slammed into the lintel over the door, an enormous hand pushing down on it, as if at any moment the entrance itself will collapse. Everything is grotesque, exaggerated, disorientating, as if one is in the middle of an earthquake.

'Your most illustrious Ladyship!' The steadying hand on my arm and the voice seem to come out of nowhere. 'I'm sorry I was not there to meet you.' Caught in the jumping shadows of candlelight, Giulio's own dark features seem deformed. 'I thought it would be better for you to experience it on your own, without the artist to prepare you. Welcome to the room of the Giants. What do you think?'

'I have no idea,' I say breathlessly, 'I can't stand properly.'

He laughs. 'The floor tilts by a few degrees, enough to take you off guard. And, as you see, we have built up the walls so they curve to meet each other and the ceiling at an angle. The gods are sending thunderbolts to defeat a gross rebellion against them and it's fitting we experience the panic along with the victims.'

I look past him to a foreshortened arm forcing its way out of the rubble, so close that it might grab me, and somewhere above are the bulging eyes of its trapped owner, matted hair and beard, face frozen in fury.

'In which case, I would say you have succeeded admirably.'

'But it's not all horror. Now, please!' he shouts up into the darkness.

As oil lamps now light up the ceiling, I see a great ring of white storm clouds circling the room, and above, a throng of people - gods and goddesses - gathered, as if over a balustrade, launching rocks, thunder and lightning bolts on to the attackers below.

Giulio Romano: Ceiling of the Fall of the Giants, Palazzo Te, Mantua.

'Behold the power of the gods.'

'Ha!' And as I gaze up, I realise I am smiling. For though it is mad, it is also magnificent. 'I would most certainly prefer to be up there.'

'Ah! I had hoped you would say that. You've come at a most opportune moment, Your Ladyship. I am overseeing some alterations to the perspective of the goddess's horses as she plunges through the cloud line.' And now I see a wooden scaffold reaching up to a corner - except there is no real corner - with a few figures standing on a platform at the top.

'You can perhaps just make out the heads of the beasts pulling her chariot, yes? It's a tricky business, as they are partly sunk into cloud. I thought you might like to see how we do it.'

'Are you mad?' I say fiercely. 'I would need a chariot myself to get up there.'

'Once again, your wish is my command. I have devised the nearest best thing. See!'

He leads me to near the base of the scaffold, where a bulky object is covered in cloth. Revealed beneath is a huge basket, tightly woven with thick saplings, high sides and chains connected to its four corners.

'It is perfectly safe. I have tried it myself more than once. It operates on a winch and pulley system. You can travel as slowly as you like and I will meet you at the top.'

I stare at him and realise that he is completely serious. He intends to hoist me halfway up to the heavens in a basket! The last time I rode to the hunt, it took two men on a platform to get my leg over the horse.

'I would rather die than go up there,' I say, focusing on a giant's leg sticking out from a fallen column, his foot almost in my face.

'I am sorry to hear it. I've spent hours on the designing of it. It is based on the calculations that Brunelleschi used to hoist up himself - as well as a good many heavy slabs of stone - when he was working on Florence's dome. Raphael copied a version of it to show the banker Chigi the wonder of his newly painted rooms. I hope to do the same when the emperor Charles returns to Mantua. Since, as you know, it is an allegory to show how he has defeated all those who seek to rebel against his rule. I think he'll appreciate his view from the heavens looking down, don't you?'

'You intend to take the Holy Roman Emperor up there?'

'If he agrees, yes.'

'And you are sure about Brunelleschi? And Raphael?'

'Your illustrious Ladyship, would I lie to you? How else did Agostino Chigi verify that the features of the lovely Galatea were indeed a faithful copy of the face of his mistress?'

'Hmm.'

'Should I get the men ready?'

My whole life, I have never liked being denied an experience simply because I was a woman. They say Julius II hitched up his robes and risked the scaffolding in the Sistine to see more clearly how God was parting the waters to make the land, and I have no doubt he groaned and grumbled all the way. This may be a more frivolous creation, but it is the nearest I would come to such a connection of patron and artist/architect.

'I shall stand in it. To get a sense of how it feels. And then we will see.'

He has indeed put thought into its design. There is a gate that allows me to step in and then close after me, fastened with a dozen leather straps and buckles to hold it in place.

'You can use the edge as a handrail,' he says, checking that each of the straps is tied securely. 'I like to think of it as a kind of throne for art lovers.'

'Do not joke, Giulio. If the pulley breaks or I fall ...'

'If such a thing should dare to happen, I will run down the ladder and catch you. You know me to be committed to the glory of the Gonzagas. Not their extinction.'

'Ha. Rather, I know you as a master of mischief.'

He shrugs. 'It is better than being a master of gloom.'

The men are now on the ground. The rope pulls against the winch and wheels connect and start to turn. For a moment, nothing happens. The humiliation will be insupportable. I think of my Uncle Borso, padded with a lifetime of good living, of Leo X, his bulk overflowing from the papal chair.

'I think, perhaps –'

But now I am jerking off the ground. I give a squeal. Another jerk. Gradually, the movement smooths. The pace of the rise is mercifully slow. I glance down and see another man has joined them at the winch. This is my punishment for a lifetime's passion for marzipan and honey cakes. Well, it is too late for such regrets now. I have heard it said that Egyptian kings put to death the slaves who worked on their tombs, so that no one would be alive who knew the ways in. Should I cut out the tongues of those below so they will be rendered silent on my weight?

The idea makes me smile. I pass the snarling face of a one-eyed giant. I am so close to the wall now that I can touch the sloping sides, see the brush strokes of what from below had been a bulging rock face, while a small town, the size of Mantua, nestles in far perspective in the landscape. The battle of the giants may have been the mythological beginning of the world, but it is we Italians who have given glorious rebirth to such stories in our own time.

Detail from the room of the Giants.

I am above the devastation now, passing upwards through the clouds that support Mount Olympus. The winching slows down and I take a few deep breaths to look around me: a muscular god lies naked on his side, a pose owned by Michelangelo's copies of ancient river gods. Billowing winged angels with men's faces and women's breasts stand next to young goddesses carrying heavy urns on their heads to add to the barrage of weapons. Higher still there is a small gleaming cupola, so impossibly distant in perspective that the sky seems to go on for ever. For a moment, I am lost in the heavens.

'Magnificent,' I say under my breath, as the basket comes to a halt. I wait till the swaying stops, then turn to greet Giulio on the platform. Except he is not there. The scaffolding is in place, but the platform is empty.

'Giulio?' The room is silent.

'Giulio!' I say louder, my voice echoing in the bright acoustic. Still no answer. I grasp the basket edge grimly and peer over the edge. The door is closed and I can see no sign of anyone below. 'Where are you? Giulio!'

Nothing. A hot stab of panic runs through me. I concentrate my eyes on something to stop the dizziness: Jove wielding a sheaf of lightning like a spear to drive through the clouds on to the rebels below. I feel a gentle wind on my face, not enough to rock the basket, but enough to make the oil lamps flicker.

'Oh, my God. Ha! Oh, look at it!'

The woman's voice comes from below. My knuckles are white with their grip on the basket. I grip the edge even tighter as I move my head to look down again.

The door, which I know was closed, is open now and two figures have walked in. In the scant light I can just make out the shock of curls around her head and the flash of a bright-yellow scarf. She is standing in the middle, turning round and round, her head thrown back, and laughing, that infectious gurgling laugh that comes from spontaneous delight.

'It feels as if both heaven and earth are coming down upon us.'

'*I thought it would amaze you.*' And as he looks up, I catch a glint of thick black spectacles. Of course. The retired art expert.

'*Oh, it's outrageous.*'

'*As he intended it to be.*' They are both staring upwards now. I am directly in their vision and yet they do not see me. Not me, not the basket, not the scaffolding, nothing. I am invisible. '*An early masterpiece of mannerism: realism exploding into wild exaggeration. He painted it –*'

'*I know. As an allegory of how the emperor had vanquished rebel princes who dared to rise against him. Except ...*' She throws up her hands. '*I keep thinking back to Mantegna's* Triumphs of Caesar. *You couldn't get more grandiose than those, and they were meant to show off the military prowess of the Gonzaga? Yet this is done to cosy up to Spain. In the what –? forty years that separates the two, her own adult lifetime, Mantua has suffered a major loss of status and independence.*'

'Is that so?' I mutter crossly. 'Even though the Gonzaga family now holds the title of Duke in perpetuity. I would say, given the state of Italy, ours was a triumphant outcome.'

But, of course, they don't hear me.

'*And you think she knew that?*'

'*There's nothing in her letters to say so, but then there wouldn't be. And you could argue Mantua did better than many states. Urbino, Bologna, Milan, Florence even ... they all went under at one point or another. If she'd been less adept politically, it could have gone much worse.*'

'Exactly!' I say loudly. 'The whole of Italy shook during those years. You were at the sack of Rome with me, you know that.'

'*It's always the drawback of letters. Having to fill in the gaps. But yes, I think she knew. She's too smart not to.*'

'*What do you think she would have made of this then?*' He waves his arm around the room.

'Yes,' I join in. 'You, who claim to know me so well. What do I make of it?'

She blows out a noisy breath. *'Oh, that's difficult.'* She turns herself around again, taking it all in afresh. *'Part of me thinks she would have resisted it, as the grotesque was never her thing. But I think his sheer imagination would have blown her away. She so yearned to be patron to a great artist. Mantegna would have none of it and she was too young anyway. Others resisted her. But she and Giulio worked together on bits of the ducal palace. In a strange way, I think they got on.'*

Not bad, I think. If you'd been younger and prettier, I could well have had you as a lady-in-waiting. In the silence, it strikes me that her 'expert' art scholar may be equally impressed. *'What else do you think about her?'*

'Ah! how long have you got?' She gives her attention back to the walls. *'Clever, greedy, competitive, imperious, bloody-minded, cunning. She can behave so badly when she wants something, then lie barefacedly about it. Yet she is also, well, glorious. A force in the world in a way that few women were then. History throws so much at her and yet she never falters. Or if she does, she picks herself up immediately. She refuses to be anybody's victim. And I love her for that.'*

Compliments. Barbed or otherwise, I could never resist them. If I had a basket of rose petals, I would tip them out now so they floated down around her. But for once in my life, I can do nothing.

'Though right at this moment, I must say I'm starting to feel like one of these giants: a never-ending avalanche of boulders of facts and dates raining down on me.'

'Oh, Sweet Mary. This is not the time to lose your nerve,' I shout down to her. 'I've told you everything you need to know.'

She turns for a final time, drinking in the madness of Romano's imagination. '*I wonder,*' she says slowly, and now I swear she is staring right at me. '*- you don't think Giulio Romano might have put her up there somewhere, do you?*'

'*If he did, no art historian has identified her. The most reliable portraits in this palace are Federico's horses with their names attached. Come, I'll show you.*'

Her laugh is the last thing I hear, then the space below goes dark. I close my eyes, and all that I feel for a moment is the thud of my heartbeat in my ears.

'Your Ladyship?'

When I open my eyes, Giulio is standing by the railing of the platform, one hand out, steadying the basket.

'Are you all right?' His voice is anxious.

'Where have you been?' I say angrily.

'Nowhere. Here, ready for you. It was a smooth journey, yes? Perhaps you looked down too much. I should have told you not to.'

'Yes, yes. I did look down. What do you see there?'

'Just my men at the pulley. Why?'

'Nothing.'

'Would you like them to winch you down?'

I stare at him. A good-looking man still, though work is ageing him fast. He has kept his promise to the house of Gonzaga. Mantua will stand tall because of him, whatever the future. And I have played my part in that. 'No, no. I have come all this way. I shall at least look at something. But make it brief. What is this problem you are having with the horses?'

He grins. 'Just a small correction to the size of their flanks. I wanted you to see who was driving them. In mythological terms it is Diana, of course, the huntress who commands the chariots of the moon. See how fearless she is with the horses. Gonzaga Barbary steeds all of them, of course. I hear you were a famed horsewoman when you were young.'

I study her. Caught in dramatic motion as she drives the horse through the clouds, she is a most sturdy figure, handsome, plump shoulders and thick thighs, with a mane of rippling chestnut hair down her back. (False, some of it, surely?) I had all those attributes once.

'Is this meant to be a portrait of me?' I say.

He grins.

I would not put it past him to be making it up in order to flatter me. In fact, I am sure he is lying. Still, I find myself a little pleased. 'At least I am wearing clothes. Or enough of them. Still, it's fitting that the house of Mantua is represented somewhere on Mount Olympus. Our Holy Roman Emperor is not the only one to triumph over vicissitudes. Speaking of which, I would like to go down now.'

He whistles to the men below, and inch by painful inch I descend from the heavens towards the ground.

XXXIII

I am sixty-four years old.

When I was young, it seemed impossible that anyone could reach such an age, except perhaps my grandfather in Naples whose breath stank of the grave. My size no longer surprises me, which is just as well, since there is nothing I can do about it. I don't miss dancing: though I loved it, it was never my forte. I can no longer play music with the same ease - the body of the lute sits too high over the mountain of my stomach so that I have to elevate my elbows at an impossible angle to reach the strings, and that, yes, is a sorrow to me. I still pay attention to my appearance and my wardrobe garners compliments, yet I no longer make fashion. I favour candle glow over the harsh light of the day and when the satirists sharpen their blades on me - which they do, calling me *the monstrous marchesa* and accusing me of being mutton dressed as lamb - I turn to the great poet, Ludovico Ariosto, whose master-piece, *Orlando Furioso*, showers me with such praise - *Graceful, beautiful, wise, discreet, open-minded and magnanimous* - that I am almost embarrassed to quote it here. I offer it in case she hasn't come across it yet. The insults, I am sure, she can find for herself.

Ariosto's words would be a fitting epitaph. Except I've no intention of dying on the page. No, I shall leave that to her, as it is only a few years till the final mark on my timeline.

I've been looking forward to seeing her again after our communion in the room of the Giants. My last letters - they are many fewer, but there is still juice to be squeezed from them - are waiting for her on the trolley. Yet she has been absent now for two days.

My grandchildren, who continue to drop like ripe fruit from Margarita's womb, bring me unexpected joy with their fat ruddy cheeks and strutting mischief. I think I like them more than I did my own children, for I am always willing to be delighted by their antics with no need to mould and judge, and as a result they seem happy to see me. I take pleasure in my governing of Solarolo, a town to which I recently bought the rights and where I spend a few months each year, overseeing the courts and dealing with petitions in the way I did when my husband was away. I believe I am liked as much as it is possible to like any ruler, since justice must always favour one side over another.

There have been dramatic moments. Like the time when my astrologer, having spent weeks poring over his charts, announced that God would be taking me into His arms on a particular day in November. He said it with such conviction that I revisited my will and made my farewells to my family, before eating a hearty last meal and going to bed early. Only to wake quite refreshed the next morning. For weeks afterwards, the man was too mortified to come into my presence. It was never an easy job, divining the precise movement of the stars, and I have had to forgive him before.

Of course, there is physical suffering. For every day I feel well, I endure another when the steels jaws from my childhood are at work in my stomach. I have long had gastric upsets - protests at the excess of rich food, no doubt - but they are constant visitors now. Gout takes further advantage of my girth to torture me, making it increasingly hard to travel. I accept I will never see Rome or Florence or Venice again and I have made my last visit to Ferrara, for the funeral of my beloved brother Alfonso.

Then there is the other kind of ache, one that eats away at the mind. I know now that Federico is suffering from the same disease that killed his father, a realisation that brings further fear as to what will happen if he dies before his own son is of fit age to succeed him. May hell swallow up 'that woman' who kept him from his duty for so long. Though I think she has a taste of it on earth now, for she is a nobody these days.

These are the things I can do nothing about. Instead, I concentrate on what I can achieve. I pray every day as ever, but with, I think, a little more sense of purpose than I once did. And should I feel in need of spiritual support I visit Ippolita in her beloved convent of San Vincenzo, where she has lived for over twenty years now with her younger sister, Paola, and they both seem content with their lot. As for my collection, I have made the decision to leave it to my daughter-in-law. Not so much for her appreciation of art as for her innate sense of family responsibility, as I know she will act as its faithful custodian and keep it intact. I acquire less these days: a dinner set of majolica plates and bowls new from a master craftsman in Urbino who is making a name for himself, and a few antiquities. From Rome, my splendid cardinal son, Ercole, sends a newly unearthed silver medal with the head of Aristotle (or so they say), along with the sweetest letter you can imagine. Such taste he has inherited from me.

And I have indulged in a final commission: a portrait of myself.

*

I've been reasonably honest about both my virtues and my faults. But they are all portraits painted with words. Ours was an age of art, yet the truth is that there is no image of me anywhere in existence that captures me as I really was. Which, as she must have realised by now, is exactly what I intended.

That fat-faced child that went as a betrothal gift to Francesco 'disappeared' early. Mantegna's effort, as we both know, was a disaster, and thus long gone. A crime against art history, or a patron's right?

The portrait Raphael's father did to compensate was not much better and that too has been lost. I later commissioned Francesco Francia, that second-rate artist who turned Federico into a ten-year-old angel, as I knew he would dip his brush in the same sentiment for me. I was never happy with my eyes, but other than that he made me exceedingly pretty. Sadly, it does not seem to have survived, or certainly not with my name attached, which is not surprising since it looked nothing like me.

There are Leonardo's sketches, of course, done to pay for his supper when we offered him succour on his flight from Milan. One or two, I think, still exist but they were all much of a much-ness. To be honest, I only valued them as a collector because his star was rising so fast and would only soar higher with his death. It seems he is now revered as something close to a god, making any half-finished, decaying work that might be attributed to him the excuse for a feeding frenzy of buyers. But if you didn't know his name, I doubt you would spend any time on his sketches of me. Certainly, he spent no time on them himself. They were rushed little things, the lines of my hair and dress smudged where he was pricking out the outline for what might have been a future portrait. More importantly, they lacked his hallmark when it came to painting women: endowing them with a kind of ethereal beauty over character. Though later, on a visit to Florence, I noticed he'd given my face to a passably graceful angel.

No, for those who asked for a copy of my likeness - and many did - I sent a medallion designed after Francesco's victory at Fornovo. There's not a lot one can do with a miniature profile, and under the elaborate decoration of my hair, my face was barely visible, so that it could be any young woman of around twenty-four or -five.

Gian Cristoforo Romano: Isabella d'Este.

But, again, it is not me.

I doubt she will be shocked by this - if she is, she's not been paying attention. I only did what other women did, with more success. It was how it was then. While we worshipped images of the Virgin and aspired to golden-haired goddesses with smooth foreheads and cupid lips, we were bred out of power and intermarriage, which, over the years, turned many family likenesses into something close to deformity. Lorenzo de' Medici and Charles V both had protruding slabs of granite jaws, and the Gonzaga family specialised in pop eyes, hunch backs and monstrously hairy torsos, like satyrs. In contrast, there was a standard women could not fall beneath. So, painters lifted chins, enlarged eyes, smoothed out pockmarks and did what was demanded of them, their fascination with realism confined to the flamboyant reproduction of fashion and fabrics. Never mind the face, marvel at the drapery. Suffice it to say that I met a great many noblewomen who were ugly in life, yet one does not see their likenesses on any walls. And what is wrong with that? We were offering the future a new kind of art, and beauty and grace were its hallmarks.

Which brings me to Tiziano Vecellio. Soon after he visited Mantua to paint Federico in full armour, he completed a portrait of me, taking advantage of the fashion of the day to hide some of my considerable girth in glorious scarlet plumped-up sleeves that made my shoulders and breasts appear less of a mountain of flesh. I was unimpressed with my likeness, but the wonder of the fabric told me he was the right man.

I was sixty when I commissioned Titian, as he is better known now, for a last portrait of me: something to celebrate the richness and influence of Mantua as personified by its marchesa. How better than by showing me as a leader of fashion? The woman whom everyone sought to emulate. I sent him a copy of the Francia portrait of the pretty young thing and gave him extremely explicit and detailed instructions, none of which involved me sitting for him.

I must say, he took his time. His reputation then was growing faster than his output - how many times did I suffer from that in my lifetime? - which left his patrons hungrier than he was. The Emperor Charles had been so impressed by his portrait of Federico that he bombarded him with commissions of his own, which meant lesser mortals like myself fell to the back of the queue.

As the sand in the hour glass of my life ebbed away, there were moments when I wondered if I would expire before it was finished.

*

If she doesn't come for my folders today, I will be taken back, wheeled through the heavy wooden door into the echoing silence of the old church. Until the next request comes.

'I'm starting to feel like one of those giants.' I hear her voice again, rising up towards me. *'Too many boulders of facts raining down on me.'*

Does that mean I won't see her again? I had expected her to at least stay with me for this last adventure in art. I've kept her place free, but I cannot save it for ever. When she does arrive, barely an hour or so before closing, she is dressed - as ever - splendidly, but seems preoccupied. She takes her files to her desk, then approaches the ageing owl.

'Are you all right?'

'I'm fine. That visit gave me a lot to think about. I've, I've decided to go home and start writing. I'm here just to check a final few letters. And say thanks to the archivists. And to you.'

He shrugs. *'It has been a pleasure. It seems the teacher in one never dies. So, how is the marchesa today?'*

'Close to death. Waiting on her last commission.'

'Ah yes. Titian's masterpiece portrait in Vienna.' There is a pause. *'Well, I wish you luck. You're sure you won't miss all of this ...'* he says, waving a hand around the room. *'... this soulless chamber with its rock-hard chairs and criminal opening hours.'*

She laughs. *'You know what I will miss most? The smell of dust from the ink and paper. Breathing in the past.'*

'And Isabella blowing in your ear?'

341

She smiles. *'I have a table fan at home for when it gets too hot in summer. I'll put it on to remind me.'*

*

She settles herself at our desk for the last time. And together we take delivery of the final portrait of me.

Is it really in Vienna now? Of course. The unstoppable rise of the Spanish Hapsburgs. It is just as well that I have become inured to the vicissitudes of the futures I cannot inhabit. In my lifetime, I picked my way through enough Roman ruins to know that no empire, however great, lasts for ever. I've read the correspondence on other desks from agents haggling over the sale of my collection a hundred years after me. I know that the paintings from my studiolo, my instruments, my silver, my busts, my coins, even Mantegna's great triumphs of war - all of it will be crated up and shipped out to cover the bankruptcy of profligate Gonzaga dukes, and that the greed of an invading imperial army would do the rest. *For soldiers*, as my mother once said, *do so enjoy the destruction of art.*

Ghosts, I have discovered, cannot shed tears. Instead, I take comfort in the fact that some of my greatest treasures found a home with a cultivated king of England and the most powerful cardinal in the whole of France. I can do nothing more to ease the pain.

*

Which makes this final portrait of me even more important. Because yes, they are right. Together, Tiziano and I created a masterpiece. I knew that from the moment I set eyes upon it. I made no attempt to hide the deliberate artifice. Indeed, when I wrote to compliment him, I told him as much.

We doubt that even at the age in which we are depicted, we have ever been as beautiful as you make us in this painting.

Ah, the sweet mendacity of letters. Well, she is an expert in that art by now.

Titian: Isabella d'Este, 1534.

The arrival of the portrait in Mantua was cause for great celebration. The day after it was mounted, alongside other memorable works in Giulio's new castle wing, Margarita brought the children to see it (she was fat with another one at the time, I remember), and they stood with me, studying it with mouths

343

half open. Especially little Isabella - close on six years old and already most fond of her own voice and opinion.

'Oh, I like her dress and her hat. Who is she, Nonna?'

I laugh and put my hand on her head.

'She is the spirt of the Mantua,' I say. 'A tribute to the power of family and good government.'

She nods solemnly, then her mother nudges her a little. 'Go on,' she whispers. 'Remember the words you are learning with your tutor. Your nonna would love to hear them.'

She wrinkles up her nose in intense concentration; though she is a natural performer, study, it seems, does not come easy to her. Alas, it is too late for that now.

'Est pulcherrimum domina me—' She stumbles. '... mea umque?' she finishes haltingly.

'"*The most beautiful woman I have ever seen.*" Perfect,' I say. 'What a very clever little girl you are.'

And those are my last words on the life of Isabella d'Este.

It is a quite unfamiliar place I find myself in.

Small, more like a water closet than a room. White walls, with a lamp like a paper balloon hanging from the ceiling. A window, half open, gives out to a view over a valley dotted with strange little stone houses, half hidden by trees. Everything is in full leaf and vibrant green.

What am I doing here?

One of the walls is made up entirely of books, another has a large board covered in miraculously clear small images, thanks to this mechanical revolution in the future that I have gradually become accustomed to. Here are views of both Ferrara and Mantua: their two handsome castles with their moats still intact (both designed by the same architect – did I mention that at the time?). Then there are pictures of the seasons of the year from the Palazzo Schifanoia: peasants in the field, my uncle Borso's plump face and cascading chins. The Palazzo Te: outside and in, the life-size paintings of Federico's favourite horses, the creamy plump skin of naked Psyche stepping out of her bath into her lover's arms, and the open-mouthed screams of giants crushed under boulders. There is even an image of the ruined ceiling from my first studiolo in the castle, while Mantegna's great painted chamber is everywhere: the trompe l'oeil ceiling, the Gonzaga horses and hounds, the court, Barbara, her husband, her sad hunchback daughter and her favourite dwarf, and underneath, a less distinct image that stabs me to the heart: the tiny room in which Osanna Andreasi lived, prayed and died, its wooden panelling - we had it painted after her death - faded but intact. I wonder, does any trace of the aroma of sanctity remain?

It seems my whole life is in this room. Yet it still does not explain why I am here.

The only other piece of furniture is a wooden desk, and on top the same kind of writing machine some scholars use in the archive, only larger. She is sitting in front of it, staring at its glowing empty face. She looks well. Her hair is pulled up high in a band, a few curling strands falling carelessly (deliberately, I am sure) on to her face, and her skin has caught a touch of the sun, which gives her a gentle glow. She is wearing her harem trousers, which I recognise from her first day, and a brightly coloured chemise, with a looping silver necklace, lithe as a snake, resting on her collar bone. As ever, she is dressed for company. Or at least dressed for me, since there is no one else here.

The rich green of the landscape outside the window suggests a place more familiar with rain, yet it is hot in here. To the side of the desk is a small machine with metal blades that whirl fast when she presses a button, sending a breeze into the room.

She starts to tap - that slightly metallic sound I always find so irritating in the hallowed silence of the archive - and a string of words appear; but before I can take them in, she shakes her head, and after more insistent tapping, they are gone.

She puts her elbows on the desk, joining her hands together as if in prayer as she stares at the empty screen, blowing out a noisy breath of frustration.

Her notebooks are spread around her, one - the last, I think - open somewhere in the middle. The breeze from the fan flutters the pages and she watches them move, as if in memory of me, then reaches over and flicks further through the book.

Suddenly, I understand.

I am here because she has brought me with her.

Nestled deep between two pages is a slip of folded paper, barely big enough for four or five lines of script: a secretary's hand, though not Benedetto, one of those many postscripts dashed off at the end of the day, which when folded and sealed for dispatch is reduced to the size of a communion wafer. I catch only a few words, an extra bolt of cloth added as an afterthought to an agent, the name at the top so faded one might never know whom. I remember watching her as she played with similar postscripts in the archive, entranced, like so many, by their miniature perfection and intimacy, as if someone from the past was whispering a few extra secret words in your ear. A scrap of paper so small, so unimportant, that it might easily be missed if it had been sitting on a notebook, closed in haste at the end of the day.

Except, its presence here is not a mistake. No. This is surely theft, the stealing of history. A small, mundane, repetitious example, of little use to anyone else, possibly. But theft nevertheless. And we both know it.

I think about the criminal whose second hand I once saved from amputation and send out my own breath of wind, this one sharp enough to lift the paper off the desk and launch it on to the floor. She flinches, as if someone has struck her. She turns off the fan, her eyes going back to the open pages of her notebook, which are still fluttering, though more gently now. She brings a hand down on to them and holds it there, smiling. I know everything she is feeling. I can read it from the look on her face, taste the tang of perspiration on her skin; a touch of guilt, yes, but mixed with exhilaration.

'*Don't worry, I'll send it back,*' she says brightly, and her tone is so conversational one might think she is talking to herself, except I know differently. '*I just needed you with me a little longer, to help ... I don't know, push me out of the plane so the parachute could open!*' She laughs. '*And I've no idea how to explain that to you. Though when you were younger I think you might have liked it.*'

She retrieves the letter from the floor and smooths out its tiny paper folds with her fingertips, then brings it up to her nose and inhales deeply. The smell of the past. Eventually, there will be nothing left: no ink, hardly a smudge of the wax seal; only the fragments of a disintegrating piece of history. Still, I will remain. In Titian's honestly dishonest masterpiece of a ravishing young woman in a headdress and ermine, who art lovers now hail as Isabella d'Este. And in all the portraits that others will paint of me with words.

I have favoured her with a great deal of my attention: it is time she offered me something back. *Get on with it,* I think. She turns back to the screen. *Go on.*

I have always had the most sensitive nose. Even as a child I registered the way perfumes and bodies fused together ...

Tap-tap-tap ... her fingers lift and hover over the raised letters as we both read them back. She taps again.

As an adult, I could identify each of my ladies with my eyes closed and smell my husband when he was two rooms away ...

Through the open window, I hear the sound of bird song over the clatter of the keys. The tapping is faster, more insistent now, until it feels as if a woodpecker has entered the room and is hammering rhythmically on the tabletop.

Though as he grew older so could everyone else, for by then his body was rotting and even the strongest of my concoctions failed to disguise his rankness. Still, I am not to blame for that.

The sky is busy with scudding clouds, their underbelly violet with the beginning of sunset. Mantegna would have given more drama to the moment, but it feels peaceful enough to me. So much to tell ...

I was an expert in perfumes, designed and gifted scents for women of good families all over Italy and beyond. Though if I am honest rather than modest (a necessary distinction in a woman's life), I never met anyone who smelled sweeter than I did ...

Mine has been a most exhausting afterlife. I think I would enjoy a little rest, now the record is set straight.

AUTHOR'S NOTE

Best to set the record straight immediately. While I once trained as a historian and have spent time in the State Archives reading room of Mantua, I do not, alas, have the ability to decipher and translate correctly more than a few sentences of fifteenth-century court Italian. (And certainly not the temerity to 'borrow' one such priceless document for a while.) So while I may share the dress sense of my scholar and her deep commitment to bringing alive this remarkable woman, I owe the bulk of the historical research to others. First and foremost, my thanks must go to Professor Deanna Shemek, for her deep knowledge, her unflagging support of this project, and her terrific translations of the many of Isabella's letters that I have used here, as well as her inspirational work on a digital reconstruction of Isabella's studiolo, to be more fully enjoyed here: (https://www.isabelladestearchive.org/virtual-studiolo).

I am indebted to Molly Bourne for her study of Francesco Gonzaga's correspondence, which opened a valuable window into his mind, and to Marie-Louise Leonard's research on plague conditions in Mantua. My appreciation of the Palazzo Te was much enhanced by its conservator, Roberta Piccinelli, and it is to her, Deanna and the custodians of the archive, who were unfailingly helpful to me on my visit, that I also owe thanks for certain of the images reproduced here. The photos of the interior of the archive were taken by a local photographer and lawyer, Marcello Tumminello, who I would liked to have met personally, but sadly he died in 2021.

I am exceedingly grateful to Whitefox for helping me birth this experimental hybrid of novel, biography and art, and to its earlier readers, Clare Alexander, my agent, Eileen Horne, Sue Woodman, Katri Skala and Lucy Jago. Their enthusiasm and advice all fed into the final product and kept me going - along with Isabella's unflagging determination to tell her own story - when the going got rough.

For those wanting further information, either on the extraordinary Isabella or any other of my novels, please visit sarahdunant.com or Email me at hello@sarahdunant.com. I would love to hear from you.

As the text makes clear, Isabella's collection suffered greatly at the hands of history. Her descendants did not share her tendency to thrift and the Gonzaga family fell increasingly into debt, necessitating the sale of the bulk of Mantua's court treasures in the 1620s to Charles I in England, then to Cardinal Richelieu in France. At some point in this timeline, Michelangelo's cheeky copy of a Roman sleeping cupid gets lost. The last Gonzaga heir, Vicenzo II, died in 1627, leaving the state open to contesting forces and the siege and sack of Mantua by the Spanish.

As an early pioneer in the art of photoshopping her own image, Isabella did a pretty thorough job. Though possibly not quite thorough enough. It seems something approximating to Titian's earlier portrait of her actually passed into the hands of later collectors, though by then it did not have her name on it. Instead, it was called simply *Lady in a Red Dress*. Alas, that too got lost somewhere along the line.

But as luck - or justice - would have it, we think a version of it was made by no less an artist than Peter Paul Rubens, a great fan of Titian, who was himself briefly court painter at Mantua, where he is known to have copied at least two of Titian's portraits.

His painting is currently housed in the Kunsthistorisches Museum in Vienna. And I offer it now as an affectionate visual postscript to this most extraordinary of Renaissance women.

Peter Paul Rubens: Isabella in Red,
copy of a portrait by Titian.

LIST OF ILLUSTRATIONS

All reasonable efforts have been made by the author to trace the copyright owners of the material quoted in this book and of the images reproduced in this book. In the event that the authors or publishers are notified of any m mistakes or omissions by copyright owners after publication, the author and the publisher will endeavour to rectify the position accordingly for subsequent printings.

BIBLIOGRAPHY

Sarah Bedford, *Cesare Borgia*, London: Little, Brown, 1981.

Maria Bellonci, *Lucrezia Borgia*, Milan: Mondadori, 1939.

Molly Bourne, *Francesco II Gonzaga: the soldier prince as patron*, Rome: Bulzoni, 2008.

Molly Bourne, *Male humour and sociability from Erotic culture*, edited by Sara F. Matthews-Grieco. Aldershot: Ashgate, 2010.

Clifford M Brown, *Isabella d'Este in the ducal palace of Mantua*, Rome: Bulzoni, 2005.

Julia Cartwright, *Isabella d'Este: A study of the Renaissance in 2 volumes*, London: John Murray, 1903.

Luigi Guicciardini, *The Sack of Rome*, translated and edited by James H. McGregor. New York: Italica Press, 1993.

Sheila Hale, *Titian: His Life*, London: HarperPress, 2012.

Carolyn James, *A Renaissance Marriage: The Political and Personal Alliance of Isabella d'Este and Francesco Gonzaga, 1490-1519*, Oxford: Oxford University Press, 2020.

George R. Marek, *The Bed and the Throne: the life of Isabella d'Este*, New York: Harper & Rowe, 1976.

Christine Shaw, *Isabella d'Este: A Renaissance Princess*, London: Routledge, 2019.

Christine Shaw, *Julius II: The Warrior Pope*, New Jersey: Wiley-Blackwell, 1993.

Deanna Shemek, *Isabella d'Este: Selected Letters*: Volume 54 (The Other Voice in Early Modern Europe: The Toronto Series), Arizona: Arizona Center for Medieval & Renaissance Studies, 2017.

Deanna Shemek, *In Continuous Expectation: Isabella d'Este's Reign of Letters*, Toronto: Toronto Centre for Renaissance and Reformation Studies, 2021.

Leonardo da Vinci: *Nei documenti dell'Archivio di Stato di Mantova*, 2019.

Kathleen Walker-Meikle, *Medieval Pets*, Suffolk: Boydell Press, 2012.